Still Reflections

Still Reflections

Stories of the Heart...

Steven Fletcher

Gentle Place Publishing
Capistrano Beach, California

© 2003 Steven Robert Fletcher. All rights reserved.
Gentle Place Publishing, P.O. Box 7601,
Capistrano Beach, California, 92624-7601 U.S.A.
www.gentleplace.com

Manufactured in the United States of America

Publishers Cataloging-in-Publication Data

Fletcher, Steven
Still Relections: Stories of the Heart / Steven Fletcher

1. Fletcher, Steven—Spiritual Life—Fiction.
2. Inspiration—Fiction.
3. Parables.
4. I. Title

813'.54

ISBN 0-9749138-0-4 (pbk.)

Cover Photograph by Axel Mertens

First Edition

This book is dedicated to all the teachers of the world, be they those who work in classrooms, under trees or those less-known, unsung educators who work on streets, in fields, and in factories. To those who give of themselves and share their hope for a better world, to them this book is dedicated.

Acknowledgements

There are many people who helped bring this book to birth. There are those who said just the right thing, at just the right moment and then stepped back. To all of those who encouraged me along this path I am deeply grateful. There are others who gave much more than encouragement.

I would like to thank three people who gave their time freely to read and edit all of these stories. They are David Bowie, Thia Neitzke and Irma Nyby. The generous service they offered will always be remembered. You may read more about them on the Gentle Place website.

I'd like to acknowledge Axel Mertens of Canberra, Australia (http://www.axozphotography.com), whose wonderful picture, *Grass Sunset*, illumines the cover of this book.

When the editing was for the most part done, many other issues raised their heads. At this point, Janey Frazier stepped forward with love and encouragement. It is impossible to describe all that she has contributed to this work.

Lastly, I want to thank my wife, Makhosazana, who risked homelessness to make this book a reality.

Table of Contents

Introduction	10
Foreword	13
Preface	15
African Daisies	19
Angel Blockers	24
Animus Gravis	29
Attar of Rose	34
Burning Bridges	39
C or G	44
The Cedar Flute	47
Coal City	50
The Compass	58
Cooked Carrots	63
A Cure for Loneliness	69
Dandelion Coffee	72
Desert Walk	77
Dream Focus	83
Dream Works	88
Early Ones	93
Far Too Precious	96
The Flood at Flat Rock	100
The Gift	106
Glowing Embers	114

Gold Fever	119
Graduation	125
A Grain of Sand	131
Grandpa's Feather	135
The Harvest	140
The Healthy Planet Bookstore	145
Jacaranda Carpets	151
Jalapeno's Fast Tacos	155
Knee Pads	160
Lava Bricks	165
The Leaves Before Winter	171
Lemon Dreams	176
Line of Sight	183
The Marathon	191
The Middle of Nowhere Truck Stop	197
Money Talks	202
Mongolian Breakfast	207
Morse Code	212
The Motorbike	219
The Mutual Compatibility Act	227
My Father's Hands	234
A Nail With No Name	238
Northern Lights	243
Orange Blossoms	248

Oxygen Masks	254
Pacific Sunset	261
Piano	265
Quaking Aspen	270
Raspberry Yogurt	278
Roasted Corn	283
Running Late	289
Satellite	295
The Silk Scarf	300
The Sounds of Hidden Lake	305
Story Tellers	310
The Sunflower Mug	314
The Swallows	319
Trying Too Hard	322
Victoria Falls	327
Watermelon and the Rose	333
West Street	337
The White Flag	344
Who Are You	348
Wooden Wheel	353
Your True Colors	357

Introduction

As with many books, this one is a labor of love. Each of us follows his own path and mine has led me to many places in the world. I have had the good fortune to live and to work with people of many different cultures and faiths and I have learned that all people share the same fundamental beliefs and emotions.

Over the past thirty years, I felt a growing desire to capture the common threads that move through and connect our lives, and as a result, I began to write. It was my goal to create a collection of short stories that would inspire and motivate a reader to think about things spiritual. The result is the book you hold in your hands.

The stories in Still Reflections are intended to be universal in nature and to speak to any open heart—regardless of the source and strength of one's belief. They address the commonly-accepted values of men and women of good will—wherever they might reside, whatever their ages might be and whatever the nature of their beliefs. The stories illustrate our shared values of good will, struggle, simplicity, courage, and love in its purest form.

Those familiar with the terms of literature might classify many of the stories in this anthology as "vignettes," while others will more appropriately be classified as "short-short stories." Regardless of the technical classification, I hope you find that these stories are a stimulus to your emotional, spiritual, and mental growth. Given their length, they leave much to the imagination of the reader, and that is—the intent. My wish is that you will easily find yourself in these stories, create your own next chapters—and in the process move along your own, unique path.

There is a line in a song that says, "On his search along the road, dancing and stumbling—trying to carry his load." All of us, to a greater or lesser degree, are dancing and stumbling on our own paths. Each of us can use a little food for thought. These stories do not seek to supply answers or advice—but rather to supply some qualities and concepts for contemplation. Beyond the most obvious personal uses of these stories in areas such as a stimulus to meditation and thought, or as an aid to journaling or a primer for dreams, I hope these stories will also find use in a number of other formal and informal situations.

One such area is in the field of education. These stories have been tested against target audiences at college and high school levels and, to a lesser extent, with younger children. They can be used in a variety of disciplines. Their primary benefit is to help students think at more fundamental levels about human behavior and about our relationship with the world that surrounds us. At younger levels there are a number of stories that can help start the process of individual thought, encouraging both empathy and personal responsibility. The stories in this book may serve as an adjunct to almost any lesson where carefully selected stories are read and then discussed in an open-ended fashion—to illustrate the theme of the lesson. When the stories are used in conjunction with the lesson text, students, whether young or old, will be able to extract deep meanings from the stories—even those beyond the conscious knowledge of the author.

Another area is the realm of counseling. Counselors of all types may use these stories in their work, both with individuals and with groups. The stories provide a mechanism to unearth and to address painful subjects in a non-threatening manner.

Another area is that of the family. Mothers and fathers are the first educators of a child. They have an innate love for their children and wish for them only the best. All too often, however, they find themselves without materials that teach values in an indirect manner and are forced to use materials that preach to a young child's heart, often doing more harm than good. When these stories are read to children before they have the cognitive skills to grasp complex concepts, they will still be attracted unconsciously to the characters and themes that the stories present. As a result, values, which most parents seek to teach their children, will be taken in as easily as mother's milk. And since it is now suspected that children "hear" us and take in information when they are still in the womb, I would recommend that parents consider reading some of these stories to their unborn children.

In the process of writing these stories, I have grown a great deal. I hope that you will also find many avenues of growth from reading them.

Steven Fletcher
March 2004

Foreword

A visit to a gentle place...

It was a hectic day in late summer. The team was putting together the preliminary budget for the new financial year and everyone was scrambling to meet the deadline. Steve had asked me to read some of his newly-written stories and to provide my impressions. I planned to start the review on my lunch hour, but I began to doubt if I could find a mental space where I could really give them a good read. I decided to try anyway and if necessary, I would reschedule the reading for later.

As I read the first story, I felt my tension begin to ease. Because each story is short—just a few pages—I finished the actual reading quickly and spent a few moments absorbing the meaning of the tale and the insight of the main character. As I progressed into the next story, it became very quiet around me. I was still physically in the office, but mentally I had moved into the stories. At the end of the hour, I felt peaceful.

I know the truly important things in life don't include budget deadlines, but it's hard to remember that when you're immersed in the process. After I finished my first reading session, I sent Steve an email message and described the stories as "a visit to a gentle place." They had removed me from my harried surroundings and reminded me of the things that count. The little stories were infused with themes of peace and tolerance—tolerance of all cultures, faiths and ways of life. People in the stories met their challenges with courage, respect, understanding, kindness and forgiveness. At the core of each story was an insight that subtly demonstrated the power of looking at life with an honest and accepting heart.

We all seek insight at different times in our lives. We may be searching for ways to help our children grow to be both strong and loving. Perhaps we're facing a serious emotional or physical challenge. We might want to explore a deeper understanding of our own spirituality. And sometimes we make choices that do not serve us well and reach a point where we want to make new and different choices.

All of us, young and old, need to be able to take time out to focus on what matters as we continue our lifelong process of discovery and growth. Rather than preach or scold, the stories in *Still Reflections* let you visit with people you'd like to know and perhaps learn from spending a short time in a gentle place you'd like to be part of.

Enjoy your visits…

Janey Frazier

Preface

You do not need to be a rocket scientist to understand that there are several processes of an immense magnitude taking place in the world today.

The Internet is expanding with knowledge at a rate which is incomparable to anything in the history of the world. And the phenomenon is not limited to the Internet—radio, television, films, books, newspapers, and magazines all offer information on ever imaginable subject.

Simultaneously, global travel and migration are taking place on a scale not previously seen, bringing opportunities for cultural interchange the likes of which mankind has never before witnessed.

In the scientific realm discoveries continue to fill our minds as man reaches ever deeper into the realms of understanding. The potential is there to eliminate hunger and poverty, to have a world where all have ample opportunity for quality education—an education that goes beyond intellectual and scientific knowledge. We have the ability to ensure that every child develops his or her potential and contributes to an ever more caring world.

But we are not there yet. Outwardly, there seems to be little progress towards these goals. Wars and conflicts continue in families, in the workplace and between countries. People still fight in the name of religion, for money, for power or for reasons that they have long ago forgotten. In many parts of the world, we have far more than we need, and yet we thirst. We thirst for the commonality in man, the commonality in our diverse beliefs, and for a genuine understanding that we are all one.

There is hope. At the same time that greed and ego seem to rise to levels never before seen, philanthropy seems to be multiplying at an ever-increasing pace. Educational institutions multiply, search intensifies, people everywhere long for a better world.

This is my contribution, my attempt at making the world a little better, my offering of hope. If this book touches just one person, if one person is moved to intensify his or her efforts, then my labor will not be in vain.

I wish each and every one of you success in all of your endeavors.

Steven Fletcher
March 2004

African Daisies

I had become accustomed to the passage of the sun at the end of each day. I had even seen an eclipse. But this was neither the end of the day, nor was it an eclipse of the sun.

At the same time, there was a rumbling noise and it was not thunder. The low rumbling noise got louder and louder until at one point there was a swishing noise, and then the darkness came. Suddenly, I was in a big container with many other seeds, which just a few moments before had been basking in the late summer sun.

"What happened?" I asked.

"Darned if I know," someone replied. "I heard this noise, then it all went dark. Next thing I know, I'm here huddled up next to you."

The rumbling noise continued for an hour or so, and then we all started moving. There was a flash of sunlight, and then we were all laid out on a long belt. There was light again, but it wasn't sunlight. I heard some voices talking.

"What do we have here?"

"Dimorphotheca aurantiaca."

"Come on, Jack, you know I don't know all those Latin names."

"I'm sorry—they're African daisies."

"Really? We still have a bit from last year; we'd better mix it in with this batch. I'll go and get them."

After that, we just kept moving down this big belt. Nobody was particularly worried; we knew we'd get planted sometime, and that's all that counted. After a while, more seeds got added to the belt. That's how I met my new friend who greeted me saying, "Howdy."

"Hello," I replied, still somewhat stunned at all that had happened.

"How are you?" he asked.

"I'm fine, thanks. Do you know where we are?"

"We're in a seed factory. They clean, sort, and package seeds here," he explained.

"Really! Have you been here long?"

"About a year."

"Wow! That's a long time!"

"Yes, it is a long time. But it has helped me to develop patience. I've had lots of time to think."

"Do you know what's going on now?"

"Yes, I went through this last year. We are going to get cleaned and sorted. Don't worry; it doesn't hurt. They have some way of knowing which seeds are not going to germinate. They pull those out and make compost of them."

"Interesting. You think I'll make it?"

"I think so. You look pretty healthy."

"What's going on up ahead there?" I asked.

"I was never physically there before, but I tapped into some memories, and I think this is where we get packaged," he replied.

"You tapped into memories?"

"Yeah, it's a little hard to explain, but I'll try. You've had dreams before, right?"

"Yes."

"Well, when you have dreams, you see all kinds of stuff that you don't see when you are awake. Are you with me?"

"Yes, I follow."

"Well, some of what you see in dreams is in the future, and some of it is in the past. Other dreams are neither past nor future. And some dreams don't have any purpose."

"Okay… I'm sort of with you."

"From those dreams, you sometimes tap into memories. You see places where you've never been."

"Wait a minute. You just said you can remember things in the past; doesn't that mean you were there?"

"Not necessarily. Think of memory as a big, collective pool, containing lots of memories—yours, mine, and those of people we haven't ever met. Maybe your great grandmother has some memories there. I can't really be sure about all this. All I know is that I have seen that machine up there before, and I remember that it is going to put a bunch of us in little packages with pictures on the outside."

"Interesting. Hey, look. Are those the packages you were talking about?"

"Yes, I think so."

"Those are pretty pictures."

" Yes, that's what we look like when we become flowers again."

"Wow, that's something."

"Okay, here we go. Stay close, and I can tell you more after we get packaged."

We were pulled up by a reverse wind and then put into one of those packages with the nice pictures on it. The lights went dim, but it wasn't completely dark.

"So, what happens next?" I asked my new friend.

"Well, I expect we have some waiting to do. I think we'll get put in boxes and then sent to a place where people will buy the packages. Then they will plant us in soil, give us water, and we will start to grow."

"Does that hurt?"

"Not at all. From my understanding, that's the most thrilling part of being a seed. The ground is warm and is packed around you on all sides. Then the water comes. Something inside of you starts to remember its purpose in life. The life force is so strong, it sends out something to become roots and something else to become a stem. Then, you keep growing until you turn into flowers—like those on the seed packages."

"That sounds exciting. Can we talk about this some more tomorrow? I'm feeling tired now."

"Sure, that'll be fine."

Over the next few months, I spent lots of time talking to my friend. That seed package became a classroom where all the new seeds like myself heard all these fantastic things from the older seeds who had been around longer. I remember the excitement as our seed package was put out for people to buy. Each day we would move closer and closer to the front. I remember the thrill of being picked up and taken to a place where someone paid money to take us home. From there, it all happened very quickly. I saw the soil as we were sprinkled into little holes. I felt the warmth and the moisture, and then I could feel the magic. Just as my friend had promised, I could feel my life force start again. I was reaching out—ending one cycle—while starting another.

Now, as I stand here before you, telling you my story and showing you my orange and yellow colors, I remember those times and those places. But from all this speaking, and all the standing here in the hot sun, I'm feeling thirsty. Will you not offer me a little water?

Angel Blockers

Zinggggggggggg pit

"Wow—who are you?"

The man standing in front of me didn't answer my question but said, "Welcome, Mr. Chandra."

"Thanks, but where am I?"

"It has lots of names; you'll figure it out soon."

"Last thing I remember there was a big truck headed towards me," I said.

"Yes, that's right."

"What happened?"

"Wanna see?"

"Sure."

He walked over to a computer-like device, typed in my name and then said, "Take a look." He pointed to this telescope-like thing that went through the floor. It had a handle sticking out the side of it. The handle looked like a gearshift and had several positions. He went on to explain, "G is for general information, D is for destiny, P is for present state, H is for history, and S is for send." Then he said, "Set it for history."

I moved the lever into the H position. Then, he went on to explain, "If you turn the handle in this position it will advance forward or backward in time. Go ahead, take a look."

I bent down and looked through the eyepiece. "All

I can see is white clouds."

"Try rotating the knob." I turned it one way and all I saw were more clouds. I turned it the other way and saw a freeway. "Can you see it?" he asked.

"Yeah, I see a freeway, a car like mine, and a truck like the one that was coming towards me just before I came here."

"What else do you see?"

I twisted the knob again and started to explain. "I see that big truck is headed right towards that car and … oh my, the truck hit the car."

"Yes, that was your car."

"I don't think so. That guy in the car must have died."

"Exactly."

"No, you don't get it. I'm here, so I didn't die. The guy in the car is either in a lot of pain or is dead."

"It's okay, sometimes it takes a bit of time to re-adjust. Come, I'll show you around."

I followed him out through the door of his office. Outside, it was a beautiful, sunny day. We were in a very large courtyard. There were lots of flowers and fountains. He walked over to a very large, round card file and pressed a button. The cards and index tabs started to spin. He pressed a stop button and the cards stopped spinning. The index card read, "A1619."

"What's the number for?" I asked.

"Oh, 1619 is your number."

"And what's the A for?"

"Angel," he said matter-of-factly.

He said, "Let's go in," and he walked straight into

the exposed card and then he disappeared.

I followed him, and we entered a big room with lots of people. There were many machines like the one I had seen in his office. In one corner, about ten people were gathered around one machine. One was operating the eyepiece. I noticed he had it in the send mode and all the onlookers seemed especially happy.

"Good afternoon, everyone, I'd like to introduce Ravechandra, son of Sinatombee. Mr. Chandra has just arrived and is still adjusting." All the people except for the one operating the machine turned and smiled.

"Welcome, welcome," said an elderly woman.

Someone said to the machine operator, "You should let him take a look."

The man, who had been intently looking into the telescope, leaned back, stood up, and then motioned for me to look. The others made way for me to walk to the machine. The man whose machine it was, had an extremely happy and radiant look on his face. He went on to explain as I looked into the telescope, "This is a model 28X bi-world interface. It allows us to send messages to those who are open. Each of us is given a large caseload. It's okay, we love our work, but we have a certain amount of frustration when the person for whom we have a message is not open."

"Not open?" I asked still trying to focus the machine.

"Yes, there are many types of angel-blockers. There is a whole list of things that can prevent us from sending messages destined for various individuals. The most common is the IGTFSE Syndrome.

"What's an I-G-T… F-S-E Syndrome?"

"Sorry, it already seems like you've been here forever. It stands for I'm-going-to-fix-someone-else."

"What's that mean?" I asked, still trying to get the machine to show me what I was supposed to see.

"It's when one person tries to fix another. They spend so much of their cosmic energy trying to fix someone else, that we can't break through to give them a message that will help them on their way. It happens in all kinds of situations: between friends, spouses, people who work together, and even children."

"Hey, this looks like my father," I said without raising my head. "Some messages are going to him while he is sleeping. I can see the messages and many of them are about me. He seems to be content now. I can see sorrow draining out of his heart and joy going in."

"Yes, that's why we were all gathered around. Even here, we have to celebrate our victories."

"May I change the settings?"

"Actually, your machine is set up over there," said the elderly woman. "I'm in charge of training. I'd be happy to show you what to do."

"Okay, but will it take long?"

"No, it won't take long, but don't worry, we have plenty of time here."

"I'm just a little concerned that I may need to wake up and go to work soon."

"Son," she said in the loving way that grandmothers often speak, "I know it is a bit hard to understand, but you are not asleep, and this is your new home."

The situation finally began to sink in. "But what about my children and my dear wife? Who will take care of them?"

"You will!" she said. "You will take far better care of them now than you ever did before." Then she gave me a big, grandmotherly hug.

We walked over to what appeared to be a brand new machine and she said, "This machine is pretty easy to use. I think you already have many of the basics. If you feel tired or saturated, as we call it here, you can rest here or wander out among the flowers. If you need anything, just ask anyone for help."

I nodded my head and smiled more deeply than I knew I could.

"And one last thing," she said. "Welcome home, Ravechandra, son of Sinatombee." With that she gave me another grandmotherly hug and then she walked away—just like in a dream.

●

Animus Gravis

"Welcome to Biology 605. In this class, you will learn about the deeper workings of the human ear."

"I heard this guy is a real hoot," whispered one of the two young women in the back row.

"Yeah, I wouldn't be taking this—except it's required," whispered her friend.

"Now how many of you are pre-med students?" Most of the class put up their hands. "And how about you?" he asked, indicating to a young man in the front row. "Why are you taking this class?"

"Well, sir," he said, struggling to his feet, "I had a friend who took this class and said it gave him a different outlook on life." A light rumble of laughter passed through the lecture hall.

"And how about you?" asked the professor, gesturing to a young woman in the third row. "Why did you sign up for this class?"

"I heard it was a spiritually-oriented class on diseases caused by the human ear." There was more laughter—especially from the medical students.

The professor ignored the laughter and continued, saying, "Fine, fine. Then, let's get started." He went on to explain the required reading, his attendance policy, the requirements for the term paper, the final exam, and his overall grading scheme. There was nothing very unusual. He asked if there were any questions and, seeing there were none, proceeded with his first lecture.

"Most of you are medical students," he said. "Many of you will become medical doctors, some will become wealthy, and some of you will become real healers of mankind."

"Watch, now, here is where it gets funny," whispered one of the two friends in the back.

"Who can detail in very simple terms how the human ear works?"

One of the pre-med students explained, "Vibrations moving through the air strike and vibrate the eardrum, which, in turn, passes the vibrations to a set of very delicate bones that are connected to nerves. These nerves transmit the representation of the sounds to the brain."

"Excellent, excellent," shouted the professor. The slightly embarrassed student sat down, as the professor continued. "Now what happens to the various parts of the ear if a person is repeatedly exposed to loud noises such as the firing of guns, the noise of heavy machinery, or the sounds heard when standing directly in front of a powerful amplifier at a rock concert?"

Another student got up and gave a detailed explanation about the damage and degeneration of hearing abilities. The professor then extracted information from various students about brain damage, genetic defects, and damage from various diseases.

One of the two friends in the back whispered, "This seems pretty straightforward to me."

Her friend replied, "Just be patient; he'll go off at any moment."

"Now, who can tell me about animus gravis?" asked the professor.

One brave soul raised his hand timidly and offered, "Is it Latin for an ear-ache?"

"Well, that's pretty close. It is Latin. One might best translate it as a spiritual pain, originating in the ear, that spreads throughout the body."

A number of students shifted their feet to new positions, while others cleared their throats. Some were busy taking notes.

One of the two in the back whispered, "You see, here he goes."

"Animus gravis has two primary causes," continued the professor. "The first is when the human ear is consistently and repeatedly subjected to gossip from external sources. The second cause is self-inflicted and occurs when the person concerned makes a habit of speaking negatively of others. In both cases, when the nerves of the inner ear transmit the sound to the brain, it is interpreted as intense pain. The result is confusion and a wide variety of maladies, such as headaches and ulcers."

"You see, what did I tell you? We won't learn much in this class," said one of the two whispering young women.

"Next, I will play a simulated conversation between the inner ear nerves and the brain." Then, the professor switched on a tape recorder and asked if everyone could hear it okay. He adjusted the volume and said, "The first speaker is the brain. It is speaking to the left inner ear nerve."

"Why do you send me this stuff?" asks the brain. "You know that all this gossip gives me a headache."

The nerve responds, "Look, I'm sorry. You know we've been through this at least a thousand times. My job is to pass on what I get. I am not supposed to edit or modify anything I send."

"Yeah, I know. Can you talk to the bones down there or to the ear drum; maybe they can do something?"

"Well, I have tried that, but they told me the same thing that I told you. The last time I tried, they said I should mind my own business."

"I sure wish you could do something," says the brain again, in frustration.

"Actually, I think there is something that you can do?" says the nerve boldly.

"Oh, really," says the brain, somewhat sarcastically, "And what is that?"

"Well, whenever you hear gossip, you could just move away and get out of range."

"You mean, like make the body react with involuntary motions?"

"Yes, something like that. Or maybe you could just shut down everything and have a blackout. Sooner or later, the person will figure out that listening or talking about that stuff is worse than burning rubber tires near an open window."

"Interesting! I'll give it some thought."

The professor switched off the tape recorder to a wave of nervous laughter. The professor ignored the laughter, assigned the reading for the next week, and then dismissed the class.

"Let's get out of here," said one of the two girls who had been talking in the back.

They both stood up and walked quickly through the double doors. "You see, I told you this guy is one very strange professor."

"Yep, I do agree with you now. And I think the ventilation in the lecture hall is bad too—I have a terrible headache."

As they walked away together, they were both determined to get a passing grade—even though, they were both equally sure that—they would learn nothing.

♦

Attar of Rose

Grandma had been sick off and on, for six months. She refused to go to a special home, and didn't want to move closer to us. She said she didn't want to become a burden on anyone. I wanted to use my summer to stay with her. My parents agreed, as did my dear grandmother. A week after school was out, I arrived and set myself up in her spare room.

Grandma went through a number of cycles that summer. Her health would improve, then worsen. When her health was good, we went for walks. When it was real bad, she'd stay in bed for a week.

During one of those bad times, she asked me to remove two candles from a drawer near her bed. She smelled the two candles, and then handed me one, saying, "This one is for you, Anne. When I depart, you light this candle and burn it to the end."

The words seemed too strange for me to absorb and I did not like the thought of her departure. I had come to help her get well, not to be there for some mystical send-off.

Seeing I was troubled, Grandma said, "You know, Anne dear, I am ninety-two years old. I have had a full life here on this earthly plane. The time of my departure is near. You should not be saddened by this."

Well, I was saddened, but I put the candle she had

chosen for me in my room and agreed that I would light it when she departed. I placed the other candle on a small table near her bed. Before sleeping that night, I unwrapped the candle and read the label, "Rose Candle. Made with genuine attar of rose. Guaranteed to burn at least eight hours. Ever Glow Candle Company. Satisfaction guaranteed or your money cheerfully refunded. Lot number 2894."

Several weeks passed, and thankfully, neither candle was lit.

One afternoon I felt especially tired and went to bed very early. That night I had a dream. In the dream, Grandma was burning her candle and then called me to her side saying, "It's almost time to burn your candle. I am almost free." In the dream, her voice was so clear and so loud that I woke up. During the dream, I had felt very peaceful seeing Grandma's radiant face. Now, being awake, I felt concerned. I walked to Grandma's room and noticed a faint light under the door. I knocked softly and then walked inside.

Grandma was there, just like in the dream. The candle that had been beside her bed was now burning and it was near its end. She smiled and spoke softly, "Anne, my candle is almost gone. Soon it will be time to light yours."

My eyes filled with tears. She motioned for me to come closer. Then, without words, she put both her hands on my face and while smiling radiantly, she wiped my tears. The candle by her bed flickered and then went out. Grandma closed her eyes and took one very deep breath. That was her last. I sat there stunned, not knowing what to do. Somehow, I did not feel the grief that I had expected. I walked slowly into my room and lit the candle as I had promised. Then I started making the necessary phone calls.

The next few weeks were very busy. Family and friends came to town to pay their final respects. I was asked me to stay on and help with things that needed to be done. At the end of each day, I was amazed to find that Grandma's candle was still burning.

Finally, on the morning of my departure for home, the candle flickered and went out. I was a bit sad and yet very relieved. I had promised Grandma that I would let it burn until the end, but there was no way to take a burning candle on an airplane.

Back at home, while I was unpacking my suitcase, I came across the wrapping from the candle. I re-read the label and was amazed that the candle, though only guaranteed to burn for eight hours, had burned for a full twenty-one days.

I decided to write to the manufacturer and let them know how long the candle had lasted and tell them a little about my wonderful grandmother. Barely a week later, I got a reply. The letter was dated August fourth and was from the Quality Control Manager of Ever Glow Candle.

Dear Miss McKay,

It was with great interest that I read your letter. Your grandmother sounds like a fascinating woman, and I am pleased that our products were used and valued by such a wonderful soul.

With respect to the exceptional length of time that your grandmother's candle burned, I can share the following information:

Because of environmental and safety concerns, we keep comprehensive records on each batch of candles we produce. From every batch we select a sample and run a destructive burn test. In other words, we take a few candles from each batch and burn them under average conditions, and insure that they meet the advertised minimum. In the case of batch 2894, our records indicate that the samples lasted between nine and eleven hours each. This is nowhere near the twenty-one days you reported in your letter.

Because of my strong desire to ship quality products, I checked with our Customer Service Department to find out if their records contained anything similar to your experience. They did not. Additionally, I checked the manufacturing records for the day the batch was produced and did find that a new employee had dumped two, one-ounce bottles of attar of rose into the batch, instead of the two drops, which the process calls for.

Not being able to identify the cause of your experience, I became somewhat obsessed with this particular batch of candles. I began dreaming about an elderly woman, and about candles that would burn forever.

Finally, I located some candles from the same batch in two different retail shops and purchased a total of twenty-seven candles. We ran exhaustive burn tests under a variety of environmental conditions, and the longest any of them lasted was fifteen hours and twenty-eight minutes.

In short, there is no earthly explanation, for the experience you had. I wish you all the best in life.

Sincerely yours,
Mr. Ron Edwards,
Quality Control Manager

💧

Burning Bridges

"It's a lovely day for a picnic, isn't it?" said the lady in the bright yellow dress.

"Yes, it is," said Cantara.

After a little more small talk, the lady in the bright yellow dress came to the question she had been longing to ask. "So, Cantara, what gave you the courage to build this school?"

Cantara smiled, glanced slightly to the right of the lady in the yellow dress, and then started her story. "Another teacher and I had dreams of building a school like this. Her name was Ameera. We wanted to create a place of refuge for children where they could be slowly opened to the world, and where they could discover within themselves their own unique qualities. We never made formal plans as to how we would bring this all about, but we certainly had the passion for it.

"When she died, it was very hard for me. We had been friends for most of twenty-eight years. Attending the funeral was difficult, not just because of Ameera's passing, but because of the mixture of emotions that her family and friends displayed. After the service, I went directly to the hotel, planning to visit her resting place again the following day.

"Because of the emotional exhaustion, I went to

bed early. I lay on my back for a long time, thinking about our dream of a school, and how that dream had been shattered. The school was our project, and now I was alone. Eventually, sleep won over emotion, and I drifted off.

"Just before dawn, I had the most vivid dream. I was sitting near her resting place when Ameera came to me, wiped the tears from my face, took the flowers from my hands, and placed them on her own grave. Next, she motioned for me to follow her to a grave with a large, flat slab of red granite. It had a lot of writing on it. In the dream, I could only read the words, 'To Be Successful.' Ameera pointed to some of the words and was speaking to me. It was as if she were explaining the words and their many meanings. I could feel the power of the words she was saying, but I could not understand their meaning.

"Then Ameera took me by the hand and led me back to her resting place. She sat me down, put the flowers back in my hand, and then said to me, 'Build the school!'

"I woke up to the sound of the birds that sing at dawn and lay in bed for a long time, thinking of the dream. Later that morning, I went to visit Ameera's resting place. While sitting there, I thought about the dream, and especially about the words she had said to me. 'Build the school,' kept running through my head.

"I stood up to leave, and was drawn to the same area that I had seen in the dream. I walked over and there was a large, flat gravestone with the words, "To

Be Successful" written on it. I was stunned as I stood there, realizing that Ameera had shown me this in my dream. It appeared to be a formula for attaining success. I took out a small notebook and copied the inscription.

> *Taylor Donahue*
> *1925--1985*

To Be Successful:

1 Create a burning desire.

2 Make a plan to attain your purpose.

3 Burn all bridges to the past. (Leave no possible way of retreat—win or perish!)

4 Stand by the desire until it becomes the dominating obsession of your life and   finally a fact.

"I looked back where Ameera was buried and then walked quickly away. I returned to the hotel, collected my things, and then walked to the train station. The long train ride home gave me lots of time for reflection. I thought about the dream, about my life, and about the formula for success I had just copied into my notebook.

"I drifted off to sleep and Ameera came to me almost instantly. She looked at me, handed me a beautiful bunch of red roses, and said to me, 'Now that you know how—build the school.' It was said with such power and force, that I woke up.

"I moved to a seat with a table, took out a notebook, and started making notes as to how such a school could be built. The plan covered funding, a mission statement and many other aspects of the project. My training in education made me as qualified as the next person to start such a project.

"I turned to the formula. I had the desire, and I had a plan. The next part, the burning my bridges, was hard. In order to accomplish this, I would have to resign my position at the university, give up a promising career path, and forfeit the security of my retirement and health plans. My hands began to sweat, as fear ran through my body.

"I walked back to my seat and fell asleep. Again, I had a dream, and again Ameera came to me. This time she spoke very formally and said, 'Cantara, you have the way—you only need the will. Turn aside from fear, lest like me, you leave this world before you attain the goals you were meant to achieve.'

"I realized the timing was right. My last classes would finish in a week, my contract called for two month's notice, and summer was about to begin. I opened my purse, took out my cell phone, and called the dean. I explained my situation and that I was grateful for all the opportunities the university had given to me, but that I was resigning in order to build a school. When I hung up, I felt a strength that I had never felt before. After that, the rest came fairly easily."

Cantara stopped speaking and looked deeply into the eyes of the lady in the bright yellow dress. She smiled lovingly, understanding that her listener had traveled with her on the journey of the story. Neither woman spoke for a few moments. Both were thinking about Ameera and her part in the building of the school, and both were wondering just who was Taylor Donahue—a mystery they would probably never solve.

Finally, understanding that the moment of her story was over, Cantara glanced up at the blue sky and then looked back into the eyes of the lady with the bright yellow dress and said, "That's how this school got started—and what about you? What bridges do you need to burn and what dreams are you going to fulfill in your life?"

C or G

Vancouver is a beautiful city, as long as you're not lonely. The snow-capped mountains don't help you much when you are sad. I was not just alone in a new city—I was lonely. The love of my life was not here, and I was bound and determined to feel bad. I wore my sadness like it was a red-and-black-checkered shirt. I thought she was the sun, and I was too far away to feel the warmth. I didn't realize that we were only moons circling around a sun that warmed us both.

I don't recall why I bought the harmonica, but it worked wonders on the loneliness. It was a two-sided chromatic model, with the key of C on one side and the key of G on the other. To me, all that meant was that it sounded real good no matter how you played it.

I wasn't really trying to learn to play music; it was more like I was learning to listen to the sounds the harmonica made, and I liked what I heard.

Each evening in the springtime, I'd go down near the harbor and sit on a small hill under a tree. I'd lean against that tree and watch the sun go down. After it got dark, I'd pull out my shiny, new harmonica and play different sounds. After playing for a half hour, I would completely forget about how sad I was supposed to be feeling.

Little by little, more rhythm crept in to my playing. The notes started blending together into beautiful phrases. Pretty soon, I felt good enough about what was coming out of that harmonica to start playing before the sun went down. The next thing I discovered was walking and playing at the same time.

Since I hardly knew anyone in this big city, I started walking down the street playing simple little tunes that I'd repeat over and over again. How nice that was. I'd walk past people, or let people walk past me, while I'd play the harmonic and stroll along in time with the music. I became a self-appointed, one-man marching band. Walking this way started to feel normal to me, and walking without the music seemed odd. Walking to the bus became a pleasure. Going to work was fun; coming back from work was even more fun. Sometimes on the weekends, I'd start out walking and find myself in a new place, not even knowing where I was.

Then one day, quite by accident, I played some notes that sounded like part of a popular song. I made the notes again, and then played the rest of the song. I played it again. Just like that—no strain, no understanding—I just played it. I looked around to see if any one else noticed what had just happened. No one did. I went back to my random notes and marching sounds until I could be alone.

A week later, after several experiments, I found I could play pretty much anything. Sometimes, it didn't sound quite right on one side of the harmonica, so I'd flip it over. If the key of C didn't sound okay, I'd try the key of G. I still had no idea what the difference was. To me, it was just the other side of the same harmonica.

I made a little leather pouch for it and after that, I never went anywhere without it. Funny enough, I started to actually enjoy being alone, and Vancouver is, after all, a very beautiful city.

The Cedar Flute

Al started making dulcimers about the same time I started making bamboo flutes. He was one of those people who was a joy to watch. He was quiet and methodical, and he concentrated so much you'd almost think he was praying. He taught me how to tap a piece of wood with my knuckle and listen to how it resonated. Doing this created a feeling of love for the wood and the sounds it could make.

There was plenty of old, fine-grained, red cedar around and it created a very mellow sound when used in stringed instruments. I often wondered how it would sound if you could make a flute out of it. The trick was to figure out how. Bamboo has a hole down the middle, which made it ideal for making flutes. Cedar doesn't have the same advantage.

One day, I was there with Al, and he was working quietly away. I picked up one of the partially completed dulcimers. I could feel the sound of the wood as I tapped it gently. I don't know why, but I raised it to my lips as I had done many times with a new bamboo flute. I blew over one of the round holes in the top of the dulcimer. At first, there was no special sound except for the moving air. Then, I tilted it back and forth and blew again. Suddenly, a warm mellow sound resonated from the dulcimer.

Al stopped working and looked in my direction. I blew again. My mind started turning fast. Al didn't speak, but I could tell we were sharing the same thoughts. If this made such a wonderful sound, why not change the shape, add finger holes and then play it like a flute.

A fire of enthusiasm burst forth from my heart. Al went back to his work, as I walked quickly out the door. Then, I walked, skipped, and ran home, though my mind was already at home working. I could picture it all. The love for this unborn instrument was about to become a reality. All that remained were the details. What size should it be? How long? How many holes? How thick should it be? How could I glue the pieces together? The answers came quickly. Since cedar has such a mellow sound, I decided to make the flute large in order to bring out the lower notes. I'd make it about an inch on each side, and about fourteen inches long. Five finger holes would be fine.

There were a few false starts, but the love was strong and the flute was going to be born. I was far too excited to eat, so I skipped lunch. By four in the afternoon, the unfinished shell with fresh setting glue was hanging from the rafters. Now I needed patience. The glue would not be fully dry until tomorrow. I carved a mouthpiece to make blowing easier. And then I needed to wait. I cooked supper and sat by the fire for a few hours.

Sleep did not come easily that night, and when it finally came, the love of this unborn child turned into dreams. All night long, I was playing the new flute in my sleep.

The next morning, I woke up early and wondered if the whole thing had only been a dream. I glanced up at the rafters, saw the half-finished flute, and knew it was real. I removed the string from around the flute, burned the holes it needed and then glued the mouthpiece over the first hole.

Again, I needed to wait for the glue to dry. I waited until late afternoon and then sanded the flute all over. After wiping off the dust, I rubbed some linseed oil into the wood. At last—it was time!

I picked up the flute and held it between my two hands. I looked at the narrow grain of the wood running from end to end and then looked at the creases in my soiled hands. All remnants of doubt were gone. There it was, ready to play. The power of love had brought forth this flute, which now looked somewhat foreign as I held it between my hands. I turned my hands over and closed the finger holes. Lifting it gently to my lips, I blew warm air inside the flute. I rocked it back and forth against my lips, took a deep breath, and then blew over the mouthpiece. The flute came to life and resonated in my hands. I played and listened and allowed the sound to entrance my heart, knowing that this too was part of the process. I played for a very long time. When I finally stopped playing, I had a great sense of inner peace, proving to myself once again that heartfelt love is strong enough to bring about a new creation.

Coal City

It was Friday afternoon. All the children had gone home, and the halls were quiet. Tosha was walking by Katerina's open door, when she stopped, walked back, and said, "Hey."

"Hi! Come in. How was your first week here?"

"The kids are great, but the town...well let's say that there might be more appropriate names for this place than Coal City. It hardly even qualifies as Coal Village. I don't think this is the place to find a husband and settle down."

"You'll get used to it, Tosha. There's more here than meets the eye."

"I'll keep an open mind, but there's no movie theater, you only get three channels on TV, and the nearest place you can hear poetry is two hundred kilometers away."

Katerina waited for a few seconds and then spoke, "Are you very busy now? I have something I'd like to share with you."

"No reason to rush home—it's just an empty house."

Katerina ignored the negative comments and then spoke again, "Do you know Aleshka, the one who's in your class?"

"Yes, she's a very bright little girl."

"Well, three years ago she was in my class. Since most of the children will grow up and live their whole lives here, I wanted them to have some understanding of the issues that surround them. We did a month-long project on coal mining. For part of the project, each student had to interview someone in town and find out something about their life history—and then they were supposed to write a report on it."

"I see," said Tosha.

Katerina continued to talk while she opened and closed some cupboards, obviously looking for the thing she wanted to share. "It seems that Aleshka had a grandfather with quite a thrilling story of rescue and romance. She wanted to write the story but she was only in the third grade, so I encouraged her to tape record it instead. She wasn't very skilled with the tape recorder, but she got most of the story. I'd like to share it with you." Katerina removed a tape recorder from a shelf and placed the cassette she had found inside. They both sat down at a table made for third graders, and Katerina pressed the play button. There were a lot of clicking and banging noises and then they heard Aleshka's third-grade voice speaking, "Are you ready, Grandpa?"

"Yes, Aleshka, we can start now."

After a discussion about where to start, Aleshka's grandfather, Slava, began telling his story. "My name is Slava. I am the grandfather of little Aleshka. I am eighty-six years old. I have lived here in Coal City all of my life. I started mining coal when I was seventeen. By the time I was twenty-five, I was a safety inspector at the mine. I was still not married then and I was lonely—but I didn't really know how lonely I was."

Katerina and Tosha exchanged knowing glances as the tape continued.

"I was working with another man named Aaron. We were sent down a side shaft that we had come across. The shaft wasn't shown on any of the maps we had. The first thing we noticed inside the old shaft were some tracks with an old cart that ran alongside it. The equipment looked like it was about fifty years old.

"We had only walked about fifty feet inside that shaft, when we heard a noise that changed my life forever. There was a cloud of dust and a hail of rocks. I was hit and half buried, but old Aaron, he wasn't. The only thing I could hear was Aaron saying, 'We'll get you out okay. You haven't seen enough of life yet to skip out so easy.' I thought it was a pretty funny thing to say at a time like that, but he was older and somehow I believed him. Aaron used his big hands to lift the rocks off my left side and then dragged me to the track near where the cart was. He took off his coat and rolled it up like a pillow. He put it under my head and then he turned the cart upside down on top of me. He said if there were another cave-in, I wouldn't get hit in the head.

"So there I am, lying in the middle of this narrow track, with the cart covering most of my body and with my boots sticking out from one end. It is pitch black and all I can hear is Aaron working, and Aaron singing, and my own mind thinking about stuff that I should have thought about a long time before.

"Well, anyway, old Aaron he is working away and singing, sort of chanting like—saying things like, 'May this young man live to learn to love a good woman, and to have children that he loves, and that love him.' And then sometimes he would talk to me, asking me questions and all, to keep me awake, you know, in case I had a concussion. He was asking me things like, 'You ever think about getting married?' And it's real funny 'cause just before he asked me that—well, that's exactly what I was thinking about. And especially I was thinking about this one girl I met in school by the name of Berta."

At that point, Aleshka's small voice could be heard asking, "Would that be Grandma Berta?"

"Now don't go spoiling the story, Aleshka. You just wait till the end and you'll find out. Some things take time to work themselves through." Then Slava continued his story, "I was kind of drifting in and out of consciousness. There was quite an echo inside that old shaft. Every sound that Aaron made went out and then came back as an echo three or four times. I wasn't altogether uncomfortable in there, I was warm and I was lying on my back, and listening to all that Aaron was doing. He asked me a lot of funny questions like, 'Have you ever had anyone rub your head—like when people rub the head of a cat?'

"Then, at one point, Aaron says he is going to sing me this song that he sings at home with his wife and children. The song went something like, '…'tis a gift to be simple, 'tis a gift to be free; 'tis a gift to come down where we ought to be. And when we are in the place just right, we will be in the valley of love and delight.' And then he sings another part of it that goes like, '...when true simplicity is gained, to bend and to bow we will not be ashamed, to turn to turn 'twill be our delight, 'till by turning and turning we come round right.'"

"That's a nice song, Grandpa. Will you teach it to me?"

"Yes, Aleshka, I will, but not right now. Remember we are doing work for your school. So let's continue with the story first."

"All right, but teach me later—Okay, Grandpa?"

"I promise. Now, in the meantime, half the town of Coal City has gathered at the mine. Some are digging, some are praying, and some are crying. And all the while, I'm lying on these tracks in pitch blackness, listening to Aaron singing and hearing his deep voice echoing all around. Now, as it turns out, one of Aaron's kids, who was about your age, was supposed to be by his mother's side, but he wasn't! His mother was standing near the opening where the men went down to dig. Well this little boy went wandering off where he shouldn't have gone. It seems there was a place he'd been to before—that 'had a nice echo.' So he went up there to play and when he got close he thought he heard his daddy singing, so he stuck his head inside the shaft and shouted 'Daddy, is that you in there?' Now, I heard it the first time, but old Aaron he didn't, so I shouted to Aaron and I said, 'Listen,

Aaron, isn't that your kid?' And we both wondered if I was dreaming till the words came again, 'Daddy, is that you in there?'

"Well, Aaron started shouting so loud, and got so excited that I thought the noise would cause another cave-in. All I could hear, through all the noise, was pieces of, 'Daddy, is that...' and '...get back, Son...' and '...go back and find your mother...'

"Well then Aaron came and sat with me really close, and we talked for a while and put our heads together and figured that the opening to this old shaft must be where his little boy was shouting from.

"And it turned out that little boy went running back to his mother shouting, 'I heard Daddy! I heard Daddy!' Well, you can imagine the commotion that it caused. First, he had to answer questions about why he didn't stay close by, then he had to try to convince his mother he really heard his daddy, and the only way he could do that was to sing part of that song about being simple and all that. His mother was still doubting, but one of the other miners understood. He walked over to that little boy and said, 'Show me.'

"Well, shortly after that, there began quite a lot of excitement as half the town ran up the hill and watched a few miners carry me out, followed by old Aaron who got lots of hugs from his wife and kids.

"Next thing I remember, I'm in the hospital with a broken arm and a broken leg and not much else wrong and guess who comes to visit—that's right, you guessed it—Berta comes to visit me in the hospital. Well, I had been doing quite some thinking, so the first thing I do is say to her, 'Berta, you ever think of getting married?' And then she says, 'Funny you should ask...'

"Click-Clack."

Tosha, who was sitting on the edge of her third-grade chair, looked at Katerina with pleading eyes, and said, "Turn it over."

Katerina smiled sympathetically and said, "That's it! There's no more!"

Tosha, who couldn't accept it, ejected the tape herself, turned it over, and pressed the play button. She turned the volume up full but the only thing that could be heard in that normally noisy third-grade-classroom was the hiss of a story that was never recorded. Then, Tosha looked towards Katerina and asked, "Why?"

"Little Aleshka didn't understand that the tape had reached its end."

"Ok, then you tell me the rest of the story."

"I can't. Just after they made this tape, Slava got really sick and passed away."

"And his wife?"

"She died before him."

"And Aaron?"

"He was quite a bit older; he was long gone."

Finally, Tosha accepted that the story ended there. The two teachers sat in silence for a few moments, understanding that they had witnessed something wonderful. Finally, the custodian, who was working nearby, began whistling as he swept the floor near Katerina's classroom.

After a long silence, Tosha started to speak, "So, there's a lot more to this town than meets the eye—that's what you are trying to tell me."

Katerina nodded and then said, "There's a lot more to every town than meets the eye."

Tosha thanked Katerina, and started her longer-than-normal walk home. She had much to think over. Like the leaves that had been covered by sand to create the coal that gave this small town its name, the slow process of change had started—in the mind of one more teacher.

💧

The Compass

I had been driving since early morning and the late summer sun was taking its toll. Grandpa and his lemonade came to mind. I needed a break, so without much further thought I turned on Highway 116 and headed that way. I pulled out my cell phone and dialed his number.

After a few rings, I heard Grandpa's distinctive voice, "Hello."

"Hello Grandpa, this is Tim."

"Hello Tim. Nice to hear from you. I was thinking about you, just this morning. Where are you?"

"I'm about thirty minutes south of your house. Got any lemonade?"

"I have plenty of lemons. We'll make it when you get here."

I started feeling cooler as I thought of the taste of his lemonade. Grandpa used lots of lemons and very little sugar—that way you understood you were drinking lemonade. A few minutes later I was at the door and being greeted by Grandpa, "Hi, Tim. Come in. Are you on your way back to school?"

"Yes, I have to buy my books tomorrow, and classes start the following day."

"Glad you could stop. You take a couple of chairs and put them in the shade of the redwood tree, while

I start squeezing the lemons."

I set up the two chairs near a small table in the shade of the redwood tree. I inhaled deeply and savored the smell of the fallen foliage that had been heated by the sun. It was good to be here. I walked back toward the house. Before I reached the kitchen door, I could already smell the lemons.

"I won't put much sugar, that way you know you're drinking something," said Grandpa.

I smiled and looked at Grandpa's very wrinkled face. It was very good to be with him.

"You're studying to be a teacher, aren't you?"

"Yes, this is my last year." I watched as Grandpa sprinkled a little sugar into the lemonade and started stirring it.

"Here, you take the pitcher, and I'll get the glasses."

We walked side by side across the grass to where the chairs were. Grandpa sat down as I poured the lemonade.

"You know, your great grandfather was a teacher," he said.

"I think I heard that."

"When he passed away, his brother made a list of all his things and asked us all what we'd like to have to remember him by. He didn't have a lot. A few tools, some clothes, and some books." Then, Grandpa took an old-looking piece of paper from his pocket and put it on the table along with a very scratched-up, old compass.

I took a sip of the lemonade. "Wow, this stuff sure is strong."

Grandpa smiled, sipped his lemonade, and picked up the folded piece of paper from the table. "After the passing of your great grandfather I went traveling overseas. When I got back, I found a package from my uncle. Inside, there was this letter, that old compass, and a redwood seedling that looked completely dead. The letter was written by my uncle and I want to read you parts of it."

Grandpa unfolded the letter and began to read, "You will recall that I wrote you several months ago about my brother's things and gave you each an opportunity to choose something. When I wrote the letter, I had no idea of the response I'd get. Here are just a few of the many replies:

'Dear Uncle, Thanks for thinking of me. If nobody has asked for it, I'd love to have his compass.'

'Dear Grandpa, I don't really want much but I'd love to have his compass. He seemed like such a directed person, that his compass is something I would treasure. If you have already given it to someone else, it's okay, but if not, please send me the compass.'

'Dear Uncle Carl, if you haven't yet decided what to do with his compass, please send it to me.'

These were just three of the twenty-five replies I got. Only one of the twenty-five didn't ask for the compass."

Grandpa and I both sipped some more lemonade, as I glanced at the old compass on the table. Grandpa continued to read from the letter, "I didn't know what to do. How could I choose one out of twenty-four to give the compass to? I contacted the company that made the compass and found that they still had a few of the same model in stock. I ordered enough for everyone and then arranged for them to be engraved the same way the original was. Then, I took my brother's old canvas knapsack and put all of the compasses inside. I threw it in the back of my pick-up truck and left it there for a few months. My thought was that the original compass would teach the others all they needed to know, and they would all get scratched up together. Now I have enclosed one of those compasses chosen at random from the knapsack along with this redwood seedling. My brother loved these trees; please plant it some place in his honor."

Grandpa folded the letter and continued with his part of the story. "The tree looked so sickly I was sure it would never grow. I was feeling all kinds of emotions and I started to cry. I took the seedling and put it into a basin of water. Still crying, I got a pick and shovel, went outside, and started to dig. I dug until after it was dark. I wasn't totally sure why I was even digging. I was sure the seedling was already dead, but maybe digging the hole would make me feel better. Around eight o'clock at night, I filled the hole with the best soil I could find and, then, set a sprinkler near it.

"I took the redwood seedling, and with the sprinkler still spraying, I planted the tree in the hole. I watered it every day for a month and sure enough, it started to grow."

Grandpa paused, wiped his eyes, and sipped his lemonade. I looked at the redwood tree that was now tall and providing us with shade.

Grandpa smiled at me and said, "Yes, this is that

tree and these are for you." With that, he handed me the compass and the letter.

I rubbed the compass between my thumb and my fingers. I looked up again at the tree and then looked back at the compass. I turned it over and opened the cover. The needle spun around and settled—pointing to the north. A multitude of emotions surged through my mind. I could feel tears welling up in my eyes. I gazed at the redwood tree in anticipation of something I could only dimly feel. To keep from crying, I sipped my lemonade. I looked at Grandpa, and then looked back at the compass that I was holding in my hand. A tear fell onto the compass. Suddenly I felt like this special redwood tree was calling me to sleep at its feet. I looked at Grandpa and tried to put words together to describe everything I felt. Grandpa just smiled, leaned forward, and handed me a pillow from the back of his chair.

Then, without words, he walked toward the house. I laid down on the grass facing the redwood tree. The warm summer wind blew over me as I put my head on the pillow and then set the compass in front of me. As the compass needle swung and settled pointing to the north, my head felt heavy against the pillow. Soul-refreshing sleep came quickly, promising fresh dreams of old places, and of ancestors I had never met.

Cooked Carrots

Mrs. Albright was a nurse, so she had plenty of reasons to worry. Willy had been a sickly boy as long as she could remember. Colds, ear infections, anemia—you name it, Willy had it at least once. Dr. Jordan spent lots of time with the Albright family, but most of it was centered around Willy. One fine day in June, Dr. Jordan ended his consultation with ominous sounding words, "I need to see you and your husband together—as soon as possible. Please arrange an appointment for later this week."

Mrs. Albright, who was a bit taken aback, responded with, "Can you tell me exactly what is the problem, and I will explain it to my husband? As you know, I am a nurse, and my husband is a very busy man."

Dr. Jordan smiled once, as he looked up from Willy's thick file. He peered over his round glasses and said, "I'm afraid I need to see you both together. Please find a suitable time as soon as possible."

Mrs. Albright felt slightly insulted, but thanked the doctor for his time and went to make an appointment with the receptionist. Three days later, the whole family returned. The nurse called Willy first. She checked his weight, his blood pressure, and then ran a few basic tests. A few minutes later, the entire family was guided into Dr. Jordan's office.

After a few formalities, Dr. Jordan listened to Willy's chest, looked into his ears, and asked him how he was feeling. Then Dr. Jordan settled behind his paper-strewn desk, as the Albrights waited anxiously for the news they were about to receive. Dr. Jordan finally broke the silence, "Willy, can you wait in the reception area for a few minutes?"

Willy nodded his head, stood up, and then carried his slender, lifeless body out of the office.

Mr. Albright, who was a take-charge kind of man, couldn't stand waiting any longer and blurted out, "Dr. Jordan, what is wrong with Willy? What does he need?"

Dr. Jordan closed the two-inch-thick file and scanned the eyes of the two parents who sat before him. "As you both know, Willy has been sick for a long time. He is thirteen years old, underweight; he's anemic, has very little energy, and gets very little exercise as a result. He has swallowed more vitamins in his few short years than most people do in a lifetime. He has taken so many antibiotics that they now have little effect on him." He opened the file again and pulled out a small piece of paper with typing from side to side. "What Willy needs now is both unique and expensive."

"Whatever it takes," said Mr. Albright.

"Nothing is too expensive for our little Willy," echoed Mrs. Albright.

The doctor continued, "I want you to read this

prescription. I had it typed so that there can be no misunderstanding. He handed the small paper to Mr. Albright who reached for his glasses, while Mrs. Albright leaned over and started reading, "What Willy needs is more time with his father. He needs exercise, sunlight, and plenty of fresh air. He needs to go on a trip with his father to the Alps for at least three weeks. He needs to camp or stay in a simple wilderness cabin, without TV, without radio, without video games, without newspapers, but with his father alone. He needs to walk with his father in alpine meadows, to eat lots of fruit and to avoid fried foods for the whole twenty-one days."

Dr. Jordan stared at the forehead of Mr. Albright, until once again he could see into the eyes of the two loving parents who sat before him. Mr. Albright, began shaking his head, "It's impossible. I would have to take three weeks off from work."

Dr. Jordan smiled and said, "Exactly! That's exactly what Willy needs. And by the way, your health will improve also."

Mr. Albright was at a loss for words, but Mrs. Albright was not, "It's okay, Carl," she said, "I will take him. I will cook him lots of green vegetables and carrots, and he will come back better. That would be okay, wouldn't it, Dr. Jordan?"

Dr. Jordan peered over his glasses at the Albrights, smiled once, and then said, "I'm afraid not. He needs his father more than cooked carrots."

"And what if we are not able to do this?" asked Mr. Albright.

Dr. Jordan paused for a long time and then said, "I'm afraid you'll have to find a new doctor."

"You mean a specialist?"

"No, a family doctor."

"For Willy?"

"No, for the whole family. I can only help patients if they are willing to follow my advice. It makes no sense for you to keep bringing Willy here, if you are unable to accept my best opinion as to what should be done. Think it over if you like, and if you agree to the treatment, bring Willy in as soon as you return—you don't need an appointment."

Dr. Jordan started to stand up to bid the two parents good-bye, when Mr. Albright asked, "How sure are you that this will work?"

"Eighty percent. Thanks for coming in, and if you decide to change doctors, just phone the receptionist, and we will send the files to the new doctor. There are plenty of good doctors here in Stolberg; you need not feel ashamed of such a decision."

The Albrights shook hands reluctantly with Dr. Jordan and then walked out of the office. They were not yet sure if they would ever return.

A month later, Dr. Jordan was alone in his office, when the intercom buzzed. The receptionist told him that Willy Albright and his father were there to see him. Dr. Jordan replied, "Weigh him, check his vitals, and then send them both in."

A few minutes later, the receptionist knocked, and then came in with Willy's thick file, followed by a smiling Mr. Albright and Willy. The doctor greeted them both and asked them to sit down. He opened the thick file, and looked at the most recent results. Dr Jordan nodded his head approvingly, and then smiled.

He walked over to Willy, switched on his otoscope, and looked into Willy's ears. He looked into Willy's throat and asked him to say, 'Ahhh.' Then, Dr. Jordan smiled again and said, "Wonderful, wonderful! All signs of the infection are gone. The eyes look healthy, and it looks like the anemia is gone. And how do you feel, Mr. Albright?"

Willy's father jumped slightly as he had been entranced by something he did not understand. Finally, after processing the question he said, "Actually, I feel better than I have in many years. We had a wonderful time together. We walked in the alpine meadows every day. I feel healthier than I have in at least ten years. Thank you very much. Should Willy resume his vitamins again?"

"I'll leave that to you. Sometimes, common sense goes a lot further than medical science."

"Should we bring Willy back in soon?"

"Next year should be soon enough."

The two men stood up, looked deeply into each other's eyes, and then shook hands. Willy stood up slowly and looked at the two men who had helped him to feel well again. After shaking hands, Willy walked towards the door with his father close behind him.

Dr. Jordan remained standing as he watched the two well-tanned men stride out of his office. He looked at Willy's thick file, and then glanced at the wastepaper basket. He decided against his impulse, and instead sat down and took out a new file and a thick, felt pen. On the new file he wrote "Willy Albright," and then transferred only the most recent papers from Willy's old file. Dr. Jordan then took the old file and crossed out Willy's name with the felt pen. He wrapped a large rubber band around the file, and wrote in large letters, "How Not to Treat Chronic Diseases in Children." He placed the thick file on a shelf marked "research," smiled slightly, and then, while holding down the button on the intercom, asked the receptionist to send in the next patient.

A Cure for Loneliness

It was probably one of those habits we pick up from our parents—in this case, from my father. Every summer we would hike in the mountains. Whenever we'd pass a stream, we'd bend down, put our heads into the water, and then drink. For me, it became my ritual ablutions—something I just had to perform.

Now, here—halfway around the world—I was thirsty. There was plenty of tea and plenty of fizzy drinks, but there is nothing like the pure water from a mountain spring. Beyond that, I was thirsty for genuine human contact.

I was in the midst of two cultures. The first one had developed over many thousands of years as the descendants of the original inhabitants of this land adapted to their environment. The second culture grew as immigrants from other places arrived and resisted becoming part of the first culture. As a member of the second cultural group, there were clearly things you didn't do. And this "not doing" kept you apart from the native peoples. Since I had only lived here for a few months, I fell into the category of the immigrants. People in this group worked hard to acculturate any newcomers. This created more confusion in my heart. I had come here to be with the people of the land, but I was constantly being told hundreds of good reasons why I should resist getting "too close."

Drinking water from the ground was one of those things that "my group" did not do. While it is true that there are some real health risks, for the most part, the many warnings seemed far from scientific. Nevertheless, I didn't do it—at least in the beginning.

One day I was walking alone, feeling hot, tired, and very lonely. This was a loneliness I didn't really understand. I had lived by myself before, but never had felt so lonely. As I tried to find a balance between the two cultures, I was discovering that I didn't fit well into either one. On this particular day, I was walking near a small village. As I walked, the feeling of loneliness intensified. My shirt was half-soaked in sweat. The ground around me was sloping, but not steep. There were a few boulders strewn about. Yellow grass was everywhere, except for a patch of green near a group of small trees. I stopped walking near the trees and watched the water pouring out of the mountain. It ran a short distance and then disappeared into the ground again. The water came out from between a few stones and then flowed across a small shelf of rock about the length of my outstretched arms.

It was a stunning and beautiful sight. There were no people and no signs that people or even animals ever came here. My loneliness vaporized as I stood staring at this beautiful spring flowing from the mountain. All my fears of water-borne diseases disappeared as the beauty of this place overcame my heart.

I knelt reverently in front of this altar of nature, cupped my hands, and poured many handfuls of water over my head. Bending nearer to the water, I half submerged my face and began to drink. With each swallow of water, a little more of my fear slipped away. A great feeling of oneness ran through my heart and soul.

Feeling contented, I lay down with my head in the shade. Peace surrounded my body and filled my heart. I closed my eyes and fell asleep. The loneliness was gone. I dreamt of playing with the children of this land and greeting their fathers and mothers. In the dream, I visited many villages and slept in huts made of soil with roofs of yellow grass. I saw myself sharing fires in the evening and accepting food I was lovingly offered.

Waking up slowly, I realized that it was fear that had created my loneliness, and that for me, there was no more healing medicine—than the pure water—of a mountain spring.

Dandelion Coffee

I filled the kettle with water and put it on the stove to boil. I pulled opened the curtains to let the morning sun fill the kitchen with light. This was my favorite time of the day. My morning coffee was like a ritual to me. It was a time without structure, where my mind could drift—a time of transition from the world of dreams, to the world where dreams become reality. I moved closer to the window and turned to let the sunlight warm my back. I picked up the new jar of coffee and started reading the label.

This coffee is made from one hundred per cent organically grown dandelion roots. They are grown on our family farm, on Low Gap Road, just outside of Ukiah. This coffee is dedicated to the memory of my great grandmother. We have included her picture and her story. We hope you enjoy the story and the coffee.

The Story of Dandelion
I was ten years old when my grandfather gave me the name Dandelion. I had been fascinated with dandelions for

as long as I could remember. Like any other child, it didn't take me long to discover what happens when you blow on the fluffy seed balls. I spent hours in the meadows blowing the fluffy heads into the wind, and then chasing them until they landed.

Just before the time of the big removal, my grandfather came to me one day and said, "Come here, Dandelion. Grandfather wants to speak with you."

I ran to him and said, "Grandfather, while it is true that I love dandelions, my name is Yellow Bird."

My grandfather motioned for me to sit down and said, "As the wind blows, things change. Yesterday your name was Yellow Bird, today it is Dandelion."

I wasn't sure what to think about this, but I responded politely, as this was our custom. Then my grandfather continued, "The dandelion gives us many things. We eat the leaves for strength, the root is good for illness, and the yellow flowers remind mothers of the warm sun. Some tribes harvest the seeds for food, and children everywhere love to blow them into the wind. Isn't this true, Dandelion?"

I nodded my head.

"Words are like the seeds of the dandelion. When you speak them, the wind carries them in the four directions. If you speak good words and tell good stories, they travel across the great rivers and beyond the great seas. If you speak unkindly of others, these seeds travel just as far. Once blown in the wind, you cannot catch them and put them back on the stem. Do you understand?"

I nodded my head and said, "As the seasons pass, I will remember these words, and given time, I will understand their many meanings."

"Good," said my grandfather as he walked away and left me wondering if I would really be called Dandelion from now on. Later, when I returned home, my mother addressed me by my new name, confirming that it was a permanent change.

As I grew older, I often thought about my love for these plants, but I had no idea that they had spread so far beyond our homeland: to the whole of the prairies, and beyond that to the whole world.

When the time of the big removal came, I cried. I did not want to leave our home and the trees and the rivers I knew. It all happened very fast. As the strange men came, and as my father and mother put what they could in the wagon, I ran to my meadow and picked a handful of dandelions. I wrapped them carefully in a soft piece of cloth. At least I would have dandelions in the new land to the south.

When we arrived in the new land, I spent many days searching for a meadow to play in. I didn't find a meadow, but I did find dandelions. I decided that someone from the north must have planted them there.

We stayed for many summers, and though I was married there, I remember little joy. Many people from our tribe left in search of a place they could really call home. My husband and I went with a small group who were moving to the west. The old ways of life seemed no longer useful. Many took new names and forgot the old ways.

I carried dandelion seeds with me again, just in case there were none in the land to the west. We traveled through land that was full of tumbleweeds and sand. The trip was long and every day was hot.

When we arrived in the great valley, it was still very

hot, and life again was very difficult. We had no land of our own, so we followed the crops up and down the valley, as each needed planting or harvesting. The only familiar thing about life in the west was the dandelions. It seemed as if they had traveled everywhere. In spite of all that happened, no matter how bad things were, I always gained strength from the memory of my grandfather's words.

One summer, as we moved north, we heard stories of free land. The government was giving away land to those who would farm it. We traveled again, but this time it was not a long journey. When we arrived, I found dandelions — many dandelions. There were more dandelions here than I had ever seen. This was our new home. This was a good place for children and grandchildren.

We hope you enjoyed the story of our great-grandmother, as much as we enjoyed sharing it with you. All of us here on the farm, wish you true happiness, peace, and good health.

The water started to boil. I opened the new jar of coffee and put a rounded teaspoon of it in my favorite mug. I took the kettle off the stove, and poured the water into the mug. As I stirred the coffee, I noticed that the sunlight had now spread to the kitchen table. I walked across the room with my mug filled with dandelion coffee. I sat down and took a sip. I watched the steam rising from the mug and let my mind drift. Today there were many new thoughts to think. I wanted to think about health and what makes it; about gossip and why it is so common; about seeds, and how they spread; and about this interesting woman—called Dandelion.

●

Desert Walk

I bought an old VW and after six months of hard work, it was ready for anything. With extra clearance and extra wide tires, it could travel with ease through streams and over deserts. On Thursday, I studied the map. After work on Friday, I took off for my first weekend in the desert.

The plan was to head up old Route 66, camp for the night near a small town, fill up with fuel, and then head out a county road that looked like it went to nowhere. I suspected there was an abandoned gold mine at the end of the road.

On Saturday morning, I pulled into the gas station to fill up and to let someone know where I was headed. The gas station owner was my last contact before I left civilization. He said, "Ain't nothing up there but sand and cactus."

"Ever hear of an old gold mine out there?" I asked.

"Yep, I heard so and there's an Indian reservation to boot—even that's dying. The young Indians don't want to live there, and the old ones don't want to leave."

I thanked the gas station owner and pulled back onto the highway. The engine was purring along without effort. A numbered signpost alerted me to the road I planned to take. I pulled over, checked the map, and decided that this was my road.

As the early morning sun continued to rise, I pushed further into the solitude of the desert. After a few hours, I stopped to cool off. A sheet of canvas and two wooden poles made a fine place to enjoy my lunch.

An hour later, I came to half of a sign swinging on the last of four bolts. The only word left on it was "reservation." I checked the map. This was the turnoff to the Indian reservation. I didn't want to think about the sign and all the history behind it. Too much prejudice and too much hatred had led to a lot of death and degradation.

I pulled back onto the sand road and noted that the last tire tracks turned into the reservation. I tried to put these thoughts out of my head and drove towards my destination. Three hours later, I came to the end of the road. Just as I expected, there was an old mine there. A few parts of buildings stood out against the bright desert sand. The old wooden planks were smooth from the blowing sand and bleached gray by the ever-present sun. I set up camp and soaked in the solitude.

The next morning, I took some photographs and then packed up. I took a deep breath and braced myself for the return to civilization. My eyes surveyed the mine for the last time, as I turned the key in the ignition. The engine turned over okay, but it did not start. I tried again. I glanced at the fuel gauge; it read half-full. I thought the problem must be something simple. A strong smell of gasoline let me know that I had flooded the engine. I removed the large air filter and placed it carefully in the sun. I waited an hour before trying again. Better to be a bit patient than face the alternative.

I replaced the air filter and was now confident that it would start. A wave of fear went through my body as the engine turned over without firing. I pushed aside my emotions and thought through the situation. Soon the battery would die, the last phone I had seen was at the gas station, and the nearest signs of human life were the tire tracks that led into the Indian reservation. If the car would not start, I would have to walk. After trying everything I could think of, I decided that the problem was a faulty coil. All logic collapsed as my options were reduced to one.

Given that I had at least a four-day walk, I thought it was best to wait for nightfall. I sat down in the shade of one of the old buildings and tried to remain calm. I carefully selected things to take: the map, a compass, a pocket knife, a little food, a small piece of cloth for sleeping under, and all the water I could carry. Then, I lay down to rest.

Later, as the sun was setting, I got up, packed, and started walking. The first few hours were actually quite pleasant. I stopped thinking about the situation I was in, and enjoyed the cool night air. Much later, my feet started to hurt and my stomach began to cramp. There was nothing to do, but to ignore the pain and keep walking.

As the sun rose, ending my first night's walk, I

found some large cactus plants to tie my canvas between. As careful as I was, my hands still got scratched in the process.

It was not easy to sleep. By five in the afternoon, I knew I should start again. I gently brushed the sand from my blistered feet and placed them back into the same socks. I laced my boots carefully. I struggled to get to my feet, packed my canvas, adjusted my hat, and started walking again. It was very hard. The pain from my blistered feet was intense, and I could feel the effects of the sun and the insects on my face. I stopped thinking normally.

After three more nights of walking, there was nothing left on my body that didn't hurt. The sand became a magnet, pulling against my efforts to continue to stumble forward. Hallucinations were a constant companion.

Near the end of the fifth night, in the midst of some stumbling dream, I started to hear an occasional thumping sound. As I walked forward, it grew louder. Then a squeaking sound began to accompany it. I stopped and strained to look. I could see some movement. I walked towards it and realized that it was the sign to the reservation, swinging in the pre-dawn breeze.

I summoned the last bit of logic in my brain. Do I continue straight into town or turn to the reservation? From my study of the map, I remembered that the reservation was fairly small and about a mile off this road. I turned toward it without further thought. The sun was rising in front of me. Each step was a great effort. I heard the faint barking of a dog. The sun was blinding as I walked towards it. I saw the outline of a building, and I heard human voices. I saw shadows and then someone spoke to me. My legs gave way, as my mind knew I was no longer alone.

When I woke up, I was on a bed in a mud brick hut. My eyes burned. My legs and feet hurt. I looked at my hands. They were covered with scratches and blisters.

I looked to my right and saw an elderly man whose face was dark and soft like wrinkled leather. He looked at me and spoke, saying, "I am Gray Wolf. You are welcome in my house."

I felt a great sense of comfort and peace. Not the peace of being alone and not something you'd ever feel in the city. I fell asleep.

Over the next few days, Gray Wolf and his wife nurtured me back to health. I started to enjoy being there. The lack of running water and electricity was no real burden. Even the trips to the outhouse became pleasant as the desert quiet became part of me. I began to realize that if it were necessary to remain here forever, I wouldn't miss much.

The next day, the son of Gray Wolf came for a visit. He lived four hours' drive from there, and was only able to visit once a month. He brought gifts of food and soap and other basic things.

He was a mechanic and offered to try to fix my car. As we drove towards my car, we spoke about old ways and new ways. Soon after we arrived at the old mine, he discovered a loose wire into the coil. Five minutes later, we were driving back towards Route 66. In spite of the dust, I stayed close behind him. When we came to the road to the reservation, he kept going straight. I could not. I had grown very close to Gray Wolf. I had to thank him and say good-bye before driving back home.

Gray Wolf seemed surprised that I had stopped. He suggested that I stay and rest another night before leaving. I thought about my job, about the love I felt for this home in the desert, and decided to stay one more night.

The next morning, I said good-bye again and then drove off slowly. Driving on the sandy road that morning was not fun. Hot tears poured from my eyes as I drove back toward civilization, feeling emotions I didn't understand. Before turning back onto Route 66, I stopped and got out. The cars driving east and west looked odd. I looked back in the direction of the reservation, poured water over my face and hands and thought about Gray Wolf. I took a sip of water, got back into the car, and headed back to the city. Though I had only set out for a weekend's adventure, and had no real expectations, I had gained something much deeper and life would never be quite the same again.

●

Dream Focus

"Hello, I'm Mitzi Wright."

"Welcome to New Zealand, and welcome to Phoenix House. You are in room 134, here is your key, and there's a letter for you." The letter was from my Uncle Alan. I took the key and the letter, said thank you, and walked to my room. I unlocked the door, set my bags next to the bed, sat down on the bed, and then opened the letter.

Dear Mitzi,

I know you are just getting settled into life there at the university and you are likely very busy, but I felt moved to write you this letter with the enclosed article.

A few weeks ago, I was sent on assignment to Switzerland to cover the International World Music Festival in Interlaken. There is nothing special about my being sent on assignment to the festival; I have been there twice before. However, the reason I am writing to you is my meeting with a man by the name of Joe Shoemaker. I had never heard of Joe before the festival, and he is still a relatively unknown person in the international music world. What is most exciting about Joe is not his music, but the story behind his music. Take a look at the highlighted portions of the enclosed article.

I put the letter on the bed and picked up the article from World Music. There was a big picture of Joe Shoemaker playing a violin, and a small picture of Uncle Alan. The headline read: "Joe Shoemaker Wins Most Sweet Violin Award." Then the article started:

Joe Shoemaker, a resident of Alabama, has won the 'Most Sweet Violin' award in Interlaken, Switzerland. This year, the contestants had to pick two diverse tunes that are indirectly connected, explain the connection between the songs, and then play them for the judges. Mr. Shoemaker chose two songs connected with the history of African-Americans. He explained his choices in his opening remarks. "My name is Joe Shoemaker, he said. "The two songs I have chosen to play are Follow the Drinking Gourd and Amazing Grace. The first is a folk song written for slaves in search of freedom. Outwardly, it contains geographic instructions for those who considered escaping to freedom; but inwardly, it seems to contain spiritual instructions to help anyone find inner peace. It was written by a man who went by the name of Peg Leg Joe in the early eighteen hundreds. The second song is Amazing Grace. This song was written by John Newton who was, at one time, a slave trader and later became a clergyman."

After Mr. Shoemaker's explanation, and after his wonderful versions of the two songs, there were very few dry eyes in the audience. After a standing ovation, the audience forced an encore by refusing to sit down or stop clapping until the judges allowed him to play again.

I put the article on the bed and picked up Uncle Alan's letter again:

Mitzi, there is no way I can explain how moving it was. The ink from my notes ran all over the page due to the tears flowing from my eyes. After Joe finished playing, I had two things I wanted to accomplish. First, I wanted to meet him personally, and secondly I wanted to write a more extended article on his life. We agreed to meet the next morning before breakfast and go for a walk in the mountains. After submitting the brief article, which you have just seen, I phoned my editor for permission to write a more detailed article on Joe Shoemaker. As of this moment, it is not clear if the in-depth article will be published or not, but I wanted to share part of the information with you. It's an amazing story. Following are excerpts from my notes:

It was 5:30 AM when I knocked on the door to his room. We walked out of the hotel, down the street a short distance, and then turned toward the mountains.

"So, how long have you been playing the violin?" I asked him.

"A little over a year."

"Excuse me?"

"I have been playing the violin a little over a year."

"Do the judges know that?"

"They didn't ask."

"Do you understand that there are people here who have been playing for more than forty years, and they didn't play half as well as you did?"

"I had advantages that they didn't have."

"Really, like what?"

"Well to begin with, the two songs are about a theme which cries out to the hearts of humanity. The melodies entrance all but the most empty of hearts. Lastly, I had the help of a special machine."

"You mean a special violin?"

"No, I mean a Dream Focuser."

"A what?"

"A Dream Focuser. About forty years ago, I found it in a secondhand store. I didn't have any idea what it was really for. A few years later, I located a modern version of the same machine. I bought an instruction manual for the newer model and though it didn't work exactly the same, I could figure it out. After that, every month, I would tell it my dreams."

"You'd tell a machine your dreams?"

"Yes, I would speak into a microphone those plans and schemes we usually refer to as dreams. The Dream Focuser translates the dreams into a few words and compares them with previous sessions. Each month, it prints out a report that shows the seven dreams that had been repeated the most often. In other words, those things that were mere passing fancies would not be repeated, and the machine would not print them on the dream report. But there were some things that would always be there. Then the machine would ask me what prevented me from attaining each of my dreams. The most common answers were time, money, or fear.

"Eventually, one by one, I started finding ways to turn those dreams into reality. I learned to overcome the fear of failure. I learned that we humans can do almost anything. I

also learned to spend money on things that are goal-oriented. Learning to play the violin was one of my dreams that kept coming up on the report. A year ago, I bought a violin and took some lessons. That is how I started playing the violin."

After listening to Joe Shoemaker's incredible story, we turned back toward town. I was still shaking my head in disbelief as the rising sun was breaking over the mountains to the east of us. When we reached town Joe headed for his hotel, and I returned to the festival.

Now a few days later, I am on an airplane headed home. I know that you are a person of many dreams, and I thought I should share this story with you. It has given me many things to think about, and I assume it will do the same for you.

Good luck in your first year at college!

Warmest love,
Uncle Alan

Dream Works

It was 4 a.m. It was at that time in your night's rest when dreams get good and getting up gets hard. I pulled the blankets tightly around my neck and returned for the last round of sleep. Then, I had a most vivid and unusual dream.

The sign said, "Welcome to Dream Works." The building was like a large football stadium. The man near the sign gave me a ticket and said, "No charge, step right up, welcome, welcome, come right in."

Then, a friendly-looking woman dressed in a light blue suit said, "First group over here. We'll start our tour in five minutes." While waiting, I looked around. There were many walls and many floors, but you could see through them all.

"Okay, everyone, listen up," said the woman. "My name is Gertrude. I want to officially welcome you to Dream Works, where all your dreams are made. The purpose of this visit is not to make requests or cheat the system; it is just to have a tour so you can understand how things work here. By the end of the tour, you should understand how dreams are created and delivered. Please hold any questions you might have until the end of the tour. Okay, let's start by walking over here."

When Gertrude said, "walking," I have to tell you, it wasn't like normal walking. We all took a step in the direction she did, and then we were there! Even if you were not paying attention and the group moved, you moved with them. It didn't seem to matter if you were walking up or down; you always got there in one step.

Gertrude continued, "Here you see the request-processing section. The people working here receive all the wishes, desires, and prayers of those who will receive dreams. These requests come from individuals and from groups. Each day all the requests are dumped into this hopper."

"Excuse me," said an elderly man, "but how do these requests get here?"

Gertrude smiled and replied in a friendly but very firm way, "Please hold your questions for the end." The man apologized and we all moved on.

"Over here," continued Gertrude, "we divide and sort the requests into three categories. You can see that after the hopper, they get cut up into individual requests, and then they get color-coded."

"Looks like they get shredded," said a woman next to me, sparking off a murmur of laughter.

Gertrude ignored the laughter and went on, "You see when these requests are made, they often get intertwined, and this process sorts them out into individual requests."

I could see little pieces of paper that had short requests on them. Each had a bar code printed on it, which I assumed had to do with the source of the request. I restrained my desire to ask a question but made a mental note to ask about this at the end of the tour.

"Over here, you can see that these requests go through another machine, which changes the color from white to either green, yellow, or red. Basically, the green ones will get a dream, which will set in motion a process that will grant the request. Requests are granted when they are either in the best interest of the person concerned or for the whole world. The red ones will not be granted, but a dream will be created and delivered to help the person gain a better understanding of what is best for them.

"Now, the yellow ones are more complex. These requests are more situational. They may require another matching request or may need to wait for a certain event to occur before being granted. They may be put on hold for a future time. Without exception, all requests are dealt with."

Gertrude said, starting to walk again, "Now we will move to the Scripting Section. Here, these workers take the requests and write scripts for each of the dreams."

The workers were taking the requests, looking at them, and then placing their hand on a machine in front of them. Next, a paper would fly out of the machine and the operator would attach the request to the script and place it back on the conveyer belt.

"From here," Gertrude continued, "the script goes through a cultural symbolator. This symbolator translates the symbols used by the script into culturally understood symbols. I'm afraid we are short-staffed in the scripting department. We do not have enough writers with cultural experience to represent all the requests we get, so we must rely on machines.

"In a similar way, over here we have a translating machine, because we need to respond in hundreds of different languages. Over here, we have Central Casting. In this section the modified scripts are actually acted out."

The woman next to me seemed a bit frustrated and whispered to me, "I wonder how they get people with all the language experience here, if they are so short in the other section." Not wanting to miss anything, I just looked at her, shrugged my shoulders, and said nothing.

I watched as the requests came into Central Casting. Each time a request came off the belt, a group of actors appeared, passed the request around, and then like a movie run in high speed, they quickly acted out the script. Next, a man threw a big net above their heads, catching the dreams as they were created. Then each dream would be wrapped up in something like a big, transparent balloon. It was amazing to see the balloons float off in an orderly manner.

We "walked" again, and Gertrude announced, "This section is Broadcasting. This is where the scheduling and broadcasting of the dreams is done. I don't have a lot of technical understanding, so I won't try to explain exactly how it works." Then she took a deep breath, smiled, and said, "Well that's about it. We hope you have had a pleasant visit and go back with more knowledge than you had before."

A dozen hands went up. "Ah yes," Gertrude said, "question time." "I will allow five minutes for questions, so long as no alarm goes off. First, yes, you, the little girl in the yellow dress."

The little girl started to frame her question, "Early in the tour you stated that…"

"Ringggg, Ringggg."

I heard the faint voice of Gertrude saying, "Sorry, time up." My eyes opened slowly, not knowing quite where I was, or where I had been. The clock said 6 a.m. I reached over and switched off the alarm and then held my head very still-trying to review what I had seen. Finally, I sat up and put my two bare feet on the carpet next to my bed. I stared at my feet against the pattern of the small carpet. There wasn't anything else to do, so I laughed, shook my head once, and stood up to start my day. It was quite a dream!

The Early Ones

"Hello!"

"Are you talking to me?"

"Yeah, how are you?"

"I'm getting better, thanks."

"Have you been here long?"

"Long enough for them to change those things they wrap around us about twenty times."

"Oh, that's not so long. I've been here almost thirty days."

"Thirty days?"

"Sorry, I was making an assumption. You see that round thing on the wall with the black arms that go around?"

"Uh huh."

"Well each time that big arm goes around twice, that's a day."

"Oh."

"What are you in for?"

"They say I was early."

"Yeah, me too, but I was real early."

"Oh"

"Where did you come from?"

"I'm not sure, but there wasn't this much light there."

"Yeah, it's sometimes hard to sleep here - everything is so much louder here."

"You can say that again."

"Hearing seems to be very different. Before, when you heard something, it was sort of feeling and hearing and dreaming all at once."

"I never thought about it that way, but you're right. I'm sure we came from the same place."

"I think so. You remember that tree?"

"Oh yeah, that was powerful. Each time I was called, I wasn't sure if I was afraid or if I was falling in love. Those were some powerful lessons."

"And did you notice the cycles?"

"You mean like when it got real dark and quiet?"

"Yeah, that's when your mother was sleeping."

"Really, what's a mother?"

"Sorry, I made another assumption. Your mother is the one who carried you around through all those cycles."

"Oh, I remember her. She was real sweet."

"And what did you like best?"

"You mean before I got here?"

"Yes."

"Hmm, well those lessons under the tree—I don't even know how to describe those, but besides that, it was the singing and the stories that my mother would tell me."

"What do you mean?"

"Each day—it is 'days' you call them, isn't it?"

"Yes."

"Well, each day, before and after she slept, she

would tell me stories, and she would sing to me."

"Really?"

"Yes, really. Those were real nice times."

"Sounds like it."

"And then there were the science lessons and the mathematics."

"Science and mathematics?"

"Yeah, I don't think I have the vocabulary to explain it to you, but it all made sense to me."

"You know a lot for a new kid."

"Thanks, I think it was those times when my mother would sing and tell me stuff."

"Kind of like the lessons under the tree?"

"Yeah, sort of. Not as powerful, but similar."

"Oh, here come those people dressed in white. I think it's time for a change."

"That'll be nice. I think I'll go to sleep after that."

Far Too Precious

"What happened to you, Grandpa?"

"What do you mean?"

"You and Grandma used to argue over little things all the time. Now, I never see you arguing with anyone."

"It's not worth wasting your life away, it's just not worth it," said Grandpa.

I thought about his words until he started to speak again. "Do you remember a couple of years ago when I had a heart attack?"

"Yes, we all remember that. You were in a coma for several weeks."

"That's right, I was in a coma for twenty-one days, and I had one very long dream. I have no way of knowing how long the dream really took."

"Just like any other dream, I suppose."

"Yes, it was like any other dream, but this one covered the whole of my life. The dream started in a large outdoor market. There were people running back and forth and shouting to buy this and buy that.

"Suddenly, someone called my name and shouted, 'Come play the game of life.' I followed the voice and walked inside a tent where I saw a large green table with a single light hanging over it. As I stepped up to the table, someone said, 'Let's get started.' A machine on one side of the table spit out a card with a picture on it as someone said, 'Day one.' I looked closely at the picture on the card and I saw the sunrise, and then I saw my own birth. As the sun set, I heard the most beautiful music I have ever heard, and then someone with a gold-colored feather swept the card off the table into a large, golden bowl.

"Then someone shouted, 'Day two' and I saw the second day of my life. I saw the sunrise, and I saw the sunset. I heard the music and watched the card as it was swept into the golden bowl. Days flew by like this, each sunrise and sunset followed by music and then the next card.

"At card number 750, something changed. I saw the sunrise like all the earlier days, and I saw myself playing as a small child. All of a sudden, someone with a stick with a nail in the end of it speared the card just before the sunset came and then unceremoniously dropped the card into a large garbage can. In my comatose-dream state, I thought it was odd, but paid little attention. As the days rolled on, there were more and more days that didn't make it into the golden bowl. By the time we reached card number 5000, most of the cards were going into the trash. Then there was a period of time when most of the cards went into the golden bowl.

"When I reached card number 9000, I saw the day I first met your grandmother. For several weeks, all the cards went into the golden bowl. I saw our marriage, and I saw your father's birth. Somewhere around card number 9500, most of the cards were going into the trash again. I began to notice that the timing of the spearing of the cards was almost always when I was arguing with someone. Usually the arguments were over trivial things like which year we went to a particular place or arguing over politics or sports. Only rarely were the arguments over anything of substance.

"I started crying each time I saw the cards speared and thrown into the trash, realizing that much of my life was wasted. Apparently I began to cry out loud, and it gave the doctors hope."

Grandpa took a deep breath and then I said, "I remember that time well, Grandpa. I got a call from my father saying that the doctors had hope of your recovery because you were speaking—even though you were still unconscious. I came to the hospital on the weekend, and I sat with you alone for an afternoon. You repeated, 'It's not worth it, it's just plain not worth it.' You said that several hundred times on the afternoon I was there."

Grandpa spoke again saying, "That sounds very familiar. Anyway, this strange dream, with this odd card game went on until I woke up. The moment I regained consciousness, the doctor was in the room speaking to your grandmother. I opened my eyes and said, 'I'm really tired of this. I don't think I have time for it anymore.' The doctor looked very surprised and then asked me how I felt.

"Ever since then, I don't argue with your grandmother or anyone else for that matter. Life is far too precious to risk having most of your days—thrown into the trash can."

The Flood at Flat Rock

Pretty much everyone knew Jackie. But then, everyone in Flat Rock County—knew pretty much everyone else too. Jackie was here when I first came, and that was twenty-five years ago. Unlike most of us, his father, and his father's father, had lived here too. His full name was Jackie Speaklittle and if you met him more than once, you'd understand why. It wasn't that he never spoke, it was just that he used his words sparingly and with great care. Last month before the storm, I remember meeting him in town.

"Hi, Jackie," I said.

"Hi."

"How's the wife and the kids?" I asked.

"Fine ... yours?"

"They are well. One of the kids has a cold, but nothing serious."

Then there was silence, something you never shared with most folks, but Jackie made it pleasant. There was no hurry. He'd listen to you, or listen with you—but he didn't talk much.

"What do you reckon about the weather this winter? Think it'll rain much?" I asked.

"Gonna rain plenty—big flood—big, big flood."

We both walked inside the shop to buy what we

had come for. Jackie's words continued echoing around my head. Folks around here said his grandfather was a rainmaker. Jackie spoke so little, that when he did, you thought about his words.

A week later when it started to rain hard, I remembered what he'd said. A few days later, an odd story started circulating round the county. I walked into The Flat Rock Feed and Grain where two elderly men were busy talking about it.

"You heard old Jackie has slipped a cog, didn't you?"

"I didn't hear nothing."

"Well, they say, he cut down a couple of tall trees, stripped all the braches off, and then leaned them against his two-story house."

"Really? Why on earth did he do that?"

"Well, I heard he told a few folks that it was gonna flood really bad this year."

"And then? So what are the trees for?"

"Well if you drive by his place, you'll see a good-sized boat on the top of his house."

"Really?"

"Yep, I swear it's true."

Having heard much more than I wanted to hear, I bought what I came for and headed home. I didn't much like the way some folks talked about each other—especially when they were talking about someone like Jackie, who never said an unkind word about anyone.

I was almost home when the rain started again. All of a sudden, I just felt like seeing Jackie—saying hello and seeing if he really thought we were in for a big flood. I turned the pick-up around and headed north. The dirt road that led to Jackie's was already mostly mud. As I drove up, I saw it. Sure enough, at least part of the story was true—there were two big trees leaning against his house, and a pretty good-sized boat propped up like it was in dry dock—sitting right on top of the house.

Jackie walked out the door and greeted me with a question, "Come to see for yourself?"

I felt my face turning red. I was glad I had not spread the story or even thought badly about Jackie. But the truth was -- I had come to see for myself, and trying to hide it from Jackie would be a waste of time. "Yeah, it seems your boat is famous," I said, still feeling a bit embarrassed.

He didn't reply, or even change his facial expression. Just like the flat rock that the county was named after, he didn't look either sad or happy—he just looked straight at me.

"I remember what you said to me at the store last week—about the winter."

Jackie still didn't speak. "You know I trust you … and I trust your judgment. You really think the water's gonna come that high?"

Jackie nodded his head once, but still didn't speak.

"You think I should do the same?"

He nodded again.

"And would you help me get a boat on my roof, if I buy one?"

Jackie nodded his head again.

"Okay, then, thanks. I best be going now ... and thanks—thanks a lot."

"You're welcome," he said.

As I drove down the muddy path toward the main road, I was struck with how much emotion and meaning he could pack into just a few words. It seemed like he was plugged in better than the rest of us.

All of the following week, it rained, and every day I thought about Jackie. Whenever I had to go to town, I'd hear talk all over about Jackie and his boat on the roof and "what did he know anyway." Each time I heard it, I just turned away. I didn't really care if Jackie was right or wrong, but I sure was beginning to understand what words were meant for.

A couple of days later, I saw a boat for sale in the newspaper. After a brief consultation with my wife, I drove to the bank, and then went to buy it. After I got home, I filled it up with water like a big bathtub—just to see if there were any leaks. After that, I emptied it out, dried it nicely, and then packed it with some food and blankets and such—all wrapped in plastic bags. Then I drove to Jackie's to see if he could come help me put it on the roof.

As I was stopping the truck, he walked out of his front door. He had on a yellow hard hat and was carrying his chain saw. He didn't even wait for me to ask. He just swung his chain saw into the back of the pickup, opened the door, and then climbed inside.

I couldn't think of what else to say, so I just said,

"Thanks."

As we drove along, I realized I'd never ridden with Jackie before. In fact, I'd never been inside his house, and he'd never been in mine. I wanted to change that soon. This was a good, kind man—the type of person who adds something to your family, instead of taking something away.

Jackie didn't even ask which trees he should cut. He just selected two that weren't far away from the house, cut them both down, and started clearing the limbs. I got my axe and helped with the branches. After about four hours of hard work, we had the two tree trunks lying at an angle on the roof. We got the boat into position and with the aid of some ropes, got it up on the roof. We covered it with a tarp, tied it all securely, and then came back down.

Jackie didn't waste any time admiring what we had done. He started cleaning up the branches and then put his chain saw in the back of the truck. He was just reaching for the door-handle of the pickup, when I asked him if he'd like some coffee.

"Nice," he said, and with that, we turned and walked back to the house. After introducing him to the family, we sat down and let the warm liquid flow into us both. A short time later, my three-year-old son walked over to Jackie, put his hands on his knee, and then looked up at him with pleading eyes. Jackie bent down, picked him up, and sat him on the table in front of him. There they sat, looking eye to eye, as Jackie started asking him questions. In those three minutes, Jackie spoke more words than I'd ever heard in the twenty-five years I've known him.

A week later, the talk of the town had dampened down. The river was rising fast and everyone knew that Jackie had been right. A few days after that, the river rose to the highest level in recorded history. Jackie and I spent two full days out in our boats, picking up people off their rooftops and out of trees. I felt honored to be there and to be helping out. I felt like I was a sergeant in Jackie's special army. I noticed that each time I picked up another family, the adults spent most of their time giving excuses or asking for forgiveness. I also noticed I didn't feel like saying much.

Since the time of the flood, I had discovered a new friend—a friend who had always been there. It wasn't like Jackie smiled at me any more than he did before, and he didn't greet me any more warmly than he greeted anyone else. But at least once a month, I'd go to his house, and we'd share some coffee—mostly in silence; and then every once in a while, he'd come by our house and add so much—to our small but growing family.

The Gift

After he was introduced, the president of the academy stood up and walked toward the front of the large concert hall. Each step seemed to be taken with an extra dose of thought and purpose. After reaching the podium, he removed a few note-cards from his pocket, cleared his throat, and then without any clear indication of what he would be speaking about—he began telling us a story.

"I was twenty-one when my grandfather died. That was over thirty years ago. It pains me to admit that I didn't really know him. I received an invitation to the reading of his last will and testament. It came from Peter Mackenzie and Partners, a legal firm that my grandfather used. I assumed Grandpa had left me some money, and since the trip was paid for—it seemed worth attending.

"Most of us didn't appreciate what he was trying to do for us; all we wanted was a check with a lot of zeros on it. We were all in for a shock.

"We sat there waiting for the lawyer to come in, speculating on who would get Grandpa's house, his car, his boat, and, of course, how much money we would each get. When Peter Mackenzie walked in, we cooled off a bit. He looked around the room with his penetrating eyes and made us all feel a little guilty about why we had come.

"Then he started speaking. 'You have all come here because you are a friend or a relative of the late James T. Conkey. If you came with expectations of a check, you can collect it now—it's on the table at the back of the room. That check is for your travel expenses in coming here and that's all. If you came expecting a large check, and if that's your only motivation to be here, you may as well leave now. But, I would encourage you to stay and hear the words of Mr. Conkey. He definitely cared for you. He went to a great deal of effort to create institutions for the betterment of mankind, and is now giving you an opportunity to be part of his vision.' Then Mackenzie warned us that my grandfather's will and testament was more like a medium-sized novel than a normal will. 'Since it is long, we have provided for lunch, dinner, and breakfast. We estimate it will take about seven hours to read the complete will, so we will take frequent breaks.'

"A lot of us started grumbling, asking out loud why we had to sit there if there wasn't any money for us. Some suggested that maybe it was a trick of my grandfather's—maybe if we sat through till the end we would get something special. Most of us stayed. Two of my cousins stood up, walked to Mr. Mackenzie, handed him a business card, and said, 'If there's a check for me—please send it.'

"The lawyer looked at them with his penetrating eyes, smiled and said, 'If there's a check for you, you can be assured—I'll send it.'

"After Mackenzie's eyes silenced the noise that resulted from the departure of my cousins, he started to read, 'The Last Will and Testament of Mr. James T. Conkey. To all my friends and relatives. I have lived a full life. I have had my share of tests and difficulties, but I tried my best to live a good life.

"'First of all, I want to thank and sing the praises of those who guided me along the way. There have been many. My mother and father who brought me into this life gave me all they could. They gave me food, and clothes and shelter. Given the level of understanding that they had, they educated me. They sent me to school where most of my teachers tried their best, and I thank each and every one of them for their efforts. There are some, however, who gave me a special gift. Those teachers helped me to find something deep inside. Those were the real educators in my life.'

"We sat there for over two hours, and listened to the wonderful things that my grandfather's teachers had done for him. I was bored stiff, but I thought that if I waited long enough, there would be gold at the end of this rainbow. Others were not so patient. They stood up, walked to the back of the room, collected their checks and left.

"Then there was a section about the informal teachers who had helped him at various times in his life. He spoke about a man named Dwight who, on a summer night, had given him the gift of music on a beach in Canada. He spoke of a farmer in Kenya whom he described as 'an Angel.' There was a lady he met on a bus in Israel, and a man he referred to as 'HD' whom he called a 'saint.' He spoke of people in places that I had never heard of.

"After lunch Peter Mackenzie continued with the reading of the will. 'Some of you claim a belief in the Almighty, while others of you claim that you have no belief. In my short time on this earth, I haven't found a great deal of correlation between what a person claims and what that person really does with his life. There are some whose actions are equal to their words, but these are one in a million. These are the real angels. They create harmony wherever they go. There is one in the room with you now.'

"Somebody mumbled something about Jessica and many of us scowled at her. Jessica looked straight ahead like she didn't even understand what was going on. We all figured this is where most of his money would go. Mackenzie had to ask us to quiet down and when we didn't, he stood up and announced that we were done for the day. Then, he slowly walked out of the room. It was only three-thirty and most of us felt insulted by his departure.

"Poor Jessica. She took a lot of abuse that evening. Everybody assumed that she was the 'one in million' referred to in the will. And we were all sure that she would get millions while the rest of us would get nothing. Those who were not openly criticizing her were trying to make friends with her. Finally, she burst into tears and left dinner early. We didn't see her again until the next morning.

"The next day not everyone turned up for breakfast, and there were even fewer who were on time for the reading. Peter Mackenzie walked in and acted like nothing had happened yesterday. Jessica, who sat close to the front, apologized for all of us. Mr. Mackenzie continued with the reading and went on for over an hour about people who were the real angels of this world.

"Then there was another hour or so about money, and about how having too much is deadly. He said, for many it was like a poison, and it had spoiled many friendships and been the cause of many wars. Then he went on and on about how he would not want to give us poison and that's why he didn't leave us each a big chunk of money.

"There was more grumbling, and we took a short break. When we came back in, Mr. Mackenzie said that the reading was almost over and that soon we would each understand how much James Conkey loved us. Then he told us that many of us would be offered a special gift. After that he began reading a long list of names. My name was among those he read. Then Mackenzie read the conditions of the gift: 'I have provided a significant amount of money in a general trust fund. Funds will be released to each of you for specific purposes against preset criteria and based on the best judgment of the executor of the trust. There are funds for travel, for further education, and for support of a non-profit organization of your choosing.'

"We found out that if we traveled around the

world on foot or by bicycle, there was an almost limitless pool of money. If you wanted to travel and live it up, you would get enough for a few months. None of this made sense to us, but we were promised a summarized version of the terms and conditions prepared by Peter Mackenzie and Partners.

"Then he explained about the money for studying. There was money to attend even the most expensive of schools for a year. But if we chose less expensive schools, there was an unlimited supply of money to study anything we wanted.

"And then we came to the part about the formation or support of a non-profit organization for the 'betterment of the world.' The conditions were that we had to set up such an organization based on solid business principles and it had to be of genuine use to mankind. Of course, Mackenzie would be involved in the approval of any such plans.

"Most of us really didn't get it. When Mackenzie said we were all done with the reading of the will, most of us just collected copies of the documents, picked up our checks, and walked away. There were a few who stayed and were still speaking to Mackenzie when I left.

"From there I went home and tried to forget about my grandfather—and his will. Much later in life, I decided I wanted to travel. One night, I had a dream, which reminded me of the time we had spent listening to my grandfather's will. The next morning I found the phone number of the lawyer and made a call to enquire if the money was still available. To my astonishment, Peter Mackenzie was still there, and he took my call. He told me the money was still available and encouraged me to use it.

"I set out on a trip that took me through all of South America, to many islands in the Pacific, to Australia, and then to Africa. I felt a strange attraction to the islands in the Indian Ocean and so I traveled to Madagascar. From there, I went to Mauritius and then to the Seychelles.

"While in the Seychelles, I fell in love with their music. Eventually I found there was a very small institute of music run by a man whose eyes reminded me of Peter Mackenzie's. His eyes sparkled when he spoke of music and sparkled even more when he played. I remembered the will of my grandfather and wondered if studying music in the Seychelles would be covered by its conditions. A phone call to Mr. Mackenzie confirmed that it was.

Four years later, I had learned to play a dozen instruments and had mastered two. I could read music and began composing songs. I began to understand the beauty of my grandfather's gift and started having dreams of him. In many of those dreams, Grandpa kept showing me buildings that looked like the ones that you now see outside. I saw gardens and fountains and practice rooms scattered around the campus. I saw living quarters like those in which you now live. The dreams went on for a whole month.

"Finally I made a phone call to Mr. Mackenzie who encouraged me to proceed with plans for what you see around you now. He assured me of his support. So, ladies and gentleman, that's how all this got started—it's all a gift from my grandfather.

"I would like to end with some advice for the students. I beg you to embrace this gift, to take full advantage of the opportunities that are now yours, to reach out with both hands and accept the gift given to us all by my grandfather, Mr. James T. Conkey."

With that, the president of the academy collected his note cards and walked slowly to the back of the large concert hall. The day could have ended there, but instead it was filled with handshakes, and chocolate cakes, and strawberries, and hot tea that finally turned cold. The students, who would be the first to study here, said good-bye to their departing families and then walked thoughtfully to their rooms. Their dreams were just around the corner, but they all realized now—that they were also a part of another dream—a dream that had begun—many years before.

Glowing Embers

It's interesting how change takes place. Sometimes you are driven away from one place and sometimes you are attracted to another. In this case, it was both.

I arrived by ferry on the east side of the island on my twenty-second birthday. My going there was a combination of search and escape. As I walked off the ferry, I had an overwhelming childlike feeling of excitement, but I had no idea why. I had a strong feeling that something wonderful was about to take place.

While I was following the directions to a friend's house, this feeling intensified. She told me about someone who was moving out of a small cabin on the west side of the island. I walked over the mountain and then turned south—just before reaching the harbor.

Meeting Stanley Jackson for the first time only added to my excitement. He owned a few acres of land that used to be a summer lodge. He lived alone now and seemed to enjoy it. I guessed his age at about eighty. He was thin and walked with a slow but purposeful gait. His blue-gray eyes had a joyous twinkle to them. Just to absorb some of his sunshine was worth the trip.

His house faced the west and had a commanding

view of the small bay. I climbed up the four steps to the porch, walked between two overstuffed, sun-bleached chairs, and then knocked on the door.

With music in his voice and a twinkle in his eyes, he greeted me like he knew who I was. "Good afternoon," he said, "And how can I help you?"

Attracted by his poetic-sounding words, I explained that I had heard he might have a cabin for rent, and I was interested in renting it.

In rhyme-like speech, he made it clear that he didn't normally rent cabins, but invited me to sit down on his porch. Though anxious about the cabin, I was excited to meet such an elevated soul and more than willing to see where this path might take me. I sat in the chair on the left, as he sat down purposefully in the chair on the right.

He glanced at me and asked my name. Then, after hearing my name, he repeated it once, gazed out into the bay, and started whistling. There was no particular melody he whistled. He would just hold a note, let it warble, and then change to another note.

Then he began mixing in questions with his whistling. At any moment, he would stop the whistling and ask me another question. I don't remember any of the questions, but I think we sat there for at least half an hour. After each question, he would squint his sparkling eyes, look out to the sea, and then start to whistle again. Eventually, he agreed to rent me a cabin. It was extremely quiet there.

For the first three days, the sound of the silence was deafening. My ears rang almost continually.

Twice each day, the ferry would come into the harbor, but the rest of the time, all you could hear was the sound of the sheltered waves, the wind in the trees, and a few birds.

This solitude is what I had sought, but, to tell you the truth, it was very hard at first. I was used to having noise, and used to talking a lot. Now, this sudden change shocked my over-stimulated system. Although therapeutic, it was also very difficult. During those first few days, sometimes I would cry, without really understanding why.

Every few days, I would see Mr. Jackson. Sometimes I'd catch a fleeting glimpse of him as I washed my dishes in the small stream behind the house. Sometimes we would talk.

Though I lived there for only three months, it seems like it was three years. His smile made a permanent imprint on my heart. He never spoke about right actions or good works; he just lived his life in a manner that left no doubt as to his inner peace.

One afternoon, I asked him about wisdom and how you gain it. He invited me to sit on his porch, and just like in our first meeting, it was a mixture of silence, looking at the ocean, and listening to his soul-entrancing whistling, sprinkled with a few words. His whistling let you know it wasn't yet time to talk and it was very soothing to the mind and spirit.

"So, you are asking me about wisdom." he said.

"Yes, I'd like to know how one can accelerate the process of attaining it." My words sounded stilted and out of place.

He looked out on the bay and began to whistle. I listened and began to relax. "No one can teach wisdom, it must be cultivated inside you," he said. Again, he squinted his eyes and started to whistle. I settled back in my chair and listened for what might come next.

"Once a desire for wisdom is planted, it's not so hard to harvest it." He paused again, as we shared the sight and the sounds of his porch. "Think of each day as a lesson in a great big school. In order to receive your lesson each day, you must be prepared. Everyone must find his own way, his own routine, and his own special method of starting each day. It may change from time to time, but without it, you are like a boat without oars."

Again, he paused. You could hear the deep rumble of the afternoon ferry boat as it came near the harbor's entrance. He didn't whistle and didn't speak. We sat in silence till the boat had entered the harbor and blown its whistle.

"You must do whatever it takes to draw enough positive energy to prepare yourself for each day."

We listened to the distant voices and sounds as people and cars moved off and then onto the ferry. We watched as the ferry backed out of its slip and disappeared from the harbor. As the sound of the engines faded, Mr. Jackson stood up and said, "Nice to share the view with you."

I understood we were done and stood up. I thanked him for his time and walked slowly towards my cabin, and let the words of the afternoon turn over in my head. I walked into the cabin and opened the front of the cast-iron stove. There were still embers peeking out of the otherwise gray ashes. I added kindling and blew the fire back to life. Adding larger pieces of wood, I thought about how everyone builds a fire differently. To me, it was a sacred act to bring the embers back to life. Though both my path and my future were unclear—somehow they seemed connected with those little glowing embers peeking through the gray ashes—begging to be rekindled—begging to create warmth, on just one more—winter's day.

Gold Fever

The day's work was finished. We walked the short distance to the cliff overlooking the sea and watched the sun set on the Pacific. As the sun changed the clouds into shades of red and orange, I remembered about how searching for gold had brought us all together in the first place.

In 1850, the world was alive with news. Comets in the heavens and gold in California—it was all intertwined, just like the beans growing up the corn stalks on my father's farm. Beans and corn, these things I understood; but as for the rumors, I left it to those who knew better.

The constant news of men leaving for gold eventually had its effect. I don't know if it was the temptation of the gold, or the longing for change, but I found myself on a ship, passage paid, sailing from London.

My father had been a farmer, and his father had been a farmer, and looking back as far as we could see, we had all been farmers—but at the age of twenty-three—I was destined to become a miner. It didn't sound that different to me: a farmer tears open the soil and plants seeds inside, while a miner digs holes and takes out gold.

I would follow the footsteps of miners gone before, sail to Panama, walk across the isthmus, and then catch another ship to San Francisco. Sailing on a ship didn't sound too hard, and as for a fifty-mile walk—that would take a day, maybe two. Then, in the goldfields of California I'd pick up a few gold nuggets, put them in my pocket, come back to England, buy a farm, and settle down. A small sacrifice for someone of my age.

Sailing on the ship to Panama, I got seasick—but I was strong and survived. After arriving in Panama, I heard they were paying good money for those who would help build the railroad. It sounded like a good idea, so I signed on. I planned to stay a month, give myself a break from the constant movement of the sea, and then carry on.

What I experienced in those few weeks was more than a man should see in his whole lifetime. There was every kind of human being you can imagine there. Death and destruction were everywhere; all for a railroad which would help miners avoid a day's walk. It didn't make sense to me. I heard that for every railroad tie that was laid—one man died. It seemed to me that it would have been more honest just to pay people to become railroad ties, instead of tricking them into thinking they were ever going home. Many died from malaria or yellow fever. Many more died from addictions and greed. Two weeks of that life, and I decided that no amount of money would keep me there, so I set out walking across the isthmus. By the time I reached the Pacific, I was covered with mosquito bites and starting to feel sick.

But, luck was with me and I soon located a ship

that was about to depart. As we sailed away, I thought about what humans will do for money. I had never seen so many men fight so hard just to find a place to be buried. On the voyage these thoughts passed through my mind as I struggled with the constant rolling of the ship. My illness changed and then got worse. Finally, I understood, it was not seasickness—it was malaria. From the next few weeks, I remember little—besides the constant dreams. The fevers were powerful, and the weakness was severe. Walking was hard, eating was hard, sleeping was hard—but dreaming, now that was easy.

Sometimes I'd lie on the deck of the ship, wishing for something else—anything else! One evening, during a storm, my wish was delivered. As the ship tilted, I slid overboard. I tried to shout, but it was of no use. Many thoughts ran through my mind as I thrashed about in the water. I tried swimming in the direction I thought land would be, but I knew deep down inside, this was my time to die. There would be no gold, and there would be no going back to England.

I have no idea how long I was in that cold water or what miracle it was that guided my body to shore, but the next thing I realized, I was awake and lying in the sand. Struggling to crawl, I pulled myself further onto the beach and fell into a deep sleep.

I lay for many hours there on the sand, until finally I awoke to the tapping of someone's finger on my shoulder. I opened my eyes and saw a dark-skinned man with long black hair who was dressed like a European. This odd mixture seemed to fit into my dreams, so I paid him little attention, lay my head back on the sand, and fell asleep again.

The next thing I remember was waking up in a Spanish mission. Over the next few weeks, I discovered that I was in Santa Cruz, only two days' walk from San Francisco. My fevers continued for weeks. When I was awake, I would hear languages I did not understand, but when I slept, I began to speak them. After a month, the fevers stopped but my body was drained. Only with help, could I walk to the courtyard and sit under a tree.

I began to see things that seemed all too familiar. In Panama, men were paid very little to work extremely hard, for the reward of a grave. Here, men of God, who were helping me, were abusing the very same people whom they had come here to save. In my case, I had little choice. I had not asked to be brought here, and I did not have the strength to leave.

After a few months, my strength returned, and I had gained a basic understanding of two new languages. Learning Spanish gave me insight into my own native tongue, but the beauty of the Awaswas language captivated my imagination.

Most of the Indians were very kind to me. One in particular was a young woman whom the monks had named Mary. She was very shy. Eventually she told me that her real name was Sun Rain.

Sun Rain became the subject of a recurring dream. In that dream, the sun was setting over the ocean as she and I stood together on a cliff. Behind us was a very small house and a field of corn. During those dreams, a feeling of peace would fill my heart, a feeling I had not felt since my earliest childhood.

One day, while I was working in the garden, one of the monks grabbed Sun Rain. He started shaking her violently, while shouting words I didn't understand. Sun Rain did not cry out, but tears were pouring down her face. My body moved into action without thought. I grabbed the monk and pushed him aside. Suddenly, there was a lot of shouting. A number of monks and Indians gathered around and all of them were staring at me. No one knew what to say. We all knew that the monk's actions had been wrong; but we also all understood that my time at the mission—had just come to an end. It was not the time for explanations. They had saved me from death, but now my presence—threatened their way of life.

"I will go now," I said. "You nurtured me back to life, and for that I am grateful, but I can no longer stand by and allow you to hurt those I have grown to love." I looked at Sun Rain and said, "I will take you back to your people." Sun Rain looked at me, but said nothing. I took her gently by the arm and started walking towards the large mission gate.

Sun Rain's brother, Oak Heart, directed a handful of strong words in our direction as we left the mission. He followed us outside and said, "You don't understand. Sun Rain has no family. Our parents were killed long ago. She only knows life here at the mission. Now that you have spoiled her life here, take her and keep her safe."

As I began to comprehend the consequences of my actions, Oak Heart looked directly into Sun Rain's beautiful, brown eyes and spoke a few words I didn't understand. Then he walked back to the mission.

It has been ten years since we left the mission. Since that day, Sun Rain and I have ended many peaceful days here, absorbing these sunsets.

The light began fading fast. Sun Rain touched my elbow. Together, we turned our attention away from where the sun had just disappeared. I glanced into her dark brown eyes and then took her gently by the elbow. As we walked past the fields, there was just enough light left to see the outline of the corn but not quite enough—to see the beans that were winding their way upward—toward the first few stars—peeking out—from the evening sky.

●

Graduation

It was a fine day. The music finished and the graduates were all seated. The M.C. walked to the podium and started to speak. "Distinguished guests, it is my honor to welcome you to Graduation 2000." After a brief welcome, the M.C. introduced the president of the university, Dr. H.T. Balboa.

As the M.C. sat down, Dr. Balboa walked to the podium and started speaking. "Distinguished guests, members of the faculty, parents, and graduates: Today, I will use my time to talk about a few of those who are graduating. I do this because their stories are far more inspirational than any speech I might write.

"It is not often that the oldest person on campus is a student, but for the last four years, this has been the case. Mrs. Martha Farrell will today receive her Bachelor of Arts Degree in the field of education. She has already secured a teaching position in a nearby elementary school. When I first heard that a woman of her age had enrolled in the School of Education, I must admit I had my own doubts. During her internship, I had the opportunity to observe her teaching style. I can tell you with certainty that this woman is not just a good teacher—she is a great teacher! I am honored to think that I was here when Mrs. Martha Farrell, at the age of one hundred and five years, was given her bachelor's degree. We are all blessed to witness this moment."

The applause overtook Dr. Balboa's story. Some people stood up and tried to locate Mrs. Farrell among the graduates. Several young men sitting near her obliged the audience by lifting her up, chair and all, for everyone to see. Martha smiled, waved to President Balboa, and then asked the young men to put her back down. Lights flashed from every direction as many people tried to capture the image of Mrs. Martha Farrell.

"Please, let's continue our program." The audience settled down as Dr. Balboa continued, "Now I would like to tell you a story of a candidate from China. Today, Deng Cheng-Ho will receive his Master of Science Degree in Physics. Cheng-Ho did not apply to the school in the normal way. His application literally dropped from the sky. A few years ago, during the summer, I invited some friends over for the evening. After dinner, we were sitting outside when someone pointed out a blinking light in the sky. A few seconds later, a parachute with a small egg-shaped container settled itself on the table in front of us. On the outside of the container, there was writing in Chinese, French, and English. Following the instructions, we removed a piece of tape, opened the container, and found a map of China and letters written in three languages."

Dr. Balboa reached somewhere under his purple-trimmed black robe and took out a well-folded piece of paper. "I would like to read to you parts of the letter that landed on our table that summer evening.

To Whom It May Concern:

If you find this, please contact me and let me know where it landed and the time and date it landed there. I launched a balloon carrying fifteen such payloads on March third, and the one you have found is number eight. The main balloon was launched from the edge of the Gobi Desert near the town of Jining. Please send me a letter if you find this.

For your information, a few months ago, I completed a degree in psychology but have not been able to secure work in my field as of the date of this letter. I am currently working in my father's restaurant. I am interested in a job in the field of psychology, or doing any type of scientific research. I am also interested in finding a wife. I have enclosed a resume with my current picture on it.

Yours very sincerely,
Deng Cheng-Ho

There was a mixture of applause and laughter as Dr. Balboa held up the parachute with the egg-shaped container hanging from it and said, "This is how Deng Cheng-Ho applied to DIT.

"The following Monday, I asked my staff to find a scholarship that would pay for Cheng-Ho to come here and study. You may not be aware that there are many scholarships that go unused because of their requirements. We found a scholarship that required,

'...evidence of a clear understanding of the unity of the world, a strong desire to travel, a major in psychology, and that the applicant be a native of somewhere outside of Europe.' A further requirement was, '...that the applicant be able to demonstrate the ability to read and write at least three languages.' That scholarship had been sitting for six years without a single application."

After the story of Deng Cheng-Ho, Dr. Balboa went on to tell the story of another graduate who was raising three children on her own. He explained that she had come from a background of abuse, which later led to a ten-year period of self-destructive behavior from which she had recovered. He encouraged everyone present to meet this remarkable woman who had so many reasons to hate, but who was so filled with love for everyone she met. Dr. Balboa then sat down and was followed by three other speakers.

The last speaker was Deng Cheng-Ho who walked to the podium with both dignity and humility. He gazed out at those in attendance and then started to speak. "Fellow graduates, most esteemed faculty, honored guests, and Dr. Balboa: Today is a wonderful day not just for those who are speaking to you, but for all those who are graduating. Today is a fine day—not because we succeeded—but because we tried, and when we failed—we tried again!

"From the story you heard earlier, you will recall that I was fortunate to have one of my payloads land in the backyard of the president of the university. For every payload that was reported as found, there were five that were never heard of again.

"One of the payloads landed just below the equator in Africa and was found by a young woman who was the first in her family to attend college. She comes from a tribe who refer to themselves as "The Efe," but who are known to most of the world as Pygmies. A few days after finding the payload, she wrote me a letter.

"As fate would have it, she also ended up here at DIT. By the end of this day she will be known be known as Dr. Efe, in honor of her tribe. But that name will not last long because on Wednesday, we will be married, and she will be known as Dr. Efe Deng."

The audience clearly wanted to see this doctor from Africa who was about to marry a physicist from China. They clapped and turned their heads trying to catch a glimpse of her. Finally, Dr. Balboa walked to the microphone and asked her to stand. There in the middle of a sea of graduates was the top of a dark head just barely visible to those nearby. Finally, after some friendly talk and laughter, she stood on her chair, bowed several times, and then sat back down.

Finally, Deng Cheng-Ho concluded his talk with, "We thank you. All the graduates thank you—because you tried. It is a fine day today because you, the parents, the husbands, the wives, the children, the grandparents, the faculty—all of us—because we tried."

Deng Cheng-Ho sat down, but the audience did not, and the clapping went on. From somewhere you could hear a female voice singing, "We shall overcome, we shall overcome..." The clapping stopped but the people remained standing. A few moments later, the whole audience, the faculty and the graduates were standing, holding hands, swaying back and forth, and singing together, "We shall overcome, we shall overcome, we shall overcome one day; oh, deep in my heart, I do believe, we shall overcome someday."

After the song had run its course, the M.C. called for the first of the graduates to stand. Then the list began, "Julie M. Akard, Bachelor of Science with honors, Ester B. Abraham, Bachelor of Arts in Music..." The list went on like that for forty-five minutes with a few breaks for standing ovations. Deng Cheng-Ho was one of those who received spontaneous applause. But the loudest and the longest applause was for Dr. Efe Deng and Mrs. Martha Farrell.

It was a fine day. Even the audience felt like they had graduated. As Deng Cheng-Ho had said before, it was a fine day—because we tried.

●

A Grain of Sand

No one ever told me that returning to a place that was once home—would cause growth. To me, it was just a place where I was born and spent a few childhood years. Now, along with my mother and my father, we all returned to see my grandfather for the very last time.

As he opened the door, I greeted him, "As-salaam alaykum,"

He replied, "Wa alaykum as-salaam."

Lucky for me, Grandfather spoke many languages. "So, is this my dear Johara?" he asked.

I smiled and looked towards the floor, feeling somewhat embarrassed. My grandfather was a jewel; he had done many things in his life, seen many places, and met many people. He seemed to know everyone in Bahrain, and they all loved him. Once you spent any time with him, it was easy to understand why. Now, eighty-six years old, he was ill with a disease that could be cured. If I could only convince him, the people of this world could enjoy him for a few more years. But Grandfather was both strong and often very stubborn. Once he said, "No," it was doubtful anyone would change his mind.

On the third day of our visit, he rented a traditional fishing dhow and took me sailing. The small crew treated me with respect, after what seemed an unusually long introduction by my grandfather. After sailing in almost total silence for about an hour, my grandfather started to speak, "Do you know the meaning of your name, Johara?"

"I think it means jewel; is that correct, Grandfather?"

"Yes, but from this day on, you will be called Jumanah."

"That's pretty; what does it mean?"

"It means pearl. Long ago, when I was younger, we used to dive for pearls in these same waters. They were worth a great deal of money at that time. Now, with the oil, no one wants to work that hard."

"Was it difficult work, Grandfather?" I asked.

"Yes it was very hard, and very dangerous too. Many families suffered when something went wrong. There was always a man in the boat whose only job was to sing. He would encourage us to go down again. We would sing with him, filling our lungs with air, and our hearts with courage. Just like the oysters suffer to make the pearl, so too did the divers who collected them."

"Were you a diver for pearls?" I asked.

"Yes, for a time. When I was young, I could dive over a hundred feet down into the sea to find the oysters. If my arms could talk, they could tell many stories."

"Weren't you afraid of dying?" I asked, hoping to reopen the subject of his illness.

"Not then and not now. Like the oyster that lives for a time, and from the fruit of its suffering creates pearls, I too have suffered and tried in my own way to create pearls. Eventually the oyster dies, the shell becomes sand, and some of the same sand is used to create more pearls. All of life is like that. Life and death are not separate like people think. When the heart stops pounding, the brain doesn't stop at the same moment. The cells in your hair don't understand death the way we humans think we do. Your dreams never die, your good actions never die, and the songs you sing never stop. In a few weeks, when I no longer walk on this earth, the words I now speak will trouble you, just like the sand in the soft body of the oyster. You will take those words, turn them over in your mind, and from them create a pearl."

I felt overwhelmed by my grandfather's wisdom. This was not the time to ask him to see a doctor, so instead I asked him how he was given his name. He explained about the roots of his name and about his pilgrimage.

Then I tried to change the subject back to his health. I explained that it was my understanding that the body was a temple and that he should try to preserve it to the end. His only reply was, "It is my time."

Who was I to say if it was, or it wasn't, his time? Surely, he should know more about it than anyone else. Still, I wasn't satisfied.

Grandfather moved from thoughts of healing and medicine, back to diving for pearls. "In some places," he said, "the divers used heavy stones to dive down. Taking many heavy breaths, they would hold onto a large stone and dive into the water. The stone would carry them down quickly and they would save their energy for working on the bottom. We never did it like that, but now, when I think about my own life—that's what I want now."

The conversation made me feel uncomfortable, so I asked if we could change the subject. Grandfather replied, "Good, you will not speak of doctors and healing, and I will not speak of death and the afterlife." He smiled and I smiled and that was that. We spent the rest of the day sailing peacefully in the gulf, avoiding the large oil tankers, and absorbing more sun than we intended.

Now, many years later, whenever I feel pain, whenever something is said that hurts, I think back to my grandfather, and I think about all the pearls he created. I see my dear mother, my children, and my cousins—and realize—they are all his pearls. Still, I felt I was the lucky one. I was the one who spent a day with him in a real dhow, heard the stories of how oysters make pearls, and how men of times past swam deep beneath the sea to recover them. And beyond all that, I knew the moment that the grain of sand was first placed inside of me—the day I became Jumanah.

♦

Grandpa's Feather

I was tired, but sleep would not come. I thought back over the last ten years, the last week, and the events of today. I especially thought of Grandpa and the summer he visited us when I was twelve.

Mom and Dad were going on a vacation alone. Something they had not done for a long time. Grandpa came to look after us while they were gone. Before Mom and Dad left, Grandpa came out one evening dressed in a red and black-checkered shirt, a black cowboy hat, and a feather hanging around his neck on a string of beads. He looked impressive as he asked that we turn off the TV, right in the middle of my father's favorite program. I thought my Dad's eyes were going to turn red. Dad didn't say anything, and out of respect, he obeyed Grandpa's request. Momma just looked at the floor and kept quiet. Grandpa then announced to us all that I was almost a man. He went on to say that our modern culture did not have a rite of passage, and that he intended to provide one for me. Dad looked at Mom, and Mom looked at me. If they didn't object now, I knew I was in for a "rite of passage"—even if I didn't know what it was. Dad glanced towards the blank TV screen, and said, "Okay by me."

Mom smiled, looked at Grandpa and said, "That'll be fine, Dad, whatever you think is best."

I sat there like I was watching myself in a movie, not knowing what would happen next. Grandpa looked at me and said, "It's settled then. We'll start at dawn."

Dad switched the TV back on, as Momma looked at the floor again. I watched Grandpa leave the room. I looked at my Dad who was watching his program, and glanced at my mother, who was still looking at the floor. Whatever was about to happen—had just been decided.

The next morning at five, Grandpa came in and spoke to me, "It's time to begin."

I opened my eyes, squinted at the clock, and said, "Grandpa, I'm tired."

He said, "You can take a nap to make up for lost sleep, but there is nothing you can ever do to bring back a lost sunrise."

It seemed an odd thing to say to a twelve-year-old kid to get him out of bed. I got up, dressed, and then went downstairs where Grandpa was waiting. He was dressed in the same shirt, hat, and necklace that he had worn the previous evening. He said, "Let's go," as he opened the door. We walked about fifteen minutes north and then headed up a small mountain. As we reached the top of the mountain, the sky changed from a pre-dawn blue, to a number of different red and orange colors. The sun rose and shot its first rays across the valley in front of us.

After a few minutes, Grandpa took a small leather

book from his pocket. He opened it and read slowly, "Life, and everything in this life, is a trust. You are loaned your body and your talents—all for a given time, and then they must be returned. Never glory in that which is not yours." Then he turned to me and said, "What do you think about that?"

I shrugged my shoulders, still feeling I wasn't here by choice, and I wasn't yet sure if I would cooperate.

"Think about it a bit," he said, and then he read it again. "What does it mean to you?"

I struggled and pulled a few sleepy thoughts out of my head. Grandpa said, "That's good," and then he started walking down the other side of the hill. I followed him and we walked silently until about ten o'clock. Then, we went home and ate breakfast. It was like that every day. He'd wake me up; we'd walk to the mountain, and then watch the sunrise. Then, he would read a passage from his book, and ask me for my thoughts. He would just listen. Then, we'd walk in silence for a couple of hours, go home, and then eat breakfast together.

The first few days I took long naps. I wasn't used to getting up that early. After a week, I started going to bed earlier and didn't take the naps. We did that for a full three weeks.

By the time my parents returned, there was a subtle change in me. I couldn't explain it, but it was there. My sister volunteered her view to my curious parents, "They get up very early, go out someplace, and then come home and eat." She also told them that I was different, but she couldn't explain to them what had changed.

Now, ten years later, I still get up early to read, and often I go out and watch the sunrise.

A week ago, I returned to college to start my final year. I arrived a day early and used the day to transform my sterile dorm room into the place I would call home for the next year. The following morning I went for a walk. There was a hill east of the campus that was similar to the one Grandpa had taken me to when I was twelve. On that morning, I found a large feather much like the one Grandpa wore during that special time in my life. I picked it up and took it back to my room. That's when I got the phone call about Grandpa's passing.

I packed a small bag, picked up the feather, and caught a train back home. I took the feather with me to the funeral, not really understanding why. At the graveside, I decided it was for Grandpa. I placed it reverently on the casket as it was being lowered into the ground.

After the burial, everyone drove back to our house for lunch. I wanted to be alone for a while with Grandpa. I sat by the graveside and thought about those special three weeks Grandpa had given me. Then, I walked back home slowly.

By the time I had arrived back home, it was late afternoon. Many of the guests had already come and gone. My mother told me that Grandpa had left two things for me. She walked into another room and returned with Grandpa's leather book and the necklace with the feather on it. I put out both hands as my mother gently placed the leather book between them, and then placed the string of beads on top. I asked my mother if she knew the story behind these two precious gifts. She told me she had seen Grandpa write in the book and she'd seen him wear the necklace, but she'd never asked him about either. I slipped the small book into my shirt pocket and then placed the string of beads around my neck.

The rest of the afternoon was strange. People were talking about Grandpa like he wasn't there, and talking about things that held little meaning to me. Almost everyone asked me about the necklace with the feather on it.

As evening fell, I retired early. Tomorrow's sunrise was one I would not miss. Now if I could only sleep.

The Harvest

It was the day after the close of the fruit-picking season. I was tired but content. I had worked hard and made more money than I had expected to make. On the bus, an elderly man from my province sat next to me. I had seen him working in the fields, but had only spoken with him briefly. After the bus started moving, he began to ask me a number of questions. In keeping with our customs, I respectfully answered them all.

"What is your name?"

"I am Shen Yong Lu."

"How old are you, Yong Lu?"

"I am twenty-three."

"And where does Yong Lu come from?"

"From the north side of the lake at Ch'ing Hai."

"And who is your father?"

"My father is Shen Si Tu."

I was becoming tired. These questions had been going on for several hours. After each question, my mind would drift and then settle comfortably, just before the next question.

"Why do you pick fruit?" he asked.

"I wish to attend a school of higher learning and the cost is considerable."

Again, my mind drifted. The sound of a chicken

squawking came from the seat behind us.

"And what will you do with your higher learning?"

I felt that he would not understand the purpose of education and my mind played with how best to answer the question. It was quiet for a long time.

"Will the higher learning help you to pick more fruit?" he asked.

We both knew the answer, but I answered politely.

After riding for five hours, the bus stopped in a small town. Most of us got off to go to the market to buy lunch.

"Yong Lu, please buy your 'grandfather' lunch," he said, handing me some money.

A few minutes later, the bus was in motion again, bouncing back onto the main road. We ate our lunch without speaking. The bus filled with the aroma of the foods from the market. It became quiet as people finished eating and were lulled to sleep by the warmth, the food, and the vibration of the bus.

I was feeling very sleepy myself and was almost asleep when he spoke again. "Yong Lu, do you have a dream in life? Are there things that you want to do besides pick fruit and attend a school of higher learning?"

"Well, I do wish to have a family one day, and I love the sound of the flute. I would love to learn to play the great classical music of our region."

"And what prevents you from attaining these goals?"

I wanted to answer. I didn't mean to be rude, but the long days of picking fruit and the long bus ride were too much for me. I drifted off to sleep. I felt my head bounce as the bus hit a bump in the road. I started to dream. The same old man appeared in the dream. He was sitting outside a small house painted in colors I had not seen before. He sat on a stool and his beard flowed down his clothes. On the house were many small signs saying, "Learn of Your Past," "See Your Future," "Solve Your Problems," and "Attain True Happiness." I walked up to the old man, bowed low, and said, "Most respected one, please tell me of my past and of my future."

He stood up slowly, walked into the house, and motioned for me to sit on a small stool. Then, he put one hand on my forehead, and the other on some large papers on the table. I felt as if everything in my head and in my heart was flowing through his hands and out onto the papers. Then he said, "Arise, Yong Lu, see your past and glimpse your future."

The papers on the table had turned into colorful maps. I was amazed to see a representation of my life. It stretched from my early childhood up to now, and it continued into the future. I was looking at the map when he spoke again. "You see, Yong Lu, here you had a wish, you worked toward that wish, and you actually went far beyond your highest aspiration and you were happy." As he pointed to different parts of my life, he repeated the same words over and over again.

"But here," he said while pointing to part of the

map, "your wish was not strong, and you started down a path with no end. Over here, is your future."

I noticed that many of the paths had names that were hard for me to understand. There were names like: "River Boat Flows Forever," "Marriage to a Kind Man," "Wealth in a Basket," "Children of a Good Woman," "Music from the Reeds," and "Eternal Rain." Each of the paths had many tributaries, and some turned back on themselves. I touched the paths with my fingers. Some were very hot, while others were cool. Some created a sense of pain, others fear, and still others created a sense of exhilaration.

The chicken behind us squawked as the bus turned a corner. My eyes opened and I began to replay the dream in my head. I looked at the old man sitting next to me. He nodded his head, smiled, and spoke again, "So, Yong Lu, what prevents you from attaining these wishes?"

I paused for a few moments and then spoke, "There is only one thing that prevents me from attaining my highest aspirations, and that is my fear of failure."

He smiled and said, "Very good."

I glanced out the window. We were passing through a small town and we were still about three hours from my home. I looked at the flowers and the trees that lined the streets. I saw a sign that said, "Regional Institute of Chinese Music."

My heart started to pound. I looked at the old man with a question on my lips. He smiled and nodded his head, but said nothing. I kept silent as the bus continued past the institute gates. I could feel my hands sweating. Alternating waves of fear and love passed through my body as my breathing sped up. I looked at him as he smiled and nodded his head again. I stood up, gathered my things, and said, "Thank you, thank you, respected one."

The old man nodded his head again. I walked to the driver and asked him to stop the bus and let me off. I glanced back at the old man, bowed my head respectfully, and then stepped off the bus.

The fall air had the smell of spring. Tears began streaming down my face. As I walked towards the institute, I found myself repeating, "Thank you, most respected one. Thank you."

The Healthy Planet Bookstore

"Excuse me, I'm looking for Lerato," said the young woman with a visible sunburn and light brown hair.

From behind a counter, a slender young woman with golden-brown skin turned slowly and said, "I am Lerato—may I help you in some way?"

The visitor with the sunburn introduced herself, saying, "My name is Kirstin. I am from Finland and I have a letter for you—from your sister."

Lerato smiled as she walked towards the counter and accepted the letter with both hands. While Kirsten waited patiently, Lerato read through the letter. While she read, the expression on her face alternated between deep concentration and outright bliss. At times, she spoke words that Kirsten did not understand—but which were filled with emotion. When she finished reading, Lerato walked out from behind the counter, looked deeply into Kirsten's eyes, put her arms around her, and said, "Thank you, thank you so much. I haven't heard from my sister for many months. Will you tell me how you met?"

"I will be happy to, but right now I am very tired;

I feel I should rest first. Can we meet later?"

"That would actually be better for me. I work until four, and then I am free." Lerato pointed to the left of the visitor's center and said, "Can we meet over there at that fire pit around five? I will bring some food and we can cook dinner while we talk."

A few hours later, they were sitting together by the fire. The gentle flames licked the bottom of two cast-iron pots. After Lerato had put her guest at ease, she started with her questions, "Tell me how you met my sister."

Kirsten started slowly. "For me, it is really a miracle that I am here. I met your sister in Helsinki. I live about an hour's drive from there. Whenever I visit Helsinki, I visit the Healthy Planet Bookstore. A few weeks ago, I went there on a Saturday afternoon. In front of the bookstore there was a sign about a talk that would take place that evening by a Mr. Molefi Saakane."

Lerato smiled, as Kirstin continued her story. "I decided to stay and listen because I have always been attracted to Africa. I never understood the attraction—it was just always there. Mr. Saakane had written a book called, *Wisdom of My Grandfathers—San Health and Healing*. I bought the book and then walked to a nearby restaurant. I read the first chapter, while I ate a light supper. Then I walked slowly back to the bookstore. As I entered, I noticed a table set up just inside the door. A sign indicated that it had something to do with travel to Africa. That's where I first saw your sister. We didn't speak then, but I did notice her sweet smile.

"I found where the talk was to take place and sat down in an empty second-row seat. A few minutes later, a woman and an elderly man walked in and sat down in the front row. Five minutes later, the woman stood up and introduced Mr. Saakane. He spoke for about an hour. The thing I remember most is how he found the material for his book. He said his grandfather had called him aside one day and given him a bundle of notebooks tied together with a piece of old rusty wire. His grandfather told him not to read them until after his passing. Then, Mr. Saakane was to read them all and '...act in whatever manner the Great Spirit moved him to.' It seems that most of his grandfather's contemporaries could not read or write, but that his grandfather could. Apparently, he had made a habit of writing in a notebook every day—much like many people do in a journal or diary. These notebooks tied with a piece of old wire were his gift to Mr. Sakaane.

"Being an avid journal writer myself, I was amazed that someone in a remote village in Africa, separated from me by several generations, had cultivated the same habit. During the talk I was making notes in my own journal."

There was a long pause as Kirstin waited for some response. Lerato got up slowly, walked around the smoke, stirred one of the pots, and then sat back down. She looked across the fire to Kirstin and said, "I see. And are there more things in your journal about the meeting?"

"Yes," said Kirstin as she opened her bag, removed her notebook, and found the pages she wanted. Then she turned the journal so that the light from the fire illuminated its lined pages. "Here it is," she said. "A man asked him what the word 'San' meant. Mr. Saakane explained that it was a polite word for Bushman. Then a reporter asked him what was the most significant part of the book. There was a long pause and many people were shifting in their seats and sipping their coffee nervously. Finally, after much thought, Mr. Saakane explained that his grandfather had chronicled a few generations of a particular family who would not allow the words 'I can't' to be spoken in or near their home. Apparently, when the children would say 'I can't,' the parents would correct them by saying, 'You can, but you just find it difficult.' He said many of the children from that family became lawyers, and doctors, and teachers. He attributed this to the early cultivation of positive attitudes."

Lerato smiled again and then stirred the contents of the larger of the two pots. "Supper will be ready soon," she said. "And so, how did you actually meet my sister?"

"The events of the day had a trance-like effect on me. When Mr. Saakane was about to sit down, the M. C. stood up and suggested we show our appreciation. Everyone started clapping. The sound of the applause tore me abruptly from my thoughts. I was a bit shaken but I wanted at least to meet Mr. Saakane before driving home. I walked over to him, shook hands, and thanked him for the evening and for the book. Then I walked slowly toward the door. That's when your sister spoke to me and asked me if I would like to visit Botswana and see the wonderful national parks.

"I explained to her that I had always wished to visit Africa—but that I couldn't. I think my exact words were, 'I just can't.'" Lerato smiled again as they both started to laugh.

"As soon as I said the words, 'I can't,' a loud noise started ringing in my ears. I took three steps toward the door and then stopped. I stood there with my back to your sister, asking myself why I couldn't? I had accumulated a lot of vacation time, and I had enough savings that would surely cover the costs. I couldn't come up with any good reason. Everything started moving in a mystical-kind of slow-motion. My hand reached almost automatically into my purse. I took out my cell phone and almost without thought, dialed the home of my supervisor. I explained to him that I wanted to take time off from work and go to Africa. He agreed almost immediately and I walked back to your sister. She arranged most of the travel details, and then wrote you the letter."

After more joyous laughter and expressions of love, the two unlikely companions ate their food. Then they shared the challenges they each faced—and spoke openly of their hopes for a better world. Each time one of them would say the words "I can't," the other would interrupt and say "You just find it difficult."

Long after most of the campfires had gone out, and long after the lights in most of the guest cabins had been dimmed, you could still hear the soft-spoken voices of these two young women. Besides this and the sounds of a few nocturnal animals, the only other thing you could hear was the gentle sounds of their sweet laughter.

🌢

Jacaranda Carpets

I don't remember when I actually realized that I was hearing things that others didn't. We take hearing for granted. Somebody moves their lips, and you hear something. I thought everyone could hear plants talking—but perhaps I was wrong.

One cool October morning I started across the campus for my morning walk. It was like every other day, except for what I heard. The jacaranda trees were in full bloom and had laid down a fresh carpet at the foot of every tree. The lavender-blue, trumpet-shaped flowers covered the ground like a fresh snow that had fallen just before dawn. No shoes had yet soiled this new carpet.

It felt almost sacrilegious to walk across these carpets that had fallen from the sky and been laid at the foot of every tree. There were places where the trees were so close together that in order to pass, you had to walk across the fresh, blue carpet. I must admit that the sound of the popping flowers under my feet brought a certain joy.

These jacaranda carpets were part of the beauty of dawn, south of the equator. On this particular spring day, at five-thirty in the morning, as I walked across one such lavender-blue carpet, I heard them talking. I couldn't exactly see which flowers were talking, but they were near the top of the tree. I stopped to listen as the first one spoke.

"I really don't want to fall."

"Why is that?"

"Well, it took a long time to get where I am, and the colors are so beautiful up here. Just look around you."

"Yes, it is wonderful and the air is crisp. But why the fear?"

"Well, I don't know about life on the ground. I only know this life. When you fall down there, you have to detach yourself from the tree, and then within hours some kid will walk by and decide that it's more fun to hear you pop, than to look at the beautiful colors."

"I do understand your thinking, but have you thought about your future?"

"What do you mean?"

"Have you considered what happens after the popping sound?"

"Well, I guess you shrivel up and lie around on the ground."

"And what might happen after that?"

"I guess, in a month or so, you dry out, and then the rains come."

"And after that?"

"You sure ask a lot of questions!"

"I'm sorry. I was only trying to help."

"It's okay, I guess I'm just under a bit of stress—thinking about all this. What was your question again?"

"What happens after you fall from the tree, get smashed flat by someone's shoe, and then dry up on the ground?"

"Oh yeah, I guess then if you're lucky, you will start to grow."

"That's it! And then?"

"I guess you grow into a tree and make more flowers."

"Uh huh! Now you're getting it! And do you remember having the growth feeling, when you first started to become a flower?"

"Yes I do. It was quite a thrill."

"Before you had that feeling, did you know what it was like?"

"No."

"Well it's the same with being a seed. When you fall off the tree, and you become part of that beautiful carpet down there, and when someone steps on you, they get the fun of the sound, and you get reunited with the soil. That reunion is about as close to paradise as seeds ever get."

"You make it sound so beautiful. I never thought about it like that before. I think I need some time to reflect on all this."

"No problem. Take your time, we can talk more later if you like."

"Thanks."

The air was still cool, even as the sun's first rays streaked across the skies. Rising at dawn did have many benefits. There was the quiet for one thing. You could hear your own thoughts better at dawn and sometimes you could hear other things as well.

As I walked across nature's lavender-blue carpet, and heard the soft popping of the flowers—I smiled. I smiled, not just for the child within me—but also for the seeds within us all.

Jalapeno's Fast Tacos

I had just settled into my seat when a young woman asked if she could get by. As I stood up and stepped into the aisle, she sat down and said, "I'm Josette. I am from Den Helder—in the Nederlands."

I introduced myself and told her that I was from Cancun and explained I was traveling to Buffalo to attend school there. After we discovered we were both headed for the Faculty of Arts at the University of Buffalo, Josette smiled and said something in Dutch which I didn't understand. Then, she smiled brightly and said something about coincidences.

I explained that I had been given a scholarship and discovered that she, too, was on a special grant program. She told me that her plane had arrived early and that was the only reason she was able to catch this plane.

I told her I wasn't so lucky and I had arrived late last night. She wanted to hear the story, so I began to tell her. "Well," I said, "it all started with a thunderstorm. We circled around Florida for about an hour. Then, the pilot told us we were going to fly into New York and land, but we'd be a little late. Just before we reached New York, we started circling again. That took another hour. Then we landed. That was around seven o'clock at night. My connecting flight was at seven-thirty. I was hungry and very nervous. The flight attendant told me not to worry, that everything would be running late and she was sure I would still make my flight.

"After landing, we sat on the ground for forty-five minutes because there were too many planes and too few places to park them. When I finally walked into the airport, it was total chaos. It reminded me of the bus station in Cancun—people shouting and waving and running every which way.

"I asked one of the airline workers for help. He looked at a TV screen, gave me directions, and suggested that I run. I ran as fast as I could with my suitcase twisting and banging against my leg. I didn't stop to remove my coat; so, by the time I arrived, I was sweating like I'd been in the hottest of jungles. When I finally got to the place where I was supposed to board the plane, there were people sitting, standing, and lying everywhere. I started picking my way through the crowd, just as they announced that my flight was canceled."

Josette laughed, shook her head, and asked, "And then what happened?"

"I didn't know what to do. I asked a woman at the desk and she said I should go to customer service. By the time I reached the desk, there were about a hundred other people already lined up. It was just before ten by the time I reached there. I was really hungry, and saw a place called Jalapeno's Fast Tacos. After a few minutes, I asked a man if he would keep my place in line, so I could get some food. I walked over to Jalapeno's, studied the menu, and then gave my order to a young girl. She told me they closed at ten. I looked at the clock and it was only two minutes past ten. I didn't know whether to laugh or to cry, so I did a little of each. I returned to the line and waited with everyone else. Finally, they put us on a bus and took us to a hotel."

Josette had tears in her eyes, but she was laughing. After looking into her eyes and seeing her tears as she laughed, I knew we'd be friends forever. As I continued my story, I noticed she was sketching on a piece of paper. "Then this morning, I got up, ate breakfast, got the bus back to the airport, got on this plane, and met you."

Josette smiled again and said, "Well, I'm glad it all happened. What I mean is, if you had made your connection, we might not have met."

"I guess that's true," I said.

Josette folded up the paper on which she'd been sketching and then handed it to me. "Here is something to remember your experience with," she said. "You can look at it later."

I thanked her and put it into my pocket. I told her that I thought the Faculty of Arts was not that big, so I assumed we'd meet again soon.

A few minutes later, our plane landed, we collected our luggage, and shared a bus with about thirty other people. I went directly to my dormitory, filled out some papers, got my key, and then dropped off my things in my room. I had promised myself that before I started school, I would go to Niagara Falls. I grabbed my sketchpad and left the dorm. The bus to the falls didn't take long.

Overlooking the falls was another Jalapeno's Fast Tacos. With a smile, I asked if they were open, bought two extra-spicy tacos, and then sat down.

There was a leftover newspaper on a red plastic chair next to me. The thunderous roar of the falls blanketed all other sounds and the light breeze blew the billowing mist from the falls over everything. I ate both tacos like it had been years since I had last eaten. I took Josette's sketch from my pocket and slowly opened it. There I was immortalized—in a line drawing at the Newark airport, standing next to Jalapeno's, looking very hungry. I smiled and thought of Josette. A little of Jalapeno's red sauce from my thumb added a touch of color to a corner of Josette's otherwise black-and-white creation. I smiled. Somehow, the red sauce seemed to fit right in. I carefully folded the sketch and put it back into my pocket.

I picked up the newspaper, put it under my arm, and crossed the street to the falls. I stood by the railing and stared at this majestic work of Creation. I was awe-struck and completely lost track of time. Niagara Falls was everything it was claimed to be, and even more.

After awhile I found a bench, sat down and thought over the events of the last two days. I opened the newspaper and started flipping through the pages, scanning the articles at random. There was all the local politics, just like in Cancun, and football scores, and lots of advertisements, and pictures here and there. My hair was wet from the spray. I felt slightly cool and decided to return to the campus. I was about to close the newspaper, when one article stood out.

"Newark Airport Fast Food Makes People Sick: The Health Department of Newark reported that it has closed the Newark Airport branch of Jalapeno's Fast Tacos pending an investigation. The spokesperson said that twenty-eight people had fallen ill after eating tacos there late yesterday evening."

I smiled, stood up, and started walking toward the bus stop. As I walked, I touched my pocket to confirm the sketch was still there and then dropped yesterday's news into a waiting trash barrel.

Knee Pads

Katrina and I had always been much more than cousins. Perhaps it was because we were the same age that we had such a special relationship. We only saw each other every few years, but whenever we got together, we did far more than just share idle chatter. It was as if we were two seeds, grown from the same flower, but planted on distant farms. When we were together, we always exchanged ideas, experiences, hopes, and dreams. Last year, however, when she came to visit, she seemed troubled.

We went for a walk and then after the normal niceties, Katrina began to talk. "You're lucky," she said, "you have your own place and you can do what you want. I'm not sure what I should do. As each day passes, my relationship with my parents goes further downhill. I feel full of resentment, and I think my parents do also."

"I think I understand," I said.

"Do you really? I mean, here you are living on your own, with your parents far away, and I am living at home and have to pay money each month for food. I can't buy what I want but I have to contribute towards the food. I don't know what I should do, but I do know that the current situation is not healthy for anyone."

Cautiously I asked, "What do you think you should do about it?"

Katrina replied that she didn't know, but that she wanted my opinion. Trying to seize the moment I asked, "Do you mind if I share a few things that might be relevant?"

"I'm ready to try anything."

"Okay, let me share a few of my own experiences and see if any of them parallel your situation. Many years ago, when I was five, I remember being in a room with my mother and father. They seemed to have forgotten that I was still there and began a serious conversation about some problem that was facing my mother. I noticed that my father didn't tell her what she should do, but that he continued to ask her, what she thought would be the best solution. A few days later, when my father told me to do something, I asked him why he didn't ask me what I thought was the best thing to do. My father laughed and then told me that in a few years he would ask my opinion on some matters.

"About ten years later, on my birthday, my mother and father sat me down and said the time had come for me to make many more of my own decisions and that they would relate to me as an adult. They told me that there were still rules to be followed and chores to be done, but that they would no longer try to mold—the way I thought.

"A few years after that, my father told me he needed my help on the weekend. He was pouring concrete for a patio and needed the whole family to help. I complained, and reminded him that I was an adult now and should be able to make my own choices. He said that as long as I lived at home there would still be chores to do and sometimes projects that required my help. By the time the weekend came, I had stopped complaining and was ready to work. Dad suggested that I wear kneepads because I would be working on my knees, smoothing the wet concrete with a trowel. I asked him with a smile if this were my choice or his. He smiled and said it was my choice.

"As the day progressed, I thought it was better to trowel in a straight line instead of in circles, but Dad made it very clear that he wanted circles. Again, I made reference to my being an adult and making my own choices. He made it clear that I was working for him, and that he would have to live with how smooth and level the concrete became. Then he said I was to use the trowel in a circular motion. We got through the day with only a few more incidents, but for me, the lessons continued into the evening. Do you remember that I talked about the kneepads?"

"Yes, your Dad recommended them, but said it was your choice."

"That's right. He actually went a little further and explained that the chemicals in the cement were very hard on the skin, and that he would strongly recommend I use the kneepads. Well, I exercised my right as an adult and I didn't wear them. Later that night, I wished I had."

"Really? What happened?"

"I was sitting in a coffee shop with a friend and I felt like something was coming out of my knees and running down the front of my legs. The first few times it happened, I thought my legs were just tired and the nerves were playing tricks on me. Finally, I took a look. It was an ugly mess. There was water and blood oozing out of my knees and running down my legs. I still have scars from it."

"Yucky. Why did he let you do it?"

"I asked him the same question the following day. He said it was my choice—that I was grown up enough to take his advice or not. He said that sooner or later something like this would happen to me and if a little scar tissue was the only result, he was quite willing to let me hurt myself. He said, in time I would come to value the scars on my knees."

"I can understand his point, but in my situation, what do you think I should do?" asked Katrina somewhat impatiently.

"What do you mean?" I asked.

"About my relationship with my parents. Should I confront them and say I don't like how they are treating me, or should I move out or what?"

"I don't know, what do you think you should do?"

"I guess I need to do some thinking about it by myself. You're not going to give me your opinion on this, are you?"

I smiled at Katrina and said, "I think you understand your situation far better than I can ever hope to. Let's walk back home now—all this walking has made my legs sore."

Lava Bricks

Our guest speaker tonight is Mrs. May Fuller. She is sixty years old, has five grandchildren and is now the director of a 'think tank' called 'Ideas on Demand.' Her topic this evening is 'Networking Your Ideas.' I know you would rather listen to her presentation than to my introduction, so without any further delay, I give you Mrs. May Fuller."

A slender women who looked far younger than sixty, walked to the podium, smiled, and then nodded her head toward the respectful audience. After the applause, Mrs. Fuller started to speak. "Before diving into the heart of tonight's talk, I'd like to ask those of you who have invented something that you believe is both unique and could be of significant value to mankind—to please stand up. Even if your invention was only in your head, please stand up."

There was a pause as most of the audience stood up and looked around. Mrs. Fuller squinted her eyes against the spotlight and said, "From up here, it looks like about ninety-five per cent of you are now standing. Now, if from any of your ideas you made more money than you spent in a year, remain standing; otherwise—please sit down." After a bit of laughter and a lot of chair movement, only three people were left standing. "Look around the room. This is why many of you have come here tonight—you want to learn how you can make money from your ideas.

"My intent tonight is not to show you how to get rich, but rather to inspire you to find ways of getting your ideas out into the world. I want to tell you a story. In it, I will use myself as the example, but I firmly believe that any one of you could easily have been the focus of this story.

"I have no idea how many ideas have passed through my head. I know that many of them might have been of use to humanity. Like most of you, I don't remember when this flow of ideas even first started. I do remember, however, the first time I blew a fuse in the house, and I remember even better what my father did after that. Because of my father's reaction, I realized that I had affected my world.

"The second time my father reacted, it was with amazement and wonder. I had a toy Morse Code oscillator that did nothing more than make beeping noises. It allowed me to imagine sending messages all around the world. I also had a small crystal set radio connected to a long antenna that was stretched between two tall pine trees. To me, without the barrier of adult fears, it all seemed very simple. I had a radio, and I had something that could send out messages. Connect the two together, and in my childish imagination, I thought I could broadcast to the whole world from a corner of my bedroom. So, that's what I tried. I unplugged the headphones from the radio, and then plugged in the code oscillator. I was busy tapping out dots and dashes, when my father suddenly appeared. I can still see the look on his face as he stood in the doorway. It was not the same as when I blew the fuse, but he was concerned. He asked me very slowly, 'What are you doing?'

"After I explained, he suggested that since he had heard my messages on his radio in the barn, the neighbors might also hear it and that maybe I should stop broadcasting. He told me that it was illegal to broadcast without a license. At that time, I was six years old. I mention this because I assume that many of you had similar childhoods.

"My next invention of note was a very simple float alarm. In high school, I had a job working in a fast-food restaurant. They had large, stainless steel tanks that were used for making soda pop. Each tank had an expensive pump under it. If the tank went dry, the pump burned out. Because of this, the employees had to continually monitor the level of the liquid in the tanks. There were no alarms. I convinced the owner that I could make something to solve the problem. It wasn't very complex, and it was not patentable, but it was very useful.

"When I was eighteen, I landed a job in the prototype shop of a company that made medical and scientific equipment. They used cam-timers to set functions on and off, to test the prototypes they created. The cam-timers were difficult to program, so I invented a timer that used chart recorder paper and a pencil to turn each switch on or off. This was the first time I actually had a patent search done. Before me, someone had made a player piano based on the same principle and therefore, my invention was not patentable. Like many of you, I had a fountain of ideas flowing, but I was discouraged. This fountain, like the lava trapped deep below the surface of the earth, longed to burst forth, but had no place or purpose. That is why organizations such as this inventor's guild are so important.

"Now let me fast-forward the story and tell you about networking, and about my first successful invention. I was traveling through Rotterdam and had stopped for the night. As it turned out, there was a meeting similar to this one being held in a conference room at the hotel where I was staying. After supper, I spoke to a man by the name of Jan Kaiser. He was the essence of the word, 'networking.' He was connected to people in many different government agencies, companies, and non-profit organizations. He had written proposals for countless government grants. We talked before the meeting, and then again, afterward.

"After the meeting, he asked me a question that changed my life. Now I want to pose that same question to all of you. Quite simply put, do you want to get rich, or do you want your ideas to be used by mankind? Of course, we all want both. But, if you had to choose between taking your ideas to the grave with you, or dedicating them to the public domain, which would you do? Most of you would choose to see the idea used. That's the choice Jan helped me to make.

"After that, I shared with him the plans I had for making volcanic bricks. It required a steel-tracked vehicle, a long hydraulic arm mounted on the front, and a conveyor belt feeding out the back. The idea was to wade into a volcanic lava flow and scoop out bricks. To me it seemed like a really good way to make low-cost bricks that would be strong, light weight, and fireproof.

"Jan liked the idea. He asked me to write up a description of how it would work and what I thought it would cost. Then he went to work, networking with various people and organizations. Six months later, the machine was completed and was on a ship headed for Indonesia. My next task was to be patient.

"First I had to wait for the machine to arrive in Jakarta and then I had to wait for a volcanic eruption. Indonesia has plenty of volcanoes, so we didn't have to wait very long.

"Interrupting the flow of the story a bit, I want to return to the goal of tonight's talk: which is to help you turn your ideas into reality. In this case, to bring the idea of making lava bricks to fruition, I essentially gave my idea away. Yes, I was paid while the machine was being built, and I was paid for the six months I lived in Indonesia, but I didn't make a fortune from the lava bricks. While it is true that I happened to be in the right place at the right time, the willingness to let go of the idea of making a lot of money, made it possible for this idea to become reality.

"After the brick-making machine arrived, we assembled the crew and started training. We took it apart and put it back together twice a week for a month. Then on July seventh, we got the news that there had been a large eruption on the island of Java. The Embassy Emergency Task Force was already in action and arranged a C130 to transport the machine to Java. A large truck took the machine the rest of the way.

"When we arrived I was completely overwhelmed, seeing this extremely powerful wonder of nature, spewing out the material which would soon become houses to replace those which the very same volcano had destroyed. Seeing the first brick come off the conveyor belt was by far the most wonderful experience in my life.

"Jan insisted we hire a photographer. After the pictures were released to the media, the news of the Lava Brick-Making Machine spread much faster than the lava did. As the Lava Brick-Making Machine became noteworthy, so did I. Suddenly I was no longer just a lady with a few interesting ideas, but a person who had accomplished something concrete. I owe my success, primarily to Jan Kaiser, who helped me to let go of my possessiveness.

"The story of the lava bricks spans only a year. By this time next year, every one of you could have a similar story. I look forward to hearing your success stories when we assemble here again next year. Until then, thank you, and good evening."

The Leaves Before Winter

I had more than a few things figured out. Everything I thought I needed, I had, or was about to get. Then, things started falling like the leaves before winter. One after another, years of planning and work fell like so many leaves that were no longer needed.

I had a good job, which paid far more than I needed to live. I was engaged to Jesse, the love of my life. We would be married soon. I had a nice apartment, with more things in it than most people ever dreamt of. I had my friends. I had surfing in the summer and skiing in the winter. I had just made a deposit on a house and the bank promised a loan soon. I was busy every day.

Then came a time in the middle of May when it all fell apart. Jesse phoned on Thursday night and said she was sorry but she had changed her mind. No, she couldn't explain it, and no, we couldn't get together to talk about it. I was devastated and confused. On Friday morning, I went to work, and when I received my pay envelope, there was a pink slip inside. A letter explained that two hundred people had just been laid off, and I was one of them. It was pretty hard to work that day. I had only two weeks left there anyway, and according to the letter, even that was "optional."

I didn't think anything else could go wrong. I went home early, put on some music and then, numbed by the day's events, looked mindlessly through the day's mail. There was a letter from the bank, saying that after serious consideration, they had turned down my loan application. Well maybe that was a blessing in disguise, because the main reason for buying a house was Jesse and she was suddenly gone.

I tried to read a book, but I couldn't keep my mind on it. I went to bed early, but I couldn't sleep. It just didn't make sense; at least it didn't make sense to me. I tossed and turned until the first birds started to sing. I dressed for my morning run. Then, I put my cell phone in one pocket, and my wallet and keys in the other.

Running felt good. The longer I ran, the better it felt. It was as if the pain in my lungs, and the pain in my legs, were burning away the pain in my heart. The salt of my sweat tasted better than the salt of my tears. After about thirty minutes, my mind cleared. I ran along the bluffs that overlooked the ocean. I heard a few sirens, glanced behind me and saw a column of smoke in the distance.

I sat down on a bench and thought for a while, or maybe I should say, I sat down on a bench and didn't think—that was really more accurate! I just let the morning run through my head. It was a pleasant sort of feeling—just to sit without thoughts. After a few minutes, the events of the last two days started to enter my head again. I got up and started running. I turned towards home and noticed that the smoke had changed from black to gray.

I ran past an elderly man who was walking his dog. I had seen him many times, but had never greeted him before. Through my heavy breathing, I choked out the words, "Good morning, sir, have a good day." It felt nice to think about someone beside myself. I passed a young boy on his way to school and much to my own surprise said, "Study hard, son, you never know where life will take you." The words coming from my mouth sounded foreign to me. I had never said things like that before. I passed an elderly woman walking out to collect her morning newspaper. I circled back, picked it up, handed it to her and said, "Have a nice day."

"You too, son. The world would be a better place if there were more people like you around."

These encounters seemed all too related to the events of the last two days to be coincidental, and I promised myself a chance to think about them. A fire truck drove passed me. They must have put out the fire and were headed back to the station.

As I turned the corner to my street, I noticed two fire trucks near my apartment complex. I jokingly thought it was probably my apartment that had burned. I ran the rest of the way back to the complex. On the way, I watched the firefighters rolling up hoses and putting them back on their trucks. When I arrived in front of the apartments, I stopped and stared. I was stunned. The whole complex was gone. What had been my home a couple of hours ago—was now gone. I saw some of my neighbors wrapped in blankets, looking at each other. I put my arm around a small child, as my cell phone rang.

"Hello."

"Antonio, it's your dad here."

"Hi, Dad, how are you?"

"Not so good, Son, it's your mom."

"What happened?"

"She has cancer. The doctors don't promise much. She wants to see you."

"I'll come."

"I know you have a busy life. And I'll understand if you can't, but she really wants to see you, and the doctors don't know how long she'll live."

"I'll leave today, Dad."

"Do you think you could get off work for at least a day or two and come up? It would mean a lot to both of us."

"Yes, Dad, I'll leave in a few minutes; I should be there by tonight."

"Really?"

"Yes, Dad, I'll be there as soon as I can."

"We're at the lake. She said she wants to see the water and sit by the fireplace."

"Okay, I'll see you there tonight."

"How about you, Antonio, how are you?"

"We'll have time for that later, Dad."

"Okay, Son. See you tonight … and thanks."

"I love you, Dad."

"I love you too, Son."

I walked over to my car. It was covered in ashes

and the paint was bubbled in a few places. I started it up and reversed out of the carport. Smoke was still coming from the ashes where the apartment complex once stood. As I drove past one of the firemen he motioned for me to roll down the window and said, "You live here, Son?"

"I used to."

"We'll need a report."

"I'm on my way to visit my parents for a few days. Can I make the report when I get back?"

"That'll be fine," he said as I drove off.

Much later, as I was driving along, I was amazed that I did not feel a sense of loss. So many things that I had valued so highly now seemed insignificant, and many things I had been ignoring—suddenly seemed precious.

It started to rain and after a short time, the ash from the fire had been washed off the car. The only thing I needed now was a shower and a change of clothes, and yet even these two could wait—just a little longer.

Lemon Dreams

The sun shone brightly on the red and white Volkswagen bus as it climbed slowly through the mountains of the Tucumán Province. Julia was returning from her annual trip to western Chile. The VW bus was ten years old and prone to breakdowns, but Julia was not just an average driver, she was also a mechanic—a mechanic who traveled with tools and spare parts. As she shifted down from fourth to third, she pressed hard on the accelerator and suddenly lost power. The engine was still running but would not respond to the pressing of the pedal. She coasted to the side of the road, happy that she always traveled with spare parts. She knew it was a broken accelerator cable. A couple of hours and she'd be on her way again. She coasted towards a small rise on the side of the road in order to create a space to work under the bus. As she came to a stop, she noticed the lemon trees lined up in straight rows, and saw a young woman walking among them.

Julia got out, waved to the woman, and removed her toolbox from the bus. As she opened the toolbox, the young woman walked towards her and greeted her, saying, "Buenos tardes."

"Buenos tardes," replied Julia.

"Car trouble?" asked the younger woman who had come from the lemon grove.

Julia smiled and said, "Yes, one of the benefits of owning a mature car."

They both laughed as Julia located the accelerator cable coiled in the bottom of her toolbox. "It's just a broken cable. It'll likely take me a couple of hours to fix it. By the way, my name is Julia," she said, extending her hand.

"I'm Ana, from Pennsylvania—in the U.S."

Julia opened the engine compartment at the back of the bus and said, "You're further from home than I am. You're not here on vacation, are you?"

"No. My grandfather was a rather eccentric man. Not really wealthy, but by the time he passed away, he owned a number of things. This lemon farm was one of them. In his will, he left something different to each of his children and grandchildren."

"And this was left to you?"

"Yes, and he left me a note saying that these sour lemons would one day change my life into sweetness—sweetness beyond anything I could imagine."

"And was your grandfather a poet also?" asked Julia with a respectful smile.

"My grandfather was lots of things."

Julia made a satisfied noise and said, "So far, so good. If the cable is broken only in one place, this should be easy."

"Can I get you something to eat or drink?" asked Ana.

"I'd love some lemonade."

Ana laughed again and said, "You know, I'm a bit embarrassed—I've never made lemonade."

"It's an easy skill to learn," replied Julia. "Just squeeze a few lemons, add some water, and throw in some sugar—it's that easy."

Ana laughed and said, "What about honey—will that do? I don't have any sugar."

"It's sure worth a try," said the older woman who was by now underneath the bus.

Ana walked back towards the small cottage in the middle of the lemon grove, while Julia struggled with the cable. It was not as easy as she had hoped. Mud and oil had built up inside the tube that the cable passed through. Not only was removing the old one hard, but threading the new one would be even harder.

Thirty minutes later, Ana returned with a pitcher and two glasses. She explained that the lemons smelled very sweet, but that the honey was hard to dissolve.

They sat down in the shade of the lemon grove and drank what turned out to be a very delicious mixture. Julia, now dirty from top to bottom, spoke first, "This is definitely the best lemonade I have ever tasted. You could sell a lot of this—it's delicious."

They both agreed that there was a special balance between the lemon and the honey. Ana told her that she was trying to decide what to do with the farm. She explained that most lemon growing in the country was done at a lower elevation near the town of San Miguel del Tucumán. "I'm no farmer," she said, "but my grandfather was very intuitive and I feel he may have known something that I don't yet see."

Ana stayed with Julia as she struggled to get the new cable installed. It was near dark when the end of the cable finally reached the engine compartment. A few minutes later, the job was done. Ana offered the use of the shower, and Julia gratefully accepted. They prepared a meal together, and talked late into the night.

Ana discovered that Julia was not only a mechanic but a professor of psychology at the University of Córdoba. After hearing bits and pieces of Julia's life, Ana said, "You're a lot like my grandfather. He did many diverse things in life. What do you think he wanted me to do? Do you think I should live here and run this as a farm? Or should I sell it and go home?"

Julia offered more questions than answers, allowing Ana to explore her own feelings and inner thoughts. Ana was more drawn to spiritual healing than she was to raising lemons. She was struggling to find a way to integrate her grandfather's gift and her own inner promptings.

Before retiring to her bus for the night, Julia offered a way to view the situation. "It's a beautiful place to live, but you don't feel motivated to grow lemons. Maybe you need to see how things play out. Like this old VW—I want to rebuild it, but it will take time. I read some place that a desire to have things done quickly prevents their being done thoroughly. Just like the cable I just installed—I had to clean the dirt and oil from the tube before I could thread in the new cable. Maybe you need to give yourself some time. Just be here a little, walk among the trees, read about lemons, travel to the surrounding towns, just explore a bit—like you were on an extended vacation. Then, if nothing turns up, you can always sell the place and go back to what you know."

Somehow hearing the words, "...go back to what you know," sounded wrong to Ana. Going back -- just did not resonate in her heart. The next morning, Ana gave Julia a bag of lemons and a few jars of honey to take home to Córdoba.

Over the next few years, the two friends kept in touch. Ana ended up marrying the farm manager and Julia continued teaching at the university. As the farm grew, so did Ana's dreams. First, there was the lemonade stand. Then, the old burnt trees were removed and replaced with fields of chamomile and spearmint. Ana was able to formulate a wonderful healing cream that she marketed all over the world. There were children of course, and Ana began to love life on the farm nestled in the foothills. But the apex of her dreams came with the building of the conference center. The center hosted retreats for people from as far away as Buenos Aires and Santiago, with an occasional ecological tour group from many places in Europe and the U.S.A.

Ten years after the opening of the conference center, there was a celebration. Julia drove up in her now fully-restored, red and white VW bus. The celebration took place on a weekend as one group was arriving and another was departing.

It was an especially hot day. There were far too many people to use the dining hall, so tables were set up in the shade of the trees. Each table had pitchers full of Ana's lemonade made with honey. The unique sound of the ice cubes sloshing in the lemonade, and tinkling in the glasses, were a constant throughout the afternoon. After a brief introduction, Ana stepped aside to let her long-time friend deliver the last talk of the day. Julia's talk was entitled "Lemon Dreams." In her speech, she explained the history of Lemon Grove. She recounted the first time she had met Ana, and told of the slow and steady progress of Lemon Grove from a lemon farm, to a place where healing herbs were mixed together into soothing creams. She spoke about the growth of the Lemon Grove Conference Center into what it had become. All the while, the guests sipped the endless supply of lemonade as the workers filled and re-filled the glass pitchers. The sound of the ice cubes against the pitchers and glasses became a gentle melody against which Julia unfolded the history of Lemon Grove.

When Julia came to her final remarks, the sound of the ice cubes came to a stop. "In summary," she said, "I want you all to know that none of this came easy. What you see here today is the fruit of patience. Ana had dreams that were destined to become manifest. She watched, and she waited. When opportunities presented themselves, she took them. I hope each and every one of you will do the same. Most of us do not own a lemon grove, but all of us have dreams. Nurture them, be patient with them, work with them, and one day, each and every one of us will have our own Lemon Dreams."

With that, she sat down, and the sound of the ice cubes dancing in the lemonade grew louder again. The afternoon, so filled with hope, drifted into the approaching sunset. Those who were leaving, drank the last of their lemonade and reluctantly walked toward their waiting cars, while those who were staying walked among the gardens—looking forward to a week filled with more lemonade, more dreams, and more hope for the future.

💧

Line of Sight

It had been over a year since they had been home. Kwang-Su missed his father and mother just as much as his wife Yoon-Hae missed hers. Though they now lived in the city, they were both still villagers at heart. In another few hours, they would be in the mountains, and soon after that—they would be back home.

Kwang-Su dimmed the headlights for an oncoming car, and then glanced at the clock; it was 9 P.M. Yoon-Hae reached over and switched the radio back on. The stations of Shanghai were far behind them. The classical Chinese music that had been with them for much of the drive, had finally faded and disappeared altogether. Yoon-Hae asked her engineer husband why the station in Shanghai was not more powerful.

"It's not just a matter of power," he replied. "With FM radio, it's also a matter of line-of-sight. The radio waves at those frequencies don't bend much—they go in straight lines. If we were on the peak of a tall mountain right now, even if we were very far from Shanghai, we might still get the station that you want."

Having received the explanation, Yoon-Hae remained silent and continued to search for another station. One station came in especially strong: "In case you have just joined us, good evening. We are broadcasting to you from our studio in Wuhan. We are coming to you on 103.8 megahertz. Our ten-thousand kilowatt transmitter covers most of the Hubei district and many places beyond. Stay tuned now for our nightly radio drama."

Yoon-Hae glanced at her husband, who nodded his agreement. They would listen to the radio drama. After a few commercials the announcer continued, "Tonight's drama is entitled, 'Your True Calling.' Without further delay, let's start our story."

Yoon-Hae and Kwang-Su listened as the drama unfolded. The story was about a young man by the name of Chan-Yu, who lived in a very remote mountain region of China. He was a good student and had won a shortwave radio in a science fair held in his district of China. As a boy, he had spent many hours listening to stations from all around the world.

During the first break in the story, Yoon-Hae asked her husband why this young man in the story could hear stations from all over the world, and yet they couldn't hear the classical music from Shanghai. Kwang-Su explained that the radio waves in the shortwave bands were capable of bending over mountains and around the curves of the earth and by doing so, their transmissions could travel for long distances.

The story on the radio continued. It seems that this young man had another interest besides his shortwave listening. He wanted to help the people in remote villages gain the technological advantages that people in the big cities have, without the problems of overcrowding and pollution. His heart was pure and he wrote down the many ideas that came to him in a special notebook.

After finishing high school, Chan-Yu received a scholarship to study at a large university. He continued to excel in his studies, and though he continued to listen to radio stations around the world, there was less time for it than before. He also became involved in many organizations whose members had interests similar to his own.

When Chan-Yu was in his second year of college, he attended a large fair in Shanghai. There were demonstrations of technologies that were very suitable to village life. Chan-Yu was there for the entire ten days and attended many of the seminars.

There was another break in the program. Kwang-Su glanced at the clock. It was now twenty minutes after nine and he wondered how much longer he could drive that night. His shoulders were sore from the many hours of driving, and he was aware that his mind was not as clear as it should be. "Maybe we should stop and sleep soon. I am very tired," he said to Yong-Hae.

"Whatever you feel is best," she responded. At times like this, she wished that she could drive. It would be a great help.

The program started again, with a description of the many fund-raising activities that took place at the fair. It seems that many of the organizations that were represented had collected more money than they had expected to. Not being adequately prepared, some of them had to carry home the money in paper bags, cardboard boxes or in flour sacks.

One such organization was raising money to spread a new strain of rice, which grew especially well in places like Chan-Yu's home. On several occasions, Chan-Yu had stopped to speak with the young couple who were manning the booth. On the last day of the fair, the couple was very fortunate. They collected three flour bags and two cardboard boxes full of contributions from well-meaning visitors. Feeling a kindred spirit in Chan-Yu, they asked if he would help them carry their things to the car.

Of course, he agreed. They folded up their banner and placed the samples and posters into a cardboard box. It had been a wonderful fair, and all three of them felt happy as they walked to the car. It was quite a sight: a man with a table and two bags of money on his head, a young woman with several boxes and bags balanced on her head and in her arms, and Chan-Yu with far more than was reasonable to carry.

They arrived at the car and, with the aid of the car lights, tied the table and banner on top of the car. They filled the small trunk and back seat with everything else. Now as fate would have it, one of the bags of money had rolled out of sight under the car. They said their good-byes, and the two new friends drove off into the night with Chan-Yu watching and thinking about all the good work these two people were doing. As their lights faded from view, he looked in front of him and realized they had left something behind.

Chan-Yu called out to them but it was too late. They were much too far away to hear him now. As he bent down, he realized they had left behind one of the large flour sacks full of money. At the moment, there was nothing to do but to take the money back to his hostel. As he walked, many thoughts passed through his mind. This much money could transform a village like his into paradise. More thoughts were running through his head than he was able to handle. There was nothing he could do or decide now, so he told himself this is a bag of flour, nothing more, and nothing less—just a bag of flour. He arrived at his hostel and put the carefully tied bag under his bed—hoping to sleep well.

During the next break in the program, both Kwang-Su and Yoon-Hae wondered what would happen to Chang-Yu. Kwang-Su glanced again at the clock—it was 9:25 now. They had started to climb into the foothills of the mountains they loved so much. Though they were both wide awake now, it would be good to stop soon. The road dropped them down over the first of the many small hills. The music from another station came in, then a hiss, then they heard the announcer come back on and say that the final part of 'Your True Calling' was about to resume. The radio hissed again and the music from another station filled their ears. Yoon-Hae spoke softly, asking her husband, "Can we turn back a little and listen to the end of the program?"

Kwang-Su glanced at the clock and thought about turning back. The thought was not appealing to him. He flicked his lights on high and strained to see how far it was until the road would rise again. "I'll try to stop on the next hill," he said.

In the meantime, the radio made an odd mixture of sounds, "Hisss...what would he do... hisss ... the news from Bejing is ... hisss ... his dreams were mixed ... hisss ... an old man appeared ... hisss ... heavy rains are ... forecast ... hisss ... could he do it ... hisss ... how could he find them ... hissss ... would they even miss the money ... hisss ... they had collected so much more than they expected to ... hisss." Then there was music—a beautiful classical piece about life and death and the struggles of families. Then another, "hisss..." and then, "...we hope you enjoyed tonight's drama ... hisss ... please join us next week ... hisss." Then the music came back on.

Yoon-Hae reached over and gently switched the radio off saying, "Maybe we should stop soon."

Kwang-Su replied, "I think so. Let's look for a good place."

As they drove, Kwang-Su wished he had turned the car around and driven just a little out of their way, so they could have heard the end of the story. His thoughts were interrupted by his wife saying, "Kwang-Su, don't worry about it. It is in the past, and it is fine—you did what you thought was best."

Kwang-Su thanked his wife for her understanding and they drove in silence, looking for a good place to sleep. Their thoughts returned to the drama and both finished it in their own ways. Finally, Yoon-Hae spoke again, "How do you think it ended?"

Kwang-Su paused for a few moments and then started to speak. "He already had the thought that the amount of money in his flour sack would transform his village. I think he keeps the money and travels home with the best of intentions to help the people in his village. But on the way home, the money begins to get a grip on him and he starts using it for his own benefit. Then he becomes very corrupt and dies a miserable old man."

"Uh, that's a horrible ending," said Yoon-Hae.

"Yes, I guess it is," said Kwang-Su, "but I think it is real. A lot of people have made decisions like that and end up just like Chan-Yu. How do you think it ends?"

"I think he goes through many struggles to find the people who lost the money. I think someone tries to rob him, and he successfully resists. Eventually he finds the people and tells them what happened. They want to reward him in some way, but they don't feel right in giving him donated money. So, they offer him a job, and he becomes interested in agriculture and eventually goes back and helps his village. He finds a kind woman, marries her, builds a nice house, and has lovely children."

Kwang-Su smiled and nodded his head, as he pulled the car to the side of the road. "How's this for a place to sleep for a few hours?" he asked.

"It will be fine," said Yoon-Hae, "this will do

fine."

Kwang-Su switched the radio back on. Because of their altitude, he was hopeful that they were now within line-of-sight of Shanghai. With a little effort, he was able to tune in the classical music that his wife loved so much. They both tilted their seats backwards and found a position that promised to give at least a few hours' sleep. After a few minutes of relaxing music, Kwang-Su switched off the radio as they both drifted into the world of dreams—a world where they would meet again and recreate their aspirations for a kinder world, a world that finds them in their villages with their families—a world that they would visit in just a few more hours.

🌢

The Marathon

Today we have a most unique opportunity. With us is Mr. Kazihito Enomoto who is the editor of the largest daily newspaper in the world, The *Yomiuri*. It has a daily circulation of over ten million newspapers. Recently, Mr. Enomoto has been promoted to the post of Senior Editor. It is my hope that his presence here today will encourage each and every one of you to reach for lofty goals—in your careers as journalists. Mr. Enomoto will give us a talk, and then, time permitting, there will be an opportunity for questions. Mr. Enomoto, over to you."

"Thank you very much. I have come today because I have a passionate belief that those who come from behind, and those who work hard, will often surpass the established leaders in any field. I expect to meet some of you again. I expect to see some of you working for the *Yomiuri Daily*. I expect that one of you might even replace me in the future.

"The essence of journalism is asking questions and listening to the answers. Just being a good writer is of no use, in and of itself. In journalism, you must be able to ask appropriate questions and listen carefully to the answers. The rest of journalism is the craft of writing and I assume you have all mastered that already. This being the case, I will not lecture you on the craft of writing, but rather I would like to go straight to your questions. I would like to invite you to ask me penetrating questions and listen deeply to the answers."

There was a long period of silence. Neither the professor nor the students was prepared for this. Kazihito Enomoto stood there in front of the class as if he were an observer. Fifteen long seconds passed. Several students cleared their throats nervously. Thirty seconds passed. The guest looked contented — as if he had all the time in the world. Forty-five seconds passed; he still looked relaxed. Finally, a young woman in the third row stood up, bowed once, and said, "Mr. Enomoto, I have two questions. First, what was the most defining moment in your life and, secondly, who was the person who had the most influence on your career?" The young woman bowed again, and then sat down.

"Excellent, excellent questions. The most defining moment in my life took place immediately before I was fired from my first job as a journalist. I was working for a small daily newspaper in the northern part of Japan. I was a sports writer and had been promoted twice. I was sent to cover the Kawaguchi Marathon at the foot of Mount Fuji. As you know, this is the largest marathon in Japan. There are more than 12,000 runners each year. The instructions from my editor were clear. I was to interview the top three finishers. Since I had covered the same race the year before, I recognized that two, out of the three, winners were the same as they were the previous year. The finish line was swarming with reporters from newspapers and magazines, as well as radio and TV broadcasters. What captured my attention was the person who placed fifth. A man I guessed to be well over sixty had placed fifth in a field of twelve thousand. This was the real story, and I was sure my editor would agree.

"By way of a small digression, how many of you would have followed the instructions of the editor? Raise your hands if you would have interviewed the first three finishers as instructed. Hold your hands up high and then look around you." The guest paused for a moment and then said, "Those of you with your hands up would have kept your jobs. Okay, put your hands down. Now, how many of you would have interviewed the old man who finished in fifth place? Hold your hands up high. No, better yet, stand up."

The guest speaker waited for all the students to make up their minds and then he said, "Congratulations, you took a chance and you are all fired. You may have written the best story in the world, but you have now lost your job. By the way, that's the decision I made. I wrote one of the best stories I have ever written and I was fired. Sit back down, and I will tell you the rest of the story."

As the students sat down, the guest speaker continued, "Of the two hundred reporters, I was the only one who went to interview the old man. His name was Mr. Akimitsu Hashimoto and he was eighty-seven years old."

Some noise rippled through the large auditorium as students grasped the fact that an eighty-seven year old man had come in fifth in a field of twelve thousand of Japan's best runners. There was an extra bit of noise near row twenty on the left side of the auditorium. The visitor continued, "Mr. Hashimoto was too tired to answer my questions, so we agreed to meet the following day. In the meantime, I finished a general story about the marathon and then sent it to the sports editor. In the article, I made reference to the elderly man who had placed fifth.

"The following day I went to meet Mr. Hashimoto for the second time. In the process of the interview, he told me he had been a baker most of his life. As it turns out, he was also a painter, a poet, a farmer, and a self-made engineer. He told me that he had been running for ten years and had been running the marathon for five. I was stunned that a baker of bread had done all of these things. He did not seem ready to stop and just watch the birds fly in the wind. I asked him how he had managed to do so many things in his life. I want to read you his exact words."

Then, the visitor pulled out a small notebook, removed a newspaper clipping from it and began to read, "Life is like a suitcase. When you are born into this world, it is empty but clean. It is lined with a thin layer of gold and has a number of special fasteners inside. The fasteners can hold things, of which we are mostly unaware. These places are for things that we are destined to achieve. Most of our lives we collect things and put them into this suitcase. Many of the things don't fit properly, so they just roll around inside and make noise. Occasionally, we have periods of introspection and we throw out things that have no proper place. And sometimes we start an activity or project that snaps naturally into place. That is how I look at life."

"Those were the words of Mr. Akimitsu Hashimoto. To return to the questions of the young woman in the third row, that was the most defining moment in my life, and Mr. Akimitsu Hashimoto was the person who had the most influence on my career. His memory continues to inspire me—just as I assume it has inspired you today. After that interview, I wrote one of the best pieces of journalism I have ever written. I explained to my editor why I had made the decision to interview Mr. Hashimoto, and then I gave him the article. He explained politely that I had gone against his instructions and that I should look for another job. I was grateful that he did hand the article to the features editor—who published it the following day.

"A few days later, I received a phone call from the editor of the *Yomiuri*, who offered me a job as their features editor. That was ten years ago. Five years later, I was promoted to the position I currently hold. Now, let's have another question."

After a few seconds, an elderly man in row twenty stood up slowly. He bowed once and then started to speak. As the elderly student thanked the professor for a wonderful class, the guest speaker squinted his eyes as if he was looking at someone against a background of a sunset. The student continued, "Instead of asking a question, I would actually like to make a statement. I trust that our honored guest will accept this and that my fellow students will be patient with me. I am ninety-seven years old. I am old enough to be a grandfather to most of you. I have done many things in my life. I have worked as a baker, and I have even run in a marathon."

The guest speaker began smiling as he left the podium and walked slowly up the aisle towards the old man in the audience. The old man continued, "Ten years ago, after running a marathon near Mount Fuji, I met a young writer who inspired me. Because of that encounter, I am now studying journalism. I hope I can become at least half the writer that he is."

The old man started moving towards the aisle where the guest speaker was headed. The class was on its feet, facing in their direction, and clapping. Many were wiping tears from their faces. The guest speaker and Akimitsu Hashimoto met in the aisle by row twenty, bowed politely to each other, and then embraced.

Sensing the moment, the instructor turned to the board and wrote, "Good luck on your final exam. I hope you learned something!" Then, turning his attention toward the scene in the aisle near row twenty, he bowed once, collected his books, and with his eyes twinkling like the stars at twilight—he walked out through the side door.

🌢

The Middle of Nowhere Truck Stop

Boyd and his family pulled off the highway and parked. The big sign described its location. "This is it," he announced to his family, "the Middle of Nowhere Truck Stop."

The two young children laughed as his wife smiled patiently. She knew how much this trip into the past meant to him, but would have rather continued their vacation some place else. As they walked toward the restaurant, Boyd spoke again, "There used to be a bench here—that's where I was sitting when I first met Al."

His wife nodded politely again, as they entered the mostly empty restaurant.

Seeing them enter, a young woman called out from behind the counter, "Sit down wherever you like. I'll be right with you."

"Thanks." Boyd chose a table near the window. There was only one other customer—a truck driver drinking coffee at the counter.

"I'm Miriam," said the waitress as she handed out the menus and glasses of water. "Can I get you some coffee?" Miriam didn't look like she belonged here, but then neither did Boyd and his family.

Boyd looked around anxiously—as if he was expecting to find something. Finally, when the food arrived, he asked, "Does Al still own the place?"

Miriam smiled and said, "You knew Al?"

"Yes, he helped me a lot and I wanted to thank him for all he did for me."

"Let me get the new owner, he can tell you more."

Miriam walked toward the kitchen and then called out, "Sanjiro, there's another friend of Al's here."

A few minutes later, a man walked slowly from the kitchen and approached their table. He bowed once, and then said to Boyd, "I am Sanjiro, long time friend of Mr. Al. I am new owner Middle of Nowhere Truck Stop. You are welcome here." They shook hands, as Sanjiro remained standing. "I made guest book for friends of Al. You want to sign it?"

Boyd took the book with two hands, still not understanding where Al was. "Yes, I'd love to sign it, but where is Al?"

Sanjiro looked at a nearby chair and then asked, "May I sit?"

"Yes, please. Please sit down."

"Honorable Mr. Al, he went to sleep with setting sun. I'm very sorry for you. You were good friends?"

"He helped me a lot." Boyd was having a hard time processing the situation. His wife took his arm and gave it a gentle squeeze. He opened the book and flipped through the many pages of well-wishing friends who had each left their stories. Boyd looked at

Sanjiro with pleading eyes and then spoke, "May I tell you my story?"

"Yes, please. Much honor listen stories Mr. Al."

Miriam, who had been listening at a distance, walked over with a small tape recorder, handed it to Sanjiro and nodded her head respectfully toward him.

"Okay I tape story? I have many stories Al. One day someone write book, *Wonderful Life of Mr. Al*"

Boyd nodded and said, "Fine," as the truck driver left his stool at the counter and pulled a chair a little behind Mr. Sanjiro. The truck driver nodded his understanding toward Boyd, as Miriam also sat down to listen. The children, feeling the energy, sat up straight—ready to listen to a story that before had seemed -- so boring. Sanjiro switched on his tape recorder and Boyd started to tell his story.

"I got stuck here once about twenty years ago. I sat down on a bench outside there. I had no money and was very hungry. Al came out, introduced himself, and offered me breakfast. I sat over there at the counter and ate a big bowl of oatmeal and about a half-dozen pieces of toast."

The truck driver laced his hands together and leaned forward.

"When I was done eating, I asked Al if I could sweep outside or something to pay for the meal. Instead of answering my question, he asked me if I was tired. It had been a long time since I had slept well, and I was very tired. Al reached under the counter and pulled out a sealed plastic bag with a blanket and a pillow in it." Boyd looked out the window and pointed to a big weeping willow tree, surrounded by green grass. "He pointed to that tree over there and said I could sleep for awhile and then he'd see what I could do to help. After I woke up, we sat down on the bench and he asked me a number of questions. I explained how down-and-out I was. I was pretty confused, and though it had been a long time since I had done any steady work, he offered me a job."

"Sounds just like Al," said the truck driver.

"I stayed here for two years. Al not only gave me a job, but he became like a father to me. He encouraged me to take some correspondence courses and eventually helped me get into college. That's where I met my wife. We are both teachers now, and these are our children."

Sanjiro, with tears in his eyes, started to speak. "Mr. Al helped hundreds of people. I was dishwasher here when he died. I promise Mr. Al help people. I try, but not the same with no Mr. Al here."

Boyd flipped through the book of testimonials. His would be number 191. After writing a brief version of his time with Al, he asked Sanjiro if there was anything he could do.

Sanjiro paused for a long time and then spoke, "You go on vacation now?"

"Yes."

"You come back this way?"

"We could. We could pass back through here in about ten days. What do you have in mind?"

"I was thinking for long time make big party for Al, invite all truck drivers, and people with stories in book. Spend whole day, tell stories, listen music, eat food—all to honor Mr. Al."

Boyd's wife spoke up first, saying, "It sounds lovely, how can we help?"

Sanjiro paused again and then said, "Mr. Boyd, you be Master of Ceremonies, you love Mr. Al and you talk nice—you be M.C."

Ten days later, Boyd and his family returned to the Middle of Nowhere Truck Stop. From a mile back there were large trucks parked on both sides of the road. There was a big banner across the road reading, "Big Day Honor Mr. Al" and the sign that used to say, "Middle of Nowhere Truck Stop" had been changed to "Honorable Mr. Al's Truck Stop."

The program included fifty-four speakers from all over the country, from all walks of life. There were musicians with wonderful music and there were three different songs called *Al*. There were a number of scholarships that were created in his honor. Every speaker had a story to tell and each one was there to pay homage to this big-hearted man, who was known to so many—simply as "Al."

◆

Money Talks

I'm sure you've heard that expression before—the one about money talking. I want to explain not only how money talks, but how it also listens. Actually, beyond listening and talking, it also jumps. In my case, I was a "twenty." I say 'was' because I am different now.

I was printed in the summer, and then I spent a few months "out of circulation." That means I sat around locked up with a lot of other money and was waiting to be called. My next stop was a bank. I was placed in a room with a very thick door. In the daytime, the door would open and people would come in and out. Throughout the day, people would walk in and take out some of the money. Then, at the end of the day they would bring money back in. At night, they would close the door and turn out the lights. That's when all the stories would start. Many of these folks had been in circulation for a while and had really seen a lot of life.

I spent a few nights next to a "fifty" who had been in circulation for sixteen years. He told me a bunch of stories that got me very excited. I wanted to start getting circulated in the worst way.

This old "fifty" told me that he had traveled in the

same wallet for a very long time, because the owner was saving him for a "rainy day." I asked him about the rainy day, and he said he didn't know what it meant.

He said he had been folded nicely and put under some credit cards in a nice brown leather wallet, and then had traveled around the world. He explained that he had ridden in airplanes, on trains, in cars, on camels, in boats, and even on donkeys. He said he had traveled throughout Africa, North America, South America, the Middle East, in China and in Europe.

One night he told me how he got here. "I was still folded and hidden under some plastic cards and was traveling every day to a new place in Europe. I was in Holland, France, Germany, and in Sweden. While in Sweden, I kept hearing conversations about running out of money and needing to go home soon. Personally, I thought it was a pretty funny concept that you could run out of money, but that's what I heard. Then one day, I was exchanged for a real warm sweater. I didn't know much about jumping yet, so I went with the money. I ended up in another bank just like this one. Then, I got exchanged for some Swedish money, and the next thing I knew I arrived here."

I asked him to explain what he meant by jumping, and this is what he said. "Well, jumping really has its roots in an understanding of who you really are. If you think of yourself as just a 'twenty,' then jumping will never make sense to you. But if you think of yourself as love that circles around the money, then jumping will be a little easier to understand."

I nodded my head and said, "Okay, I think … I understand."

He continued, "You see, you think your existence started the day you were printed."

I nodded again.

"The fact of the matter is that before you were printed, you were paper and ink. And before the ink was ink, it was a fruit on a tree. Likewise, the paper had been a tree.

"One fine day, the paper and the ink joined together in a printing press and out pops this "twenty." But your life only takes on real meaning after you get into circulation. That's when you start to see things. You see you are really not the paper, and you are really not the ink.

"You are really the essence of what surrounds the money, not the paper. Your essence is love. Sometimes the love will become overdone and turn to greed. This is not a particularly nice feeling, but it is part and parcel of being money."

"But, what about jumping?" I asked.

"Ah, jumping," he said pausing. "Jumping is when you follow the 'other,' instead of following the money."

"Hmm," I said, struggling to understand.

"Sometimes, it happens without effort, sometimes you wish for it, but one day we all jump. I have been told that it is a very pleasant thing, but I never met anyone who actually did it."

At that point, in the conversation, I told him I was

tired and needed to sleep. The next morning was my day. I became very excited because I was on the top of my pile. Then I was picked up and sat in a teller's drawer for a while. At around three, I was handed over to a woman who placed me nicely in a wallet and then put the wallet in her purse.

From that point forward, my life has never been boring. Although I never went out of the country, I did travel a bit. I often thought of what that old "fifty" had told me. I have experienced both love and greed. I spent many nights thinking and dreaming about jumping.

One day, I was in the pocket of a young man who was shopping in a hardware store. He was buying tools for making guitars. It seems that he had just quit his job and had decided to start making guitars. I had once been in the wallet of a guitar player, and I liked the sound his instrument made. Making guitars seemed like a nice way to spend time.

The thought of jumping came strongly into my mind. I felt some fear and my heart started beating faster. I felt like I was about to jump. The fear of jumping faded into the background of my thoughts, and a great longing to jump overcame me.

The young man spent a lot of time in the hardware store. He chose a very nice saw, an expensive plane, a drill, and a rasp. He walked up to the cashier to pay. He took me and some other friends out of his wallet. I told the others I thought I was about to jump. They looked afraid. He handed us to the cashier.

Then, I heard the others saying, "There he goes,"

and, "Will you look at that?"

Then the magic started! I not only jumped, but I divided. I went into the drill, and the saw, and the plane, and the rasp—all at once!

What an experience that was. I didn't have time to say goodbye to my friends, but I do think of them sometimes. Now I spend my days shaping wood into guitar tops and necks. It's a nice place to be. So I ask you, don't you think this is pretty good for a guy who was once just a "twenty?"

Mongolian Breakfast

The Trans-Siberian Railroad was one of those unforgettable experiences. I had boarded the train in Beijing and had the experience of watching the first rays of sun shining on the Gobi Desert. The following day, we changed trains on the southwestern border of Mongolia. On the trip to Ulan Batar, I was all alone in a compartment that was made to sleep four. On arrival in the capital of Mongolia, an elderly man joined me in the compartment. I greeted him but he just nodded his head and bowed slightly. Assuming he didn't speak English, I used the only words I knew. "Ba yar laa, ba yar laa," I repeated. We settled for a warm smile and my attempt at "thank you."

A few minutes passed in silence and then we were joined by a man in his thirties dressed in a slightly outgrown western-style suit. When the younger man came inside, he first asked me something in Russian, then asked, "You speak English?"

"Yes. My name is Sam," I replied.

"Hi, Sam. You American?" he asked.

"No, I am from Australia."

"Okay, good Austria. You speak German then!"

"No, I'm from Australia. You know—down under," I said pointing to the floor. My pointing to the floor didn't help with the communications, as it only caused him to tilt his head slightly and look under my seat. I took out a notebook and made a rough world map and then pointed to Australia.

"Okay, okay, good, my name Dochin," he said. "Me international business make. I go Moscow sell wool, buy dresses, come home, sell dresses."

I nodded and said, "I am a student."

"Student—very good," said Dochin in reply.

The train lurched forward as Dochin turned his attention to the elderly man. They both spoke the local language and it was nice to see Dochin more relaxed. I had learned to enjoy watching people speak languages that I did not understand. I liked riding on the music of the speech and letting my mind hover over the sounds.

After about an hour, the older man turned his attention to the samovar and started preparing tea for all three of us. I watched with interest as he unwrapped a block of pressed tea and then shaved off pieces into the teapot.

Dochin explained that the older man's name was Temuge.

Temuge lifted one of the metal cups with reverence and handed it to me, using both of his brown, wrinkled hands.

I thanked him saying, "Ba yar laa."

Temuge smiled but did not speak. Then we drank our tea in silence. After the tea, Dochin explained that the tea we had drunk was not real Mongolian tea. He also told me that Temuge was traveling to Moscow to look in the National Archives for traces of his grandfather who had been exiled to Siberia. Apparently, his grandfather was a Buddhist monk. There were many who had been taken to the work camps and were never heard of again.

I left Dochin and Temuge in the compartment and walked to the dining car for dinner. When I returned, Dochin and Temuge were both asleep on the two top bunks. I lay down on one of the bottom bunks and quickly fell asleep.

When I awoke in the morning, Temuge was already awake. He was busy making the traditional tea, which I had only read about. I greeted him, and he smiled warmly.

Dochin was still sleeping soundly as Temuge handed me a metal cup containing the tea and a large piece of bread. To me, the tea had a very strange taste—more like milk soup, than tea. I thanked him and then ate the bread with the tea. When we were both finished, I was surprised to hear Temuge speak. I had assumed that because he had not spoken to me before, that he could not speak English. I was wrong.

"For what do you search?" he asked softly.

I replied, "I am a student traveling from Beijing to Moscow."

The sun was rising from the east and splashing off the lake and flickering on the windows.

"Yes, but for what do you search?" he asked again.

I now understood that his question was more than superficial. I thought about the lake outside the window. I watched as the sun bounced off the surface and reflected its rays on the trees. I thought about what I had learned about this lake: that it contains twenty percent of the world's fresh water, has an average depth of over seven hundred meters and that once the water enters the lake, it stays in the lake for over three hundred years before draining out again. Temuge was old and deep, like this lake.

"I guess I seek happiness," I said in reply.

"And how will you bring happiness to your heart?" he asked.

I paused and then said, "While I am young, I want to travel and learn things from the many diverse cultures of the world."

"Can you feel my heart?" he asked.

"I think so," I said, feeling somewhat perplexed by the question.

"And do you trust my wishes for you?" he asked.

"I had not thought about it before, but I do trust you." I replied.

"You trust me because I wish well for all mankind. I wish the best for you. This is my path, this is the path to protection from self, and this is the path to true happiness," he said.

I glanced out the window as we passed people walking near a small village. As I looked at the people, Temuge spoke softly, "Yes, that's right, continue. Wish them well. Wish them health. Wish for them happiness and that they find what you have just found."

There was a cosmic tension in the air. It was the tension of "truth in motion," when guidance flows from one human being to another. I felt like a small child, holding on to the fingers of my parents as I was learning to walk.

Temuge spoke again. This time his voice was even softer. "Relax, don't hold it tight. It is only a path. Sometimes you will step off the path, but you can always return."

I heard Dochin waking up. I wished he would go back to sleep. My heart felt light and my head happy. I didn't want it to be spoiled.

Temuge spoke again, "You cannot create the path—you can only walk on it. You need not grip it tight. Let life come to you, and let love flow from you."

I turned as Dochin's feet touched the floor. "Good morning," I said.

"Good morning, Sam. You had Mongolian breakfast?"

"Yes, I had a Mongolian breakfast. I hope you slept well."

"Yes, I'm okay, Sam. I'm A1 okay!"

"Good, it is a wonderful day," I said.

I glanced at Temuge. He was looking out the window, and repeating ever so quietly, "Ba yar laa, ba yar laa."

And now, many years later, whenever I think of what he taught me, I picture those I have wished well and see his brown, leather-like face smiling out the window repeating, "Ba yar laa, ba yar laa."

♦

Morse Code

"Okay, everyone! Let's get started. Welcome to Communications 101. The goal for today is to orient you to the class, set expectations, and let you reaffirm your desire to take this course. There are other alternatives. As you may know, two other instructors teach this course. Professor Magdalena Gomez, who is the author of the textbook we use for this class, is an outstanding teacher. Another alternative is Professor Copeland, whose style of lecturing is one of the most intriguing you will ever come across. If you stay in this class, you are expected to participate, to think creatively, and to allow your emotions to become an agent of your own change. If by the end of today, you have not been touched deeply, or if you are not thinking seriously about the essence of communications, then it is my humble request that you drop this class. Are there any questions?"

The class was quiet. No one moved, and no one even coughed. Professor Woods smiled in the direction of the class, but remained quiet. Then he started to speak again, "Okay, let's start on today's lesson. First off, who can tell me a little about the telegraph, when the first message was sent, and what is Morse Code?"

The students, who were still reeling from the professor's somewhat stern welcome, remained silent for a long time. Finally, a young man sitting near the front of the large auditorium raised his hand.

"Yes, please... go ahead."

The young man spoke so softly that only the professor and a few other students could hear him.

"Wonderful! Now please stand up, turn towards the class, and speak as loudly as you can."

The young man stood up nervously, turned and started to speak, "Samuel Morse invented the telegraph and something we call 'Morse Code.' Morse Code uses a series of short and long sounds to represent the letters of the alphabet. Mr. Morse built the first telegraph line between Washington, D.C., and Baltimore. On May 24,1844, he sent out the first message."

"Wonderful! Thank you," said Professor Woods.

The young man, looking somewhat elated, turned back towards the professor, and then sat down. Professor Woods continued, "As the technology evolved, the basic system was automated so that these dots and dashes were converted into letters and printed on small rolls of paper tape. These were cut into strips and pasted onto telegram forms for delivery to their respective recipients. Those who created the earliest business models made the decision to charge by the word, instead of by the character. Thus, for example, the words 'happiness' and 'joy' each cost the same.

"As telegrams became part of everyday life, a style of writing developed based on the economics of the 'per word' charge. Because long words cost the same as short ones and punctuation marks were charged as a word, a new style of writing was born. In it, short, unnecessary words were dropped and the word 'stop' was used to end sentences.

"Please take out a paper and change the following sentence into telegraphic style." Professor Woods then turned and wrote on the board, "Dear John, It is my pleasure to inform you of the date of the upcoming marriage of your cousin, Josephine. She will be married on July fourteenth at two in the afternoon. You and your family are invited to the wedding. Please respond as soon as possible."

The professor turned back towards the class and gave the students a few moments to complete the task. Then he spoke again, "Who wants to share his version?" A few brave students raised their hands. "Okay, you... there, in the very back row. Stand up, speak slowly and clearly, while I write it on the board."

The young lady stood up and read her rendition of the wedding invitation:

> JOHN PLEASURE INVITE YOU AND FAMILY WEDDING COUSIN JOSEPHINE JULY FOURTEENTH TWO PM STOP PLEASE RSVP ASAP

After writing the last words on the board, Professor Woods whirled around and said, "Wonderful, you got the idea. Let's have a few more." After hearing three other versions of the same wedding invitation, he pronounced, "You are now ready for the story. When the story is over, class will be finished for today, and you may leave.

"The story begins in the 1930s with a young man named Walter and his father named Douglas. They were in the middle of an argument. It was not the first time they had argued over small things, but as it turns out—it was the last. The argument started over the definition of 'sky blue' and ended with the son packing up his clothes and leaving home. Both men were stubborn, both knew they were right, and neither was thinking about the future. It was a sad day for their families, and a sad start to a long chapter in each of their respective lives.

"Fifteen years later, Walter had married and was in the process of raising three children when another tragedy struck. Walter had ignored the pain in his chest—for far too long. By the time the doctor saw him, it was too late. From his hospital bed, he wrote a letter to his father. His dear wife, Cynthia, took the letter to the telegraph station and inquired about the cost of sending it. With the help of the operator, they cut it down to its essentials and sent it to the father-in-law she had never met.

"The following morning, the telegram was delivered. Walter's father walked slowly from the front door back to the kitchen table where he had been reading the morning newspaper. He opened the envelope and read:

DOUGLAS FONTANA 128 CLAIR AVENUE
GREENVILLE KENTUCKY

DEAREST FATHER MOTHER STOP WAS STUBBORN MOST MY LIFE NOW COMING END FAST STOP BOTTOM HEART BEG FORGIVENESS NOT CONTACTING SOONER STOP LOVE FOR YOU AND MOM NEVER DIED STOP MANY YEARS MUCH WATER UNDER BRIDGE STOP MARRIED CYNTIHA EIGHT YEARS AGO STOP YOU HAVE GRAND CHILDREN CARL BARBARA AND RICHARD STOP ONLY THRESHOLD DEATH OVERCAME MY STUBBORN EGO STOP DOCTOR GIVES TWO DAYS LIFE MAXIMUM STOP ONLY DESIRE NOW YOUR FORGIVENESS AND MEET FAMILY STOP

DEEPEST LOVE
YOUR SON WALTER

"Douglas wept and moaned as he read and re-read the telegram he had just received. He folded the now damp paper and put it into the pocket of his shirt. He walked slowly to the front door, opened it, and walked outside. He was so emotionally unsettled, he didn't remember to close the door. He walked towards town, only knowing he would send a reply. After ten failed attempts at framing his thoughts, he finally felt he was ready. A nice woman at the telegraph office helped him shorten his emotional reply:

WALTER FONTANA CARE OF MERCY
HOSPITAL SAN FRANCISCO

DEAR WALTER RECEIVED TELEGRAM WITH
OPEN HEART TEARS JOY STOP SAD INFORM
PASSING MOTHER TWO YEARS AGO STOP
DESIRE YOU UNDERSTAND DEPTH MY LOVE
BEFORE PASSING STOP TELL CYNTHIA CARL
BARBARA RICHARD VISIT SOON STOP BIG
EMPTY HOUSE HERE LONELY GRANDFATHER
STOP MY HEALTH ALSO POOR WILL MEET
AGAIN SOON STOP FORGIVE ALL PAST STOP
LOVE YOU BOTTOM HEART STOP

DAD

"Walter walked back through the park where he sat and thought about his son until late afternoon. Much later, as he arrived home, the telegram deliveryman was calling through his still open front door. He signed for the delivery and then walked inside. He went to the kitchen and put water on the stove to boil. Then he sat down and opened the envelope. He was ill prepared for the news it contained.

DOUGLAS FONTANA 128 CLAIR AVENUE
GREENVILLE KENTUCY

DEAR DAD STOP
WALTER NO LONGER ABLE REPLY STOP
READ YOUR TELEGRAM LOVE STOP
WALTER CRIED TEARS JOY STOP
REQUESTED TELL DAD I LOVE YOU STOP

AFTER TELEGRAM WALTER SLEPT THEN
RELATED DREAM STOP IN DREAM SAW YOU
MOUNTAIN BLUE SKY WALKING HAND IN
HAND STOP LAST WORDS REQUESTED ME
PROMISE VISIT YOU STOP MINUTES LATER
SMILED TOOK LAST BREATH STOP
ARRIVING TRAIN SEVEN SUNDAY MARCH
TWENTY ONE STOP

LOVE CYNTHIA CARL BARBARA
RICHARD STOP"

Professor Woods removed a handkerchief from his pocket, wiped his own wet eyes, and then looked into the hearts of his newly initiated students. Then without any further words, he walked silently out the side door. The students took time to realize where they were, and where they had been. Slowly, one by one, they got up and taking care to avoid eye contact, they walked out of the large auditorium. All but a few would return on Wednesday.

⬤

The Motor Bike

"Hey, Uncle Jeff, who did these paintings?"
"Do you like them?"
"They're great. Who was the artist?"
"Do you really want to know?"
"Of course I do—that's why I asked!"
"Then you need to promise not to share it with anyone else."
"Okay, but why?"
"Just because. Do you promise?"
"Okay, sure—I promise."

Jeff lowered his voice almost to a whisper and then said, "I painted them one summer—while I was in college. It was a very special time in my life. I don't share it with everyone."

"Really? You painted these—they're great. But I thought you were a vet."

"I am."

"So, tell me the story—especially about the motor-bike painting."

"Well, it all started after I got a scholarship to go to St. George's University in Granada. It was quite a change. I studied there for my first three years, and then I had to do my fourth year in the U.S.A. During the summer, I needed a job and wanted to do something connected with animals. A friend told me about a place called Kennedy Meadows where they hire out horses and take people into the Sierra Nevada. I applied for a job there and I got it. Two weeks before the job was to start, I arrived in a small town called Sonora. I needed to buy a car and I was thumbing through the newspaper when two things caught my eye.

"The first one was an ad for a motorcycle for twenty-five dollars. I phoned the owner and he said it had an oil leak, but except for that, it ran great. Not being much of a mechanic, I paid the twenty-five dollars and rode it back to the motel. By the time I got there, my right leg was soaked in oil. Other than that—it did seem to run all right.

"The next thing I noticed was an ad for a painting class. I still carry it in my wallet, because it totally changed my life." Jeff slid his wallet from his pocket and then removed a small newspaper clipping. Absorbed in his clipping, he failed to notice the three young people who had gathered behind him. "Let me read you what it says, 'Learn to Paint In One Week! This class, offered by the California Arts Project, is guaranteed to release your creativity and help you learn to paint in just one week. Money back guaranteed if not entirely satisfied. Twenty-five dollars plus materials. The course starts Saturday, June 6th, at 8 A.M. and lasts seven days'"

"I laughed when I thought about the cost, and hoped that this course didn't leak oil like the motorbike I had just bought. Next, I washed my oily blue jeans and wondered whether the motorbike was really worth fixing.

"The next morning I was in the park before eight. I paid the registration, and the class began. The instructor was full of enthusiasm, and I soon forgot about everything else. Her opening remarks are burned in my memory: 'If you want to do something you need four things. It doesn't matter if it is painting a picture, or building a house, you still need the same four things. First, you have to want to do it. In the case of painting a picture, you already want to, otherwise you wouldn't be here. Secondly, you have to believe that you can do it. We are going to make sure that by this time next week, you believe you can paint. Then you have to turn your thoughts into action. If you come every day—that too will happen. Lastly, you work on your techniques and improve your craft. You will find your own ways to do this, either through another class, a book, or just by more painting.

"'The assignment for today is a self-guided field trip. You need to find seven pictures that you like. It doesn't matter if they are photos, prints, or originals—you just need to like them and get them here by tomorrow morning. You also need to buy the materials on the sheet of paper you received when you registered. Please don't buy anything more than what is on the list—especially the colors. If you have questions, come see me now, otherwise I'll see you tomorrow morning at eight.'

"I headed towards a thrift store I had seen the previous day and bought the seven pictures that I needed. There was a sunset in the mountains, some waves on a beach, some wild horses on a prairie, a thunderstorm, a waterfall, some trees in the mountains, and a rider on a motorbike splashing through a small stream. I tied them up in one large bundle and then headed for the craft store to buy the supplies. After buying the rest of what I needed for the class, I walked to a motorcycle shop across the street.

"I spoke to the mechanic and described the condition of my newly-acquired motorbike. He said it sounded like the timing chain had come loose and had worn a hole in the casing. He said I could bring it in for him to take a look but that he was already sure that my only hope was 'Pratley Putty' and some 'good old-fashioned luck.'

"The next morning, I took my seven pictures to the park. After everyone arrived, the instructor wanted each of us to share his choices. When I showed mine, she said each of them was 'wonderful,' except for the motorbike, which she described as 'interesting.' For every student in the class, she put the seven pictures in an order and instructed us to number them, one through seven. In my case, number seven was the motorbike picture.

"She started by explaining that the shapes and colors in any picture create invisible lines that give direction to the human eye.

"Then she said, 'Now I'd like each of you to take out picture number one and to run your finger across the horizontal lines, as if you were painting it. Think about the color but don't worry about how you might paint it—just paint the lines in your imagination using your finger.'

"Then she told us to do the same thing for the lines that run vertically. After that, we were to do the same thing for any lines that we had not already traced with our finger. Then, she asked us to take out our miniature flashlights and do the same thing again.

"After a short break, we put tracing paper over our pictures and with a pencil followed the same procedure. First, the horizontal lines, then the vertical lines, then everything else. The whole time she walked among us saying, 'Beautiful' and 'Wonderful'. After a long lunch break, she explained that we were going to paint on the tracing paper. She reminded us that we only had three colors, so we should put the original away, because it would only distract us. By the end of the day, I can honestly say I liked what I had done. I looked at the work of the others and I liked every one of them. The first picture I painted was that one—the one with the waves."

A voice from behind Uncle Jeff said, "Wow." Jeff whirled around to see three teenagers with their mouths open. He was slightly embarrassed, as were they, but it was too late to change anything, so he just continued his story.

"After a successful day of painting, I felt really good and was inspired to give fixing the motorbike a try. I bought a small set of box-end wrenches, some Pratley Putty and then walked back to the motel.

"After supper, I removed the head from the engine and could clearly see the problem. The aluminum casing had a hole in it where the timing chain had come loose. The chain survived and was now tight, but the hole in the casing needed to be filled. I cleaned everything I could, and then went to sleep.

"The next day's lesson followed the same pattern as the day before. We ran our fingers over our pictures, then we 'painted' it with our small flashlights, then we traced it, and then we painted it with acrylics. The instructor became louder and more dramatic. Though we all knew we were being encouraged, we still felt great. She really was helping us to believe we could paint.

"On the way home, I bought a small file and some emery cloth. After eating a sandwich, I started back to work on the motorbike. Using the file, I made scratches around the hole on the inside of the casing. I scratched as deep as I could in order to give the Pratley Putty more area to bond. Finally, I mixed the putty together and pressed it into the hole. The instructions said I should wait for twenty-four hours, but I decided to wait longer.

"Two more days of painting passed before I began to put the motorbike back together. I used the emery cloth and a stick to smooth the inside of the casing where the hole used to be. After a final cleaning, I reassembled the engine. Though the sun was setting, I wanted to know if my repair had worked or not. I started the engine and then drove around the motel a few times. An inspection of my blue jeans revealed that there was no oil leak—at least not so far.

"For the next few days, I decided to continue to walk to class, but to do some driving in the late afternoon. Each day I drove a little further, and each night an inspection of my jeans gave me a little more hope.

"The week took on a quality of magic. Each day I was creating images I never really dreamt were possible, and each afternoon I went riding in the foothills of these majestic mountains. On Friday, I took my bike into the motorcycle shop and spoke with the mechanic. I told him what I had done. He just smiled and said, 'Keep the chain tight, and ride safely.'

"Saturday was the last day of the class, and the day I would paint pictures six and seven. It seemed only fitting to ride my newly-blessed motorbike to class—so that's what I did."

Pointing to the last picture on the right, Jeff said, "Over there, that's the last picture I painted."

"Have you painted since then?"

"Actually I haven't, but I keep them on my wall as a reminder that you can accomplish pretty much anything you want to."

"And what about the motorbike?"

"I rode it all summer and all the following year, without any trouble."

"Do you still have it?"

"Yep, I still do—it's out back under a tarp."

"Can we see it?"

A few minutes later from the back of the yard, there was a rumble and a roar followed by a great cloud of smoke. All eyes turned to see this well respected veterinarian in his blue jeans, straddling an old motorbike which belched out alternate puffs of blue and white smoke. Though the adults at the family gathering weren't much impressed, there were four teenagers surrounding the motorbike who certainly were. It was a day that none of them would ever forget!

The Mutual Compatibility Act

Vietnam seemed far away now. Twenty years of hard work in Vancouver had made us far more money than we needed. The shoe factory had done well and we'd been richly rewarded for all our hard work. Still, I missed the sun reflecting off the water of the rice paddies; and even more, I missed the peace and quiet of living outside a city.

The first few days of our vacation were actually hard to take. It was like trying to walk after running for a long time. Your body is still set for running and the hard breathing doesn't fit in well with walking.

The five-hour trip from Vancouver created enough excitement in the family to carry us through the two weeks we had planned. Sheridan Lake seemed a good place to stop running and start walking.

The first three nights, I didn't sleep very well. On the fourth day, I drove to Kamloops to buy some supplies. While in town, I bought a copy of the *Kamloops Daily News*, along with an assortment of sodas and food.

The drive did me good. It was like continuing to

run after the race was over—it helped me to slow down. When we returned, I set a chair in the shade of a tall evergreen tree. I cast my line out into the lake and watched the red-and-white-colored float stabilize itself. Then, I opened the newspaper and started to catch up on what I had missed in the last four days. Actually, I hadn't missed much, but somehow I felt better for having checked on the news.

I scanned the classifieds and found a variety of ads for garage sales, boats, RV's, and an assortment of used cars. All the cars were in "good shape" and all made the same claim: "no salt damage." One advertisement in the Real Estate Section caught my attention.

"Buy Your Own Lake: Twelve acres of land. Plenty of tall trees, a five-acre lake, and a waterfall. Quiet enough to bring you peace of mind yet close enough to civilization to have electricity and a telephone. Priced to sell! Near Trapp Lake, 40 km southeast of Kamloops."

I became very excited and lost all interest in fishing or reading the newspaper. After a conversation with my wife, I was back on the road, heading for Kamloops. The real estate agent wanted to go with me, but I wanted to go alone. I turned on Highway 5A, and then followed the map he had drawn for me. I found a chain across the entrance just like the agent said. The lock was rusty, but the key turned and the padlock snapped open.

I had never seen anything quite as beautiful as this in all my forty-five years of living. A waterfall cascaded out of a large rock formation on the east side of the lake. The mid-day sun filtered through the tops of pine trees from the south. I took a deep breath. Excitement surged through my veins as I realized we could easily afford this. We could build a place for vacations, and maybe even retire here. The fresh air made me sleepy so I opened all the doors of the car and took a long nap in the back seat. When I woke up, I took a last look around and then drove back to the public road. I locked the gate behind me, drove to the real estate office to drop off the key, and then took the road back to Sheridan Lake. My wife said my face looked like the sun. "Chong-Duy, I haven't seen you so happy in years. If this will bring you joy, let's buy it."

Early the next morning, I was in the real estate office when it opened. By eleven, I had written the deposit check. I bought a sandwich, some film and then headed for what would soon be our own lake. I took many pictures, and then returned to Sheridan Lake.

That night, my eyes stared at the ceiling for a long time. When I finally fell asleep, I had a series of dreams that centered around our new property.

"Come here. Come here, Chong-Duy."

I looked in the direction of the sound and saw a man dressed in ceremonial robes. He called me again, "Come here. Come here, Chong-Duy. Come and make some dreams." I was aware that I was already dreaming and wondered exactly what he meant.

Without asking, he started to explain, "This is the dream world. You can try out anything here. If you don't like it, you don't have to buy it. And even if you buy it, you can return the dream if you don't like the way it seems to be going. We aim for one-hundred-percent customer satisfaction."

I said, "Okay," but only because he seemed to be waiting for me to say something.

"What do you need? We have it all here," he said. "Come, let me show you around." We whisked by hundreds of shops and offices. We passed an office called, "Dream Architects." I must have looked interested, because my guide stopped and said, "Oh, you want to build a house? This is the best place to have one designed."

He opened the door, pushed me inside, and then left. Another man walked out from one of the many offices and asked how he could help me. I said I needed plans for a house, and showed him all the photographs I had just taken.

Then he asked, "Big or small?"

I said, "Big."

"Good, come back later," he said somewhat abruptly.

I walked outside the office and made sure I didn't wander too far away. After a short while, I returned.

"Okay, Chong-Duy, here is what we built for you."

"You built it already?"

"Well, here in the dream world, it's already built."

"I see."

"You see? How can you see when I haven't yet shown you?"

"I mean, I understand."

"Oh, okay, let's take a look. Step over here, please." I turned the corner and he unlocked the chain just as I had done the first day. I was shocked. There was a very big house just like our house in Vancouver. The lake was completely drained. Where the waterfall had been, there was now a large, gray pipe sticking out of the mountain and turning downwards.

"What have you done to the lake?" I asked.

"We drained the lake. Isn't the house nice?"

"The house is just like the one we live in now."

"Yes, we assumed you liked it."

"It's okay, but it doesn't seem to fit here. Why did you drain the lake?"

"The regulations."

"Which regulations?" I asked.

"Section 28.596."

"And what does that mean?"

"It's the Mutual Compatibility Act. You can't have a big house like this next to a lake. You chose a big house, so we drained the lake."

"It sounds like a goofy regulation to me," I said.

"The Act states that where there is an unimproved body of water within five hundred meters of any portion of a habitual structure, the ratio of dry land to the size of the house must be at least four-hundred-to-one."

"I don't like it," I said. "The whole reason we bought this property was because of the lake."

"I'm sorry you don't like it; we aim to give our customers total satisfaction. Please, come back later."

I went out again and wandered among the many interesting shops. After a while, I returned. This time, the lake and the waterfall had been restored to their original condition. There was a small cabin neatly nestled in an opening in the trees. All the windows had a view of either the lake, the waterfall, or the mountains.

The architect was very worried I might not like it and said, "How is this? Is it better?"

Before I could answer, I woke up.

I forgot about the dream until a few weeks later when I was back in Vancouver, meeting with an architect. From the photographs I had given him, he had made a rough sketch of a large house. The architect announced to me, "This should easily suit all your needs." Sensing my disappointment he said, "You don't like it, do you?"

"It's fine," I said, "But it's not possible to build a house of that size next to the lake."

He looked puzzled and said, "Not possible?"

"Yes, you know, section 28, the Mutual Compatibility Act."

Now he looked even more puzzled, "Is that a local regulation, up there in Kamloops?"

I paused, and then smiled as I recalled the source of my knowledge. "It's something I heard about while I was in the area."

"I'll make it smaller," he said.

I smiled and said, "Seven-hundred square feet should be fine."

"That's a cabin, not a house!" he said.

"Okay, a cabin that fits in with the lake and the trees, that's what we need."

He rolled his eyes, shook his head, and said, "If that's what you'd like. We aim for one-hundred-percent customer satisfaction."

Hearing that phrase again—I could only smile.

◆

My Father's Hands

Being a kid, I never found it odd. Whatever your parents do is normal, and everything else seems odd. It was only much later in life that it struck me.

My dad didn't talk much; but he did get things done. One day, I woke up and he was outside making a big rectangle with string and some sticks. Then with a pick, a shovel, and a wheelbarrow, he started. Yes, I asked what was going on; he was digging a basement. No, he did not know how long it would take. And yes, he did know how deep he was going.

Many years later it struck me just how much dirt that was. The hole was thirty feet long, twenty feet wide and eight feet deep. If you figure that's about five thousand cubic feet of dirt, and if you figure seventy-five pounds per cubic foot, it means my dad dug up, put in a wheelbarrow, and pushed up a plank around four hundred thousand pounds of soil. Now, if you are a metric-thinking person, you can figure this is about two hundred thousand kilograms—but any way you slice it—it was a lot of dirt.

Now, as I told you before, I didn't think there was anything odd about this. Every morning I'd wake up to the sound of the chunk, chunk, chunk of the pick slowly tearing into the hard-packed clay. By the time

I'd get up and go outside, he would still be looking pretty fresh. By the time the mid-day sun was shining, you could see a lot of sweat on his clothes. I don't remember if he rested in the middle of the day or not, but I do remember him still working as it was getting dark.

Of course, it didn't stop there. After the basement was dug, there were forms to build, steel to bend and concrete to mix and pour. Then he built a large living room on top of the basement.

But that seemed to be the way he'd work. There was no announcement when he started and no announcement when he was done. He'd make a plan, start working on it, and keep working on it—till one day, it was complete. If it took a day, that was fine. If it took five years, that was fine too.

Some of this rubbed off on me—even as a kid. One day, we built an airplane out of wooden planks and some old wheels. We were surprised that it didn't fly. I started to understand that it wasn't just working on a dream that would make it happen. In this case, we needed a little knowledge too.

One night, long after I had grown up, and long after I had forgotten about hard work and big plans, I had an interesting dream. That night, I woke up at two in the morning, all refreshed and ready to go. Checking the clock, I realized there were several more good sleeping hours before I needed to wake up. I started thinking about my dad and then fell asleep. I found myself side by side with him and we were digging. We were singing while we swung our picks. The song went something like this: "Swing your pick, and scoop the dirt, move the earth to change. You change it, and it does you, that is—the eternal way."

After a while, I looked at my dad and said, "Can we talk a bit?"

"Sure," he said, taking a cloth and wiping his brow.

"You have a vision here, don't you?"

"Yes," he said. "Sit down, and I'll explain it."

"Whatever we build will be very large," he said. "There are many generations that will follow. Yours is the blessing to dig with me. You will get many blisters on your hands doing this work. Each blister turns to strength. Just like this temple we are building. It will be constructed of bricks and mortar, but it is made from sweat. While we build here, someone else is building you."

He took my hand and turned it over next to his. I looked carefully at them both. Mine had a few blisters that hurt when touched. His hand was like a road map. There were no blisters but many calluses.

Then he spoke again. "At this moment we are here and the work is sweet while we swing our picks, but we are being built. Tomorrow may come and find someone else here, doing this work. You may be called to another task and may feel like a failure for not finishing this work. But the real work is happening to you. It is not something you do, but something that is done to you."

I looked down at his hands and they were glowing. He took my hand and placed it on my heart with his hand on top. I felt a warm glow spread through my body. Then my eyes opened slowly. I felt warm all over, and found my right hand was pressed against my chest, with my left hand folded over it. I lay there very still for as long as I could, absorbing the warmth of the dream. Finally, I sat up in bed and turned both hands with their palms up. I stared in amazement. These were the hands I had seen in the dream; these were my father's hands.

A Nail with No Name

It was a wonderful, warm day and we were riding in the back of a small truck. Just yesterday, we were in the store waiting around to be purchased. You should understand that though nails long to fulfill their potential, we all look pretty much the same, and we don't have a lot of choices. Unlike humans, we get made, get moved around, spend some time waiting, and then, if we are lucky, we get to be part of something wonderful like a house. Normally, that's our highest wish, and our destiny. My destiny, as I would learn later that day, was different.

We were discussing the fact that nails don't have names. I was talking to nail number 176359. She was a very shiny two-inch nail. Some people would call her a fifty-millimeter nail. I wanted to call her beautiful, but that seemed too personal for someone you just met. Calling her 176359 was too much of a mouthful, so I settled for calling her Fifty-nine. She seemed okay with that.

As for me, I am nail number 192719. Well, that's not really my full number. Just like humans who sometimes have first names, middle names, and last names, my complete number includes the date I was born, the factory I was made in, and my size and type.

I am actually a roofing nail, and the only reason I got to meet Fifty-nine was because both of our boxes were torn when they loaded us into this truck.

Now as I said before, we were talking about the fact that we didn't have names. We were doing what people call "philosophizing," but, in actual fact, we were just getting to know each other. She said to me that she had been waiting for months to be purchased, and she was happy to be going some place to be of value. She said she felt that this was the most important day of her life.

The driver hit a bump and we both fell out of our respective boxes. Other nails fell too. In total about fifty nails of various types and sizes were now in a small pile—sandwiched between the boxes. Actually, I wasn't very interested in the other nails; I was only interested in her. I asked Fifty-nine whether she thought we would still be together once the house was completed.

She said, it doesn't matter, that once you meet someone you are always with them, even if distance comes between you. I thought about her words and remembered hearing something like that in the training class we had, just before we were boxed up.

Suddenly, I felt an overwhelming desire to hop off the truck and onto the road. Being a normal nail, this was a pretty strange and somewhat anti-social thought, so I just kept it to myself. Sometimes, strange thoughts pass through your mind when you are overtired, so I attributed it to that, and just let it go.

The sun was warm and the ride had become

smooth. Many of the nails started dozing off. I felt sleepy and told Fifty-nine that I was going to take a nap. She said I had all of eternity to sleep, but that if I wanted to take a nap, it was okay with her. I don't know what school she had gone to, but she seemed to understand a lot about life. Soon, I fell asleep.

While sleeping, I saw myself jumping high into the air and then landing on the road. My sharpest end was pointing dangerously into the air. In my dream, I remembered what we were taught about safety and figured this dream was a nightmare.

Just after I hit the ground, a small blue car drove over me. I heard the air coming out of the tire, and felt the anxiety of the young woman who was driving. She pulled off to the side of the road, got out, and started staring at the flat tire and at me. She said something about being late and started crying. Next, a young man drove up and started changing the tire for her. Then, they exchanged pieces of paper with numbers written on them. I guessed that humans not only have names, but also have numbers—just like nails do.

Suddenly, the dream fast-forwarded and these same two people who met because of me, were getting married, building a house, raising children, and then showering their grandchildren with love. It all happened so fast that I woke up.

I told Fifty-nine about my dream. She said maybe I have a destiny that was different from hers. She was sure she was going to be part of a wonderful house.

The truck seemed to be traveling a bit fast for the

road we were on. More nails were spilling out of the boxes. The truck turned a corner faster than was safe. Nails were sliding all over. Then, the truck hit a bump. Everything went crazy. A lot of us went up in the air. I saw Fifty-nine do a couple of one-eighties and then land back in the truck.

As for me, I went flying high into the air, and when I came down, I hit my head on the side of the truck and then bounced out. I could see Fifty-nine watching me. She seemed to understand everything. While I was in mid-air, time slowed down—just like in the movies. I looked at Fifty-nine and she was smiling.

She shouted out to me, "Don't worry, we all have separate and very wonderful destinies. You were made for yours and I for mine. Maybe we will meet again one day in some re-cycling plant. In the meantime, you will always be in my heart and I will be in yours. Go well, my friend."

As I was tumbling on the road, I could hear Fifty-nine still shouting, "And remember to embrace your destiny."

Things happened very fast after that. I was driven into something softer than wood. I was going around in circles. There was a loud hissing sound. When the motion stopped, I could see a young woman getting out of her car.

A feeling of warmth and contentment filled my being. I thought about Fifty-nine and all she had taught me. Her voice rang in my ears, "Remember to embrace your destiny."

A man drove up and stopped. I thought about Fifty-nine and the dream I had while I was sleeping on the truck. The man started changing the tire. After he finished, he rubbed his finger gently over my head, glanced upwards towards the clouds in the blue sky and then said, "Thank you."

Though I wasn't sure if he could hear me or not, I looked into his eyes, smiled, and said, "You're welcome."

Northern Lights

I can still recall the conversation with my mother the week before I left. She couldn't understand why I was going. I explained that they would give me a Special Service Medal just for being there for the six months; and on top of that, I would get extra pay.

"Why would they give you a medal just to go and work some place?" she asked.

"I guess they have a hard time getting volunteers."

"Probably because people go there and lose their minds," she stated.

"I promise I won't lose my mind," I replied.

That was my mother's concern before I left for CFS Alert. To me, it seemed like quite an adventure. I pulled the "night shift," which meant, I'd be there for six months, from October to March, and most of that time it would be dark.

My job at CFS Alert was pretty straightforward. I collected local weather data and made sure that the machines for measuring magnetic fields and the ozone layer were working. Unlike most of my colleagues, I went outside every day. Well, to say that I "went" outside—maybe that was stretching things, but each day I was there I would prepare the weather balloon under the big dome, open the launch door, let go of the balloon, and then close the door again. After launching the balloon each day, I would monitor the data coming in and check that all the instruments were working. After that, I would normally read books or write in my journal. Sometimes, I'd play chess or checkers. The clock was the only way to know when to sleep and when to wake up. There were no chickens like on the farm, and there were no first streaks of sun, but we did have the northern lights. Sometimes, I'd wake up to a light tapping on my door and hear my friend saying, "Francois, wake up—it's show time."

I'd dress quickly and walk to the mess hall, where I'd join six or seven other people gathered next to a window. We were all entranced by this wonder of nature. The first time or two, there were lots of "uuhs" and "ahhs." After the third time, it became like a shared meditation, and nobody wanted to talk. When the show was over, we'd drink tea or coffee in silence until finally, one by one, we'd each return to what we were doing before it all started. The northern lights were as close to a religious experience as most of us would ever get.

Now, back home on the farm again, I had to settle for watching the sun rise at dawn. I'd been back long enough to have my internal clock readjusted to the cycles of light and dark. Awakening one morning, I glanced out the window and could see that dawn was at hand. I dressed quickly, jumped into the old Chevy truck, and drove to the highest point on the farm. On the prairies of Manitoba, any small hill is a "Mount Everest." Since there was no road that went up "Everest," I accelerated hard so I could drive as far up the hill as was possible. When the hill became too steep, I stopped, pulled the hand brake firmly, and then walked to the top of my own Mount Everest.

Just as the first rays of the sun rose, I heard my name called.

"Francois, what did you learn?"

I turned my head quickly to see who was joining me. I stood up and turned in a complete circle. There was no one.

"Francois, what did you learn?"

I decided it must be the return to civilization. Maybe my mother was right. Maybe people do lose their minds in places like that.

The voice came again, "Francois, what did you learn?"

"What do you mean and who are you and where are you?" I asked, turning in a circle as I spoke.

"Sit down and listen for a moment," instructed the voice.

I turned around a couple more times and then sat down facing the rising sun.

"Did you learn anything while you were gone?"

I glanced to the left and right and responded, "I suppose I did, but what do you have in mind?"

"I am wondering if you learned anything more about humility?"

"Well, I suppose so, I think I talk a little less, and maybe not so loudly. I'm not so sure about some things now."

"Did you ever think about the earth and how patient it is?"

"Not really," I replied.

"Year after year, people and animals walk across the earth, fight over it, bury their dead in it, and drive their plows deep into it in order to grow their food. Yet in spite of all this, have you ever heard the earth complain or brag?"

"I guess not; why do you talk to me now?"

A few birds chirped. The sun was halfway up. All else was quiet.

"And why do you scare me like this?" I asked again.

There was still no reply. I continued to sit there and listen, but heard nothing more. I removed my coat and stood with my back to the sun. A breeze blew gently on my face. I slowly turned to each of the four directions and thought deeply about what I had just heard. I actually did feel different since coming back.

I walked down the hill to the truck, got inside, and let it roll slowly down the hill. As I drove home, I thought about my grandfather and the little I knew of him. The smell of breakfast greeted me as I walked through the kitchen door. "Good morning, Mom. Morning, Dad," I said.

"Morning, Son."

Dad was sipping his coffee and staring thoughtfully out towards his day's work.

"Dad, you know that hill east of the corn field?" I

asked.

"The one you go to each morning?"

"Yes, that one."

"What do you know about it?"

"Well," he said, "my father used to tell me that it was a sacred place to the Indians. He said a medicine man used to go there to pray. Your Aunt Lucy used to go there when she'd visit us. She said she heard voices there. I don't know much except that it's far too steep to plant corn on."

I added Dad's contribution to my own experiences and realized that this mountain was in fact a very special place. Mom brought breakfast to the table, sat down, and asked if I was getting back on Manitoba time. I told her I was still adjusting, but that I felt fine.

Now, many years later, I still make it a point to see the sunrise from on top of that special mountain. Though I never heard the voices again, that hill always seemed far too sacred to drive up on in an old Chevy truck. Since that day, I always park the truck at the bottom of the hill, close the door with a lot more respect, and walk up the hill—with just a bit more humility.

Orange Blossoms

As my eyes opened, I noticed the banks of fluorescent lights and the crisscrossed metal beams of the ceiling. It took a minute to return from the world of sleep and dreams, to wakefulness and to the world we call—reality. As I became aware of my body, I realized that my feet were sore and I was sleeping in yesterday's clothes. I turned on my side to avoid the bright lights and noticed a young woman with brown skin who was sitting on the next cot—rubbing her eyes.

I began to remember the fog, our arrival in the early morning, and the chaos of being in the airport all day. I remembered the news that there would be no more flights and then being shown a cot with a single blanket where I would spend the night.

I sat up as the lady on the next cot spoke softly, "Good morning."

"Hi, what time is it?" I whispered.

"A little after five. There's some coffee and tea over there—do you want some?"

"That would be nice."

We both stood up and quietly picked our way through the rows of cots towards the smell of the fresh coffee. We found a table and began to chat.

"Have you been awake long?" I asked.

"For about three hours. I flew in from Mexico City—it's a six-hour time difference. When I woke up

I found all the lights still on—I just couldn't get back to sleep. I was happy to see you wake up. It's a strange loneliness when you are around a lot of people with no one to talk to."

We both smiled and then took sips of the hot coffee.

My new friend continued, "My name is Rosario Morales, and I am traveling to a public health conference in Bucharest."

"Are you a doctor?" I asked.

"Yes, I work in public health."

"Nice to meet you, Doctor Morales."

"Please call me Rosario."

"Okay, nice to meet you, Rosario"

We both laughed a little more and sipped our coffee again.

"Looks like more people are waking up. There must be several thousand travelers stuck here. By the way, my name is Linda LeClaire. I live in Saskatoon—in Canada. I'm just returning from Mozambique."

"From what I've read, the people of Mozambique have suffered greatly. What were you doing there?" asked the doctor named Rosario.

"I was working for a non-profit organization called VISIT. It stands for Volunteers in Service for International Tourism. We try to promote travel to places where the economy could benefit. And yes, you are right, the people of Mozambique have suffered greatly; but they have a strength of character you seldom find elsewhere. I'm sure in your work you have noticed the differences between children who are raised with every material advantage and those raised and accustomed to some element of hardship."

"Yes, I have noticed how people raised in adversity seem kinder and more sensitive."

"I have noticed this in many places in the world—Mozambique is only one such place," I said.

"What exactly did you do there?" asked Rosario.

I laughed and then said, "I towed old cars and trucks to a scrap yard."

Rosario laughed with me as we looked around the hall and saw that our fellow travelers were now waking up in greater numbers.

Rosario smiled and then said, "So what do you mean you towed old cars?"

"Well, they had a civil war that lasted sixteen years. Like any other guerilla war, there were lots of civilian casualties. The idea of the opposition is always the same—make the country ungovernable so that it can seize power. In the case of Mozambique, there was a lot of traffic from Swaziland to the city of Maputo. It was a short stretch of road through a variety of terrains. Workers, returning from Swaziland or South Africa, would come home for holidays with their cars loaded with food and gifts for their families. These made easy targets for the insurgents. There were also large trucks, often overloaded with goods bound for areas that had little. These too, became targets. After the war was over, the sides of the roads were littered with the remains of these cars and trucks."

"It doesn't sound like a pretty sight," said Rosario.

"It's not—these hulks of trucks and cars sit as

rusty reminders of a particularly troubled time. They are not what tourists want to see."

"That's where you came in?"

"Yes, my job was to catalog every burnt-out wreck along that road, and then put out bids to have them hauled away. My small team would spray a number on each one, and then using a GPS device, we'd position them on a map. After the contracts were signed, we had to follow up and make sure all the scrap was removed."

"Did you also have to deal with land mines?" asked Rosario.

"No! We were lucky. For some reason, there were no mines planted in that area."

"How long did the project take to complete?"

"Four months, from the day I arrived until I got on a plane in Maputo headed here for my connecting flight."

"What was the highlight of your experience there in Mozambique?"

"Orange blossoms," I said without any hesitation, "it was the lessons I learned from the orange blossoms."

"I guess there are not many orange groves in Saskatoon? Was it your first time to smell the blossoms?" she asked.

"No, but I had never had any experience like that before. On my first trip, driving from Maputo, we were about halfway along the road when suddenly the landscape changed from sand and houses made of reeds, to rows and rows of orange trees. The smell was overpowering and I asked Mashama, my assistant, to stop. We spent about fifteen minutes there, just inhaling the fragrance of the blossoms. Most days, we would stop there at least once. It became like visiting a temple to me. It was a sharp contrast to the rest of the road.

"After the third trip, we began cataloging the old cars and trucks along the side of the road. Most of these were between the orange groves and the Swaziland border. After about a week, it suddenly hit me that there were no burnt-out cars and no burnt-out trucks in the five-kilometer stretch of road that wound its way through the orange trees. I asked Mashama why this was. He didn't know and suggested we ask the farm manager.

"The following day, as my head was spinning with questions, we located the sixty-three year-old farm manager and asked him if there were really no attacks on the road inside the farm, or if the farm workers had towed all the wrecks away."

"What did he say?"

"He said there were never any attacks inside the farm. As we continued to inquire he told us that the rebel troops, as well as the soldiers, would come and help themselves to the fruit, but it was his thought that no human being who comes and smells the orange blossoms could ever possibly turn his gun on another—not here, surrounded by the smell of the orange blossoms."

"That's interesting, really interesting. And you never found evidence of any attacks inside the farm?"

"Not one. We hauled out over a thousand burnt

out cars and trucks. Not one of them was from the section of road that ran through the orange groves."

Suddenly a voice over the loudspeakers announced that the flights would resume soon. Rosario and I exchanged addresses, finished our coffee, and then returned to our cots. We gathered our luggage, washed our faces, and started to look for our respective departure gates.

We found Rosario's first. We embraced and said good-bye. As I turned to walk away, Rosario called out to me, "Next spring, when the snow is still covering your houses and you've had enough staring into the warmth of your fire, come down for a visit. My father has a small farm in the mountains. It has three guest cottages. They're in the middle of an orchard—all planted with oranges."

I smiled, knowing we'd meet again soon. Just the thought of sleeping surrounded by orange blossoms made me feel happy.

As the fog cleared, I saw the first plane take off and another one land. Even though I was tired and sore, I was grateful for the fog that had stranded me here. That fog had given me a new friend, in another country, and that friend had a guesthouse surrounded by orange trees. I could already imagine making a trip there and could feel in my heart the peace of waking up at dawn—to the smell of the orange blossoms.

●

Oxygen Mask

As I sat down in the taxi, I took a deep breath and tried to center myself. I asked myself why I was catching such an early flight and then remembered how badly I wanted to get home. As the taxi neared the airport, I handed the driver enough money for the fare and the tip. When he stopped, I jumped out, quickly grabbed my rollaboard, pulled out the handle, and started running toward the security checkpoint. I could already feel the effects of too much coffee and too little sleep. After clearing security, I ran to the gate and found that passengers were just starting to board. After a short wait, I got my seat assignment, joined the boarding line, took a deep breath, and tried to focus again. It was good that I had nothing important to accomplish today. I closed my eyes briefly and took another deep breath. This was in sharp contrast to how I normally operated, and the feeling was not pleasant.

I followed the other passengers who were boarding the plane. As I passed the first class section, the passengers in front of me stopped while an elderly lady sought help to lift an overweight bag into the overhead compartment. Glancing ahead and to the left, I saw a man who appeared to be Dr. Mitchell

Kirby, the world-famous author of so many self-help books. I couldn't tell which row he was in, but glanced at my boarding pass and noted I was in seat "16-A." What an honor that would be to sit near him and exchange a word or two.

The line started to move again. A few seconds later, I realized Dr. Kirby was sitting in my row in 16-C. I smiled, nodded my head toward my seat, and then said, "Excuse me, my seat is by the window."

He didn't speak, but smiled graciously, stood up and moved into the aisle to allow me to sit down. This was my lucky day. His books had taught me so much, and I had read them all.

As I settled into my seat, I extended my hand and said, "My name is Darlene Yury. I'm from Edmonton."

He smiled, bowed his head slightly, and said, "My name is Mitchell, and I am very happy to meet you."

Hearing the sound of his voice, and the gentle smile as he bowed his head, I was sure this was Dr. Kirby. I was about to ask if he was the author of the wonderful books I had read, when another man walked quickly onto the plane, tossed a bag in the overhead, and sat down between us. My heart sank, as I saw the opportunity vaporize before my face.

"I'm Larry Kidwell, what's your name?" asked the new arrival.

"Darlene Yury," I said, feeling very disappointed that this man was now a barrier separating me from the chance of a lifetime. As the plane pushed back from the gate, the flight attendants gave us the normal talk about the emergency exits and the oxygen masks. I took a deep breath and again became aware of how far off-center I was.

"What do you do for a living, Darlene?" asked the newly-arrived passenger.

"I'm an investment counselor. I work out of Edmonton."

"Ah, kindred spirits we are. I'm a trader. Mostly day-trading, but I'll buy anything, anywhere, and make something on it."

"Sounds risky to me," I said.

"You have to take risks if you are planning to make money," he said

Somewhere the conversation took a bad turn and became adversarial. We were not at all the "kindred spirits" he thought we were, and I did not handle the situation well. I offered him a lot of advice, which he hadn't asked for. That, coupled with the resentment I was building about how I was feeling, made for an especially miserable first leg of my flight.

As we made our first stop, Larry got off, and I was determined to find out if the other passenger really was Dr. Mitchell Kirby. Using less than my normal tact, I just blurted out, "Aren't you Doctor Mitchell Kirby, author of *Centering Your Days*?"

The passenger in the aisle seat smiled lovingly, bowed his head towards me, and said, "Yes."

"I'm so happy to meet you," I said, smiling. "I have read all your books and carry one of them with me wherever I go." I somewhat proudly pulled out *The Practice of Divine*, from my purse.

Dr. Kirby nodded his head again, smiled and said, "I feel honored to sit near someone who has benefited in some small way from my efforts."

Then the conversation drifted towards the concept of daily practice, and Dr. Kirby asked me if I had adopted one. I explained that I had, and he asked what it consisted of. I explained that every morning, I exercised for twenty minutes, meditated for twenty minutes, and wrote in my journal for twenty minutes. He told me it was a wonderful practice and asked if I managed to do it every day. I was about to explain that I did it every day, except for days like today, when the flight attendant asked if we wanted something to drink. Dr. Kirby asked for water and I asked for a soda.

"I'm sorry for the earlier noise," I said. "Something went wrong. I just couldn't manage that conversation—it was very unhealthy."

Dr. Kirby nodded his head again, smiled, and said, "I understand."

After more apologizing, I was hoping he would help me with some guidance on what went wrong. Instead, he seemed to change the conversation, "Did you hear the flight attendant before we took off?"

"Not really. What do you mean?" I asked.

"About the oxygen masks."

"I'm afraid I tuned it out. I travel a lot and I guess I don't listen anymore."

"Do you know what they normally say about the oxygen masks?"

"I think so. It's something like, 'In the event of a

cabin depressurization, oxygen masks will automatically drop from the compartment above your heads. Though the bag may not fully inflate, there will be oxygen flowing.' Then they tell us to put on our own masks before trying to help someone else—like a child, or an elderly person. Is that what you mean?"

"Yes, exactly. Now you mentioned you have a 'daily practice.' And you acknowledge that the conversation with the other passenger did not go well, and you feel slightly responsible, is that correct?"

"Yes, that's all true," I said.

"Today, you got up for this early flight, but were you able to do your daily practice?"

I felt the blood rushing to my face, as I realized that whenever I had to wake up earlier than normal, I skipped my daily practice and put myself at risk. I wanted to apologize, or say something but I was unable to speak. Then, Dr. Kirby spoke again. "There is no need to feel embarrassed or apologetic. As part of my work, I often coach business executives. The situation you are now in is a common one and is easily solved. My advice is that if at all possible, take a later flight and if it is not possible, then just wake up earlier and remember to put your own mask on before you try to help others."

I felt a tear run down my face as I realized the truth of his words. I wanted to turn the clock back and start the day over—but I couldn't.

Dr. Kirby reached down and opened a book as if he had not noticed my tears. He glanced at me briefly, smiled, and nodded his head respectfully. Then he spoke again, "There is still forty-five minutes left—before we land. Though it may be hard for you to do your physical exercises on the plane, there is nothing to stop you from your meditation and journal writing. I will be reading this novel until we land." With that, he opened the book wider and drew it closer to himself.

I started to breathe consciously, and closed my eyes. The airplane is not the best place for meditation, but under the circumstances, I was willing to try. I started to picture the bright-yellow sunflowers in my garden at home. Then, little by little, I let go of all conscious thought and drifted into a deep meditation. After a few minutes of this, I pictured the sunflowers again and then directed loving thoughts to the man who had sat next to me – the man I had probably offended. After forgiving him and forgiving myself, I opened my eyes and began to write in my journal. When the plane touched down, I closed my journal and put it back into my purse.

Dr. Kirby closed the book he was reading and asked, "Better now?"

"Much better," I replied. "I'm very grateful." I handed Dr. Kirby my business card and said, "If you ever need help with any investments, I'd be happy to do it—free of charge. What you just gave me is worth all the wealth I can imagine."

Dr. Kirby smiled again, nodded his head in that characteristic way of his and then said, "You are welcome for the little advice I have given, and I thank you for the generous offer; perhaps one day I will call you." He nodded his head once again, smiled, and said, "Good-bye and take care of Darlene—she is precious, more precious than all her investments."

💧

Pacific Sunset

The gracious host lived in a beautiful house that was well beyond the means of her writer-friend, Michael Parker. She was delighted to have the book-signing in her house, and he was happy to be there. By the time Michael was to start reading, there were thirty-five ladies and two men gathered in the spacious living room overlooking the Pacific.

A teacher was among the friends gathered for the occasion and she was not afraid to ask questions. Just as Michael opened the book, she stood up and said, "Excuse me, Mr. Parker. Before you start reading, I would like to ask why you do not mention the name of The Creator in your books. Though I have not read your most recent work, I have read all the previous ones, and as far as I can recall, you speak of many spiritual events, but you have never once directly mentioned The Creator. Would you mind explaining why?" The teacher's eyes were twinkling and you could see she meant no harm.

Michael Parker smiled at her and closed the book. "Normally, I do not answer questions at this time. However, given the nature of your question, I will respond to it now, but would request that any further questions or comments will be saved until after we read chapter one."

The teacher smiled and nodded her head. No one else spoke. After a brief pause to seal the agreement, Michael Parker continued, "This is, indeed, an interesting question. To give you some background information, there are many people on this planet of ours. There are hundreds of languages in use today, and thousands of dialects. On top of that, there are many different belief systems, all of which have at their core the same fundamental values. Additionally, there are many grades of belief. It is my wish, and the intent of all my books, to create events in the minds of the readers that might intensify their faith. I don't wish to tell people what to believe, but rather to create small rites of intensification that might help strengthen the beliefs of any reader.

"Glance out the window and notice the ocean and the clouds. If you look at the sun slowly dropping towards the horizon, it is a very moving experience. But not everyone lives on a bluff overlooking the Pacific. Not everyone has smelled the fragrances of orange blossoms. Most people are not able to travel around the world and discover how similar we all are. The events in my books are there to give each person a chance to intensify his beliefs—on a daily basis. I'd like to think of myself as a gardener or a farmer. I have planted a large field so that each reader can choose a few flowers that they are attracted to."

There was a long pause as Michael Parker looked into the eyes of the teacher. Finally, although she realized he had not directly answered her question—she smiled and said, "Thank you very much."

With that, Michael began reading Chapter One of his latest novel, *Daily Passages*. As he read, the host quietly filled glasses of iced tea, and those present added the amount of sugar they each desired. They stirred their tea as quietly as was possible while Michael continued reading. Then the host sat down and listened in earnest.

Halfway through the chapter, Michael stopped and reached for his ice tea. No one moved. The large living room was quiet except for the sounds of the ice cubes moving in his glass. The gracious host started to get up to serve him more, but he motioned that none was needed.

He continued reading. Outside the window, the clouds clustered on the western horizon and waited to embrace the setting sun. The sun continued towards them. Michael read on as those gathered sat spellbound. The first chapter of the book was almost over. The sounds of the Pacific Ocean filtered in between the words of the story. Finally, the clouds received the sun, and a great painting appeared in the sky. Orange, yellow, and gray were the main colors—but there were others too—if you looked closely enough.

The smell of earlier promised oranges began drifting into the living room. Michael read on. The teacher, who had asked the earlier question, coughed once and then shifted in her chair. Finally, Michael reached the end of the chapter, and the gracious host nodded to someone waiting in the hallway. Soon afterward, fresh-cut oranges appeared from one side of the room, while steaming hot tea appeared from the other. Those gathered, who had sat spellbound for almost an hour, now began to realize where they were. Now, it was time for conversation; it was time for questions. The room began to buzz as the oranges were eaten with care and the tea was sipped with appreciation. Books were purchased, and the color of the sunset, through the still open window, intensified. As the glass tea-cups grew cold, the guests began drifting toward the large front door.

An hour later, the sun was down and the window closed. Michael Parker was gone—as were the other thirty-seven guests, who had shared so much more—than just another—Pacific sunset.

♦

The Piano

It was just after my seventeenth birthday and my parents needed a break. Grandma had been sick for a long time. Mom and Dad had really done their best to give her all the love and care they possibly could. I had suggested that they take a vacation and go to a place where there were no phones and no children and no parents. They chose a place in the mountains of Switzerland. School was over for now, and Grandma would be fine with me.

The day after they left, Grandma ran a high fever. I called the doctor, and he said we should come in. While we were there, the doctor and Grandma had a discussion. When I say discussion, I should say that Grandma talked and the doctor listened. The short version of the "discussion" was: Grandma was tired of hospitals, and she wanted to go home. The doctor looked at Grandma, looked at me, and then nodded his head in agreement.

A few minutes later, he took me aside in the hall and said, "There comes a time when medical science really cannot do much. People live or die by forces doctors can't control. My suggestion to you is that you take her home, let her eat what she wants, sleep when she wishes, and watch what happens." I agreed to follow his advice, but the phrase, "...watch what happens," created a feeling in my heart that I cannot explain.

On the way home, Grandma spoke dramatically, saying, "I want to sleep in the room facing the east, so that I can wake up with the sun every morning. I want the curtains left open so I can see the moon and the stars at night. I only want fruit to eat. And most of all, I want you to play the piano as often as you can." She explained that she wanted to hear the piano while awake, while drifting off to sleep, and while she was sleeping. She gave me a list of books she wanted to have nearby, so that I could read them to her. I wasn't really sure what this was all about, but my heart was excited by the idea of surrounding Grandma with all these things so dear to her heart.

The first week was heavenly. I had decided to sleep on the couch in the same room. Every morning at dawn, before the sun was up, Grandma would call my name softly. Then she would tell me it was time to greet the morning. She would ask me to open the windows wide to let in the fresh morning air, and then to play the piano. After this, we would sit in silence, watching the gentle clouds playing with the sun and creating new colors. Each morning was unique and fresh.

At the beginning of the second week, Grandma's fevers began again. During this time, she would only drink water. She would wake up at different times and ask me to play something softly. I would wake up, bring myself back from the world of sleep, wipe her sweating brow, and then play the piano, while she drifted back to sleep.

Without asking, I phoned the doctor to see if I should take her back to the hospital. He said to keep her comfortable and listen carefully. Part of me wished that my parents were home, and part of me was glad they were gone. I had no control over it anyway, since I had insisted they not leave a contact phone number.

On Wednesday, Grandma awoke and said, "Come near, my child." She had never called me this before. I walked over and sat beside her bed. It was 4 a.m. I wiped the sweat from her forehead as she began to speak. "I went to a wonderful place, where lights were everything," she said. "I was given a ticket that had 'Visitors Pass!' printed on it in big, red letters. There were many people there. Some of the people I knew; others I recognized from stories. In this place, all the people seemed busy. They were all working hard but in a relaxed and wonderful way. My guide told me I could move about freely, but that I must come back to him before I woke up. There were signs that said things like: 'Academy of the Sciences,' 'Center for the Performing Arts,' and 'Musical Inspiration Society.' Each of the signs changed each time you looked at them. These people seemed to be responsible for creating all of the arts, the music, and the sciences. They told me I could share with you anything I remembered. It was very wonderful, my child."

I told Grandma it was a beautiful dream, and

asked if she wanted to wake up the sun with music. She said she did, so I began to play. While playing, I thought about her dream and failed to notice that Grandma had gone back to sleep. The music touched my soul in a way it had never done before. That day, I watched the sunrise alone.

On Thursday morning, Grandma awoke at 5 a.m. and said, "Come and sit close, angel." Just as on the previous day, she recounted the dream she had just experienced. "I went back to the place of lights," she said. "I met the same guide and I asked him where I was. He told me that this place had many names, but I don't remember them. Then, he told me that this is the place of those who had left the bells behind so that they could sing forever; the place of those who had chosen to be 'just' even when it was not in their own best interests. I asked if I could stay, but all he did was to smile." Before I could ask Grandma anything more, she closed her eyes and drifted off to sleep. I walked to the piano and played our sunrise music, knowing she was absorbing it. I was moved to tears, but failed to understand why. Then, I sat beside Grandma, holding her hand as the dawn changed to the day.

On Friday morning, Grandma awoke at 5:30 a.m. and called me her "spirit sister." The sun was already rising, and the first rays were shining upon her face. She smiled lovingly at me and told me she had again visited the place of the lights. Her face radiated like the sun as she spoke. "The same guide took me to a graduation ceremony. The speaker gave a wonderful talk, but I don't remember it. I was there for a long time and met many people. I was given a diploma wrapped in a ribbon of gold. The guide took me by the hand and told me I may return to you, but only as a visitor."

She looked deeply into my eyes and said, "Go, and play the song of the morning. I need to hear it now." I walked to the piano, sat down, and started to play. Suddenly, playing the piano became easy. Always before, it had been with great effort and concentration. Now, suddenly, it was as if I became the instrument. I glanced at Grandma; her hands were on top of the blankets with her fingers extended. A beautiful smile played upon her face. As our eyes met, she nodded her head once, looked at me, broadened her smile, and then closed her eyes. I closed mine and continued to play. A tear ran down my cheek. I started to play louder. With my eyes closed, and my ears filled with the sound of the music, I saw Grandma with her ageless smile saying, "Play, angel, play the song of the morning."

◆

Quaking Aspen

Any university campus contains a mixture of people, personalities, and events. The library captures much of it—all in one building. A few years ago, I wandered into the library of one such large university and found myself in the section where they keep the dissertations filed by various disciplines. One of the bound volumes stood out among the black, brown, and maroon-colored covers. This one was sky blue with gold lettering on its spine. As I removed it from the shelf, some folded sheets of paper fell onto the floor in front of me. I picked up the papers and walked to a long table where two students sat in the very quiet library.

I placed the book on the table, opened it, and from the title understood that it was a thesis on the nature of the quaking aspen. I closed the book and opened the papers that had fallen from it.

It appeared to be a letter and started out, "To Whom it May Concern." It seemed to have been written as a postscript to the thesis about the quaking aspen. In the upper left-hand corner of the letter was a note in blue ink which said, "I found this letter among my father's things. I thought it belonged with his thesis, so I placed it here."

The letter, written by the author of the thesis, started out quite seriously and explained the process by which he had been granted his doctorate, but by the time I reached the end, I started to laugh. Well, I should say it started out as a laugh—but it soon turned into a howl.

Soon, after I had broken the code of silence, a librarian rose from his desk and walked towards me, followed by a security guard. He bent down and quietly explained that this was a university library and they had a zero-tolerance noise-policy. He said if I could not abide by the rules, I would have to leave. I apologized, explained what had happened and handed him the letter. He started reading it and after awhile, he also burst out laughing. Two of those sitting at the table began to smile and then followed us as we walked around the corner to see the head librarian. After a brief explanation, the head librarian motioned for me to hand her the dissertation I was holding. She looked stern, holding the book in one hand and the letter in the other. Statue-like, she started reading the letter until she too collapsed in laughter. By this time, there was a gathering of about fifty people waiting to be told what was so funny. The head librarian glanced at her assistant who shrugged his shoulders and offered no help. She glanced at the security guard who looked down at the ground and avoided her gaze. Finally, after noticing the large gathering of students, she said, "Okay!" and then slipped off her shoes, and stood up on a nearby chair. The security guard walked over and steadied the chair as she held up the book and the letter and then began to speak: "This letter was found inside this dissertation. It's a pretty funny story apparently written by the same person. I'll read it aloud and then we can all go back to doing what we are supposed to be doing." She handed the book to her assistant and then held the letter with both hands and began to read:

The whole reason I came to these mountains in the first place was to study the quaking aspens. Ever since I was a child, I had marveled at how these trees had spread throughout North America. I imagined one massive root system spreading from the mountains of Mexico, throughout much of the continental United States, linking almost all of Canada and stretching its roots to the northernmost part of Alaska. In high school, I had learned that these massive trees also propagate their seeds by blowing in the wind. Though I had traveled to many places to collect data for my thesis, the Cascades remained my favorite place to visit.

I really wanted to understand why a single tree that spans many acres still contained so much genetic diversity. Finally, I began to understand that the spread of these trees was not only caused by the growth and movement of roots, but also by the occasional migration of its fluffy seeds.

After many months of work, my research was complete, the classes were all over, and my thesis had been written. Then, presentation time arrived. My stomach knotted up like spaghetti that had been over-cooked and then left out to cool.

I walked in front of my committee feeling very nervous. I started to read, "A Species Determined to Spread—The

Growth of the Quaking Aspen." I could feel my legs trembling. Something inside of me cried out that if this was a true search for knowledge, I had no need for fear. I took a deep breath, closed my eyes, and paused.

Suddenly, Dr. Balser spoke, saying, "Please continue, we don't have all of eternity."

I opened my eyes, smiled, and then started to speak, "You have all read my thesis, and understand the claims it puts forward. Now, I'd like to ask you to close your eyes and go on a journey with me."

"May I remind you that this is science and not religion?" said one of the committee members.

I took another deep breath and then said, "Dr. Green, it is my firmest belief that religion and science are as intertwined as the root systems of the quaking aspen. It was long held that these forests were, in fact, one tree. While it is true that some of the forests are one large tree, others, as explained in my research, are two or three trees with overlapping root systems."

"'And just how far does that go towards convincing your committee that science and religion are one thing, and that we should close our eyes and go on a journey with you?"

At that point, Dr. Chung spoke up and encouraged the others to keep an open mind. I thanked Dr. Chung for her intervention and noticed that most of the committee members had now closed their eyes and were prepared to hear the story of my dream. I took another deep breath and started the story. "Two weeks ago, I was in a valley fifty miles east of here. Suddenly I felt an attraction to walk in a particular direction. After about thirty minutes, I felt ex-

tremely tired. I sat down at the foot of a particularly old aspen. I felt very sleepy. The urge to sleep was intense. Finally, I succumbed and curled up next to the tree and drifted off to sleep. I had many dreams, including one about standing here before you and asking you to go where I walked, and to see what I saw.

"In one of the many dreams, an old woman spoke to me saying, 'I am a root, cut from the ancient root from which we all come. My name has long been lost, but my influence lives on. I was there when we were banished from Nubia. I watched as a small group of the Menashe migrated into China. I saw our people as they were taken in chains to new worlds where they were sold as slaves—so that others might live well. I watched as the seas froze and your ancestors walked across the frozen seas to reach new lands with more hope. And yes, I watched as your family set out upon the seas, moving from island to island in search of peace. If you think hard, you too will remember.'

"In the dream, I tried desperately to speak to her, for I had many questions. I looked intently into her face. The lines were a tapestry of age, wind, and sun. Her brown eyes looked peaceful and wise. Her hair was pure white, except for a few streaks of black.

"She spoke again saying, 'Never forget that the beauty you see in nature has always been and will always be. The sense of "us" and "them," so current among the tribes of today, is the same illusion that separates trees of the mighty aspen forests.' Her face started to fade, as she chanted, 'Sing the praises of all that is good, and ignore the rest.'

"My eyes fluttered open, and I noticed there was a light breeze blowing from the east. The leaves of the aspen forest *responded with their song. I sat with my back against a part of this mighty tree. It all seemed to mix together, the roots of these trees, the old woman in the dream, and my research. I looked to the east again, wondering where this particular breeze had started, and wondered if this was the same breeze my grandfather had felt as he walked across some desert of old."*

At that point in my presentation, I cleared my throat and scratched my head, and then looked at the members of the committee. I noticed that all their eyes were still closed. I spoke softly saying, "So, respected members of this committee, you might ask why you should grant me a doctorate based on this thesis?" Seeing that no eyes had opened, I spoke a little louder saying, "Um, maybe we can open our eyes again, now." All of them remained closed. It appeared that they were asleep. It took all the restraint I could muster not to laugh. The acceptance of my thesis was one thing, but the crisis at hand was — how to get out of there?

The librarian, who up to now had been reading with restraint, began laughing. Composing herself a bit, she continued to read.

I tried again. "Umm, Dr Balzer and esteemed members of this committee, I appreciate your time, and know that you all have busy schedules. I think I should go now." The only reaction was that a couple more heads went down on folded arms.

Not knowing what else to do, I picked up my copy of the dissertation and tiptoed out of the room. After closing the door quietly, I ran through the hall until I reached the safety of the outside door. As the sunshine and the fresh air hit my face, I burst out laughing. For better or for worse, this was over. I felt more freedom in my heart than I had in two years. By this time next week, I'd be writing letters and sending resumes—trying to get a job. Exactly what that letter would say about my academic achievements was still in the balance, but it was too late to care.

The following Tuesday, the long awaited letter arrived. One way or another, the tension would be finished in the time it took to open and read the letter. I took a deep breath and then started to read:

> Dear Mr. Vuluso:
>
> After careful consideration, and based on a unanimous decision, the committee wishes to inform you that your thesis has been accepted without reservation.
>
> Sincerely yours,
> John W Balzer, PhD,
> Department of Botany.

With that, the librarian relaxed her arms, telling all she had reached the end of the letter. The library quickly filled with a laughter that it seldom heard. Thus ended a day of study for the hundred students who then gathered their books and left the library, laughing, smiling, and talking far too loudly. The graduate students and the under-graduate students suddenly felt no separation. Those studying psychology spoke freely to the science majors and the literature students. All suddenly seemed bonded as one, as they walked outside and left the librarian to put on her shoes, get her staff back to work, and to decide exactly what she would do with the dissertation, and one—very funny letter.

◆

Raspberry Yogurt

Working as an intern in a hospital is not easy. You spend a lot of time on the night shift, and unless you are careful, lack of sleep can make you a little crazy. This week had been particularly stressful. I loaned some money to a friend, who promised to pay it back on Monday. When I saw my friend on Friday, he still didn't have the money. I stretched my remaining money by eating less and less and I complained to anyone who would listen.

"It's a pretty strange world we live in," I would say. "You think you can trust someone, so you lend them money, and they don't pay it back. You walk into a store and the salesman circles you like a vulture. You walk downtown, and if you are not careful, you'll find that your wallet has also taken a separate walk."

Anyone who would listen, and even those who would not, heard my sad view of the world. Now, it was one o'clock on Saturday morning and I was hungry and tired. There was nothing to do but wait for an emergency case—or for six o'clock—whichever came first. I walked to the lounge and rested my head on the table. I drifted in and out of sleep.

After some time, I heard Charlene speaking, "Dr.

Stone, you're needed in the O.R."

"What's going on?"

"Brain surgery, Dr. McCormick wants you to assist."

"A car accident?"

"No, a tumor."

"In the middle of the night?"

"Hey, I'm just a nurse here. I don't make the decisions."

A few minutes later, I was scrubbed and ready to work. Dr. McCormick was already there and the operation was in progress. I watched in awe as the skilled hands of this world-famous brain surgeon masterfully did his work. As he exposed the top of the brain, I saw something I had never seen before. There was a green lump about the size of a golf ball. Since I was still an intern, I felt free to ask questions. "What's that?" I asked.

Doctor McCormick looked above his glasses and then spoke, "Cosmic requestor."

"A what?"

"A cosmic requestor—lactobacillus acidophilus."

I looked at the eyes of the other members of the team. Only Charlene's eyes met mine. I had never heard of a cosmic requestor before so I was determined to ask Doctor McCormick for further information when the operation was over.

Without further questions or comments, he snipped it out and dropped it in a stainless steel tray. "This one is beyond hope," he said. "They turn green if someone spends too much time dwelling on negative things."

After the operation was complete, I asked to see Dr. McCormick. We agreed to meet in the reference library in fifteen minutes.

I arrived early and was asking myself why I had not learned about cosmic requestors in medical school. I was about to look up lactobacillus acidophilus when Doctor McCormick walked in.

"You wanted to see me, Dr. Stone?" he said.

"Yes. I was wondering if you could tell me a little more about cosmic requestors."

"Sure. The cosmic requestor is the part of the brain where all our wishes go. The only problem is that it's rather simplistic. Not only do the things we call 'wishes' go there, but also other statements end up there and are treated as wishes. It has no sense of time — past, present or future. Many of our statements go to the cosmic requestor and are interpreted as a request. Do you understand?"

"Well, sort of."

"Like you, Gerald. This past few days you were complaining a lot."

"Yes, I suppose that's true."

"You spoke about the sad condition of the world. About how there is no trust and everyone seems greedy and ready to steal your money."

"Yes, it's true. I did say those things."

"Well all those things you said go to the cosmic requestor and get translated as wishes. They come out as requests for future action. So the requestor is trying to set up things so you get ripped off, because that's what it thinks you want."

"Really?"

"Yes, really. Sometimes the cosmic requestor gets infected with all the negative thoughts and it turns green. Sometimes it goes septic and we need to remove it surgically."

"They never taught us that in medical school," I said.

"Maybe you missed that class."

"Maybe. By the way, what is lactobacillus acidophilus?" I asked.

Suddenly I felt a sharp pain in my neck. My eyes opened and I realized my head was on the table.

"Yogurt. Yogurt is also spelled yogourt or yoghurt. It is a fermented milk product, which originated in Bulgaria," said a familiar voice.

I sat up and rubbed my sore neck. I looked across the table at Charlene who was busy reading from a yogurt container. "You want some?" she asked.

"Some what?"

"Some yogurt. I have some more in the fridge. I have raspberry, vanilla, and plain."

"No, thanks. How long have I been asleep?"

Charlene glanced at her watch and said, "Two... maybe three hours."

I looked up at the clock on the wall and said, "Hey, I'm going home."

"See you tomorrow."

As I was walking out of the hospital, Dr. McCormick was walking in. "Good morning," he said.

"Good morning," I said, smiling, thinking of his

role in my dreams.

"How was the night shift? Busy?"

"No, it was pretty quiet."

"I trust you had some sweet dreams then?"

I smiled again, laughed, and then said, "Yeah—raspberry yogurt dreams."

"You'll make a fine doctor, Gerald. But for now just go home and get some good sleep."

🌢

Roasted Corn

My fourteenth year was the most interesting year of my life. In that year, I learned more about people than anytime before, or anytime since.

We were one week into a two-week camping trip, when my mother asked me what I wanted for my birthday dinner. "Roasted corn," I replied without hesitation. So, Mom and I drove the thirty minutes to town and found all we needed for my birthday dinner. Best of all, we bought fresh corn and fresh tomatoes—all straight from a farmer's field. At one point while we were in town, a policeman walked up and asked to speak with Momma. After that, she seemed a bit sad. Being curious, I asked, "Did he give you a ticket?"

Momma just said, "No," and didn't offer an explanation.

Whatever it was, she wasn't going to let it spoil my birthday. Daddy roasted the corn over the fire and we ate until we couldn't eat any more. After that, we had cake. The cake came from the store, so it wasn't half as good as Momma's was, but given the situation it was a pretty nice party. We sang a few songs and looked at the stars together and then my brother and me were sent to bed. I couldn't sleep right away because of the excitement and all the food I had eaten. Lying in my bed, I started listening to Momma and Daddy talking. I could see their shadows on the wall of the tent and hear bits and pieces of the conversation.

I heard Momma first, "… policeman in town today…"

And then I heard Daddy ask the same question I had, "Did you get a ticket?"

But Momma seemed to change the subject and they started talking about the fire. The last thing I remember before falling asleep was Daddy saying, "We'll finish our camping trip as if nothing is wrong, and turn this into a positive experience."

The next few days Daddy became like a camping preacher. Every chance he got, he talked about how good it was to camp. "Camping puts you in touch with nature and your roots," and, "It's so nice to camp; you get to see the stars every night."

Momma joined in the campaign to convince my brother and I that camping was such a wonderful thing you'd be lucky if you could do it all year round. Only on the way home did we find out, what it was all about.

Daddy started out saying, "There's something I need to explain to you both."

I remember saying, "Okay," because Daddy seemed to be waiting for a response.

"There has been a fire," Daddy said.

My little brother, who was just learning to count, spoke up saying, "Twenty-six fires to be exact."

We all laughed and then Momma asked him what he meant. My brother went on to explain, "On the day we arrived we made a fire at night, and on the rest of the days, we made a fire in the morning and another fire at night. That makes twenty-five fires. Today we made one in the morning. That makes twenty-six fires, right?"

Momma said, "Yes, that's exactly right." Mommy and I laughed, but Daddy didn't.

Then Daddy continued explaining, "Yes, that's right, those were fires we made for cooking. There actually is another kind of fire that is accidental. While we were camping, there was an accidental fire in our house." Daddy paused while we all looked at each other. Then he said, "Pretty much everything in the house is gone."

As I thought back over the last week, all the pieces fell together. "Momma, is that what the policeman told you?" I asked.

"Yes, that's when we first heard about it."

My brother asked, "Is my bed burned?"

"Yes," said Daddy.

"So where am I going to sleep?"

"In the same place you have been sleeping for the past two weeks."

"In a tent?"

"Yes."

"Oh, that'll be fun."

With that, it seemed everyone was resigned to the fact that we had no house—that is everyone except for me. I was wondering where my friends would come to visit, and I was thinking about my clothes and my books. The only thing that kept me from crying was the fact that nobody else was crying.

When we got home, Momma and Daddy took all the stuff from the car and piled it up in the back yard. The tent went up and Momma started to cook dinner just like she did when we were at the campground. A few neighbors dropped by and gave us things that they thought we might be able to use.

We spent the next week pulling down the pieces of wood that once supported our house. We piled it all up in a corner of the backyard. Daddy said the charcoal was as good as any you could buy in the store, so we'd use it for cooking. A few days later, all the work of cleaning up was done, and we settled into the business of living. Over the next year, we got to know everyone on the street. Sometimes ladies would come by with a casserole, claiming that they had more than they could eat. Sometimes we'd find little notes in the mailbox with money folded up inside. Every morning before Daddy went to work, he would cut and nail pieces of wood into what started to look like the outline of a house. Momma would work all day, and my brother and I would do what we could. I kept planting corn all summer, hoping we could still eat roasted corn in the winter.

By the time school started, Daddy had finished most of a bathroom. By the time it started to get cold, he had finished one of the bedrooms and part of the kitchen. To get warm before sleeping, we still made a fire every night. After we had washed and we were ready for bed, we'd stand by the fire for the last time to get warm. Then we'd run and crawl into our sleeping bags on the floor of the new bedroom.

Life went on like this until summer started. Daddy said we'd be ready to move into the house before my fourteenth birthday. My brother and I went up and down both sides of our street and invited every neighbor to our house-warming party. Momma made more potato salad than I had ever seen in my life, and Daddy cooked a mountain of roasted corn. Before we started serving the food, Daddy started to talk, "Um, everyone, can I have your attention for a couple of minutes?" All the neighbors turned to face Daddy. Some sat down. "First, I would like to thank you all for coming today. Second, I want to thank each and every one of you for your help. When the thing we needed most was to take a shower, one of you graciously offered us the use of yours. Those first few days were the hardest and the messiest.

"Most of you brought us food at one time or another. Some of you brought building materials. And there were some of you who put little notes in our mailbox with money inside. Each and every one of you has helped in some manner and today is our day to say, 'Thank you.'

"This day is special in a number of ways. Today is the anniversary of the day we received the news that our house was gone. Today is also special because it is our daughter's fourteenth birthday. The corn you are about to eat, she planted, nurtured, and picked. The charcoal we used to roast it with is the very last of the charcoal from the remains of our old house.

"Once again, every member of our family thanks you. Please enjoy the food."

With that, Daddy started unwrapping the mountains of roasted corn, and Momma started serving the potato salad. As the neighbors started to fill their plates with food, my little brother started walking around, singing like it was a planned part of the program:

> We went camping for a year,
> It was fun and there were no tears,
> Though the house burnt to the ground
> Many new friends—we have found.

Each time he'd finish singing, there would be another burst of laughter. About an hour after we all finished eating, I stood in a corner where I could see everyone. My brother was still singing his song; my mother was talking to a small group on one side, and my father was talking to a family that was leaving. I couldn't help but wonder, if it weren't for the fire, would we have known all these people—would we be so close as a family, and would I feel so happy—turning fourteen?

◆

Running Late

Lawrence opened the door and walked out into the morning air. He stretched his arms and inhaled the sweet smell of some distant desert herbs, mixed with the fresh sea breeze. The white stucco houses stood out like freshly-cut daisies against the blue summer sky. He inhaled again as the front door of the house opened. David came out quickly and walked to the car.

"Let's go," said David. "If we don't leave now we'll hit the traffic and be stuck forever."

Lawrence walked to the passenger side of the car, opened the door, and got inside. He had just closed the door when David pulled the car away from the curb with a jerk.

"You do plan to drive the speed limit—don't you?" asked Lawrence.

David looked at him, smiled, and then laughed. "This is L.A., Uncle Lawrence—nobody drives the speed limit here."

The older man waited a moment and then said, "If you don't plan to drive the speed limit, you can stop now and let me out."

David mumbled something, glanced at the speedometer, and slowed down. They drove in silence for the better part of ten minutes. Then, it was David who broke the silence. "What's the big deal about driving the speed limit, Uncle Lawrence?"

"I've had some pretty strong lessons, and I don't enjoy riding in speeding cars driven by nervous drivers."

David had heard a number of stories about Uncle Lawrence, and he wanted to hear this one. "I'd like to hear the story; maybe it will help me reform my driving," he said with a smirk on his face.

Uncle Lawrence, saw the expression, and just said, "Perhaps."

David pulled onto the freeway and put his foot to the floor. Then, remembering his uncle's seriousness, he backed off a bit. They drove silently like this for another ten minutes. Finally David spoke again, "So, will you tell me the story or not?"

"Okay, you hold the speed limit, and I'll tell you the story."

David backed off a little more on the throttle and moved the car into a slower lane.

Lawrence waited a few moments and then began his story. "It was mostly due to Judge Yancey. It was about twenty-three years ago. Like you, I was fond of leaving late and driving fast to make up for it. I already had two tickets when I went into Yancey's court. He looked at me, looked down at the file he had been given by the prosecutor, and then said in a quiet but very firm voice, 'Give me one good reason why I shouldn't prevent you from ever driving again in the State of California.'

"I stood up. An all too familiar trembling feeling

came over me. My knees could barely sustain my weight. Tears started rolling down my face as I braced myself on the table in front of me. The room seemed to be moving beneath my feet.

"'Well?' said the judge, 'Do you have any reasons why I shouldn't throw your driver's license away forever?'"

"Yes, sir, I do, Your Honor," I said in reply.

"'Well let's hear the sob story quickly—I have a heavy caseload today.'

"There are two reasons that I would like you to consider. The first reason is that I am a security guard at a factory in the desert. If I can't drive to work, I will lose my job. The second reason is that I am a different person now than I was a month ago when I got this ticket for driving through the red light."

"'But, you don't deny driving through the red light, do you?' asked the judge.

"No, Your Honor, I don't deny that."

"'So why should I believe that you are a different person now than you were a month ago?' asked the judge.

"I went on to explain how the events of the day I ran the red light changed my driving forever. By the time, I had finished the story, I was not the only one crying. The judge was among those moved to tears. He sentenced me to five years of community service."

David let out a loud whistle, glanced at the speedometer, and slowed down.

"Judge Yancey told me that I could keep my license as long as I told my story to the students in one hundred traffic schools during the following six months, and then to at least five classes a month after that for the remainder of the five years. I kept thinking that at some point I'd stop crying and just tell the story—but I couldn't. My eyes were red a lot during those next six months. After the five years were up, I continued getting phone calls from traffic schools requesting that I come and tell my story. Now, many years later, I still go to speak. It's such a powerful lesson, and if it can save a life or two, I'll keep telling it until I'm too old to talk."

"So what really happened that day? I mean, what really changed your driving?" asked David.

"You mean the day I ran the red light?"

"Yes," said David, whose speed was creeping up again.

"Well," started Uncle Lawrence, "I was late leaving the house. I used to stay up late, go to bed late, wake up as late as possible, and then try to make it to work on time. I lived life like that for almost two years before the day of my last ticket. There was a traffic light that took a really long time to go through all its cycles. When it changed to yellow, I was a long way from it. I accelerated hard but I didn't get into the intersection before it turned red. That's when I got the ticket. What the judge didn't know was that a car started to pull into the intersection, and I almost hit it. That was the start of my morning drive to work on that day.

"The next incident happened in a cross-walk just before the freeway onramp. There was an elderly man who was about to step into the crossing. He glanced back and saw me speeding towards him. I braked hard as I realized that I was driving very dangerously. He stepped back on the curb, bowed his head towards me, and made a sweeping motion toward me, indicating that I should go first. I made a quick wave of the hand meaning that he had the right-of-way. He smiled at me, pointed to his watch, then placed his hand over his heart and made the sweeping gesture again. Feeling somewhat embarrassed and annoyed, I waved at him and then quickly accelerated. I drove the rest of the way to work with a combination of feelings. The older man's face kept coming back into my mind, and I kept picturing his hand motions.

"I was almost all the way to work when I turned a corner onto a side street. I was still driving too fast when suddenly, to my horror, I saw a mother pushing a baby carriage, with one child in hand and another who had fallen down. I hit the brakes hard and the car stopped just inside the cross-walk with the front bumper touching the baby carriage. I got out of the car, ran to the carriage, and then stared motionlessly at the sleeping baby. The mother looked at me with piercing eyes, lifted up the fallen child, and then walked her children across the street. She didn't say anything as I mumbled, 'I'm sorry.'

"I drove the rest of the way to work, stepped out of the car, and then fell down. My knees wouldn't hold the weight of the three near-misses. I was overwhelmed. That whole day at work was torture. Something deep inside me was shaken very badly and since that day, I drive much more slowly."

"Wow," said David as he looked at his speedometer and slowed down again. "That's some story. That's really some story." David used the sleeve of his shirt to wipe the tears from his face as he parked the car in front of the tennis courts. He reached into the back seat and got his tennis racket and then opened the door of the car. He put his feet firmly on the ground and tried to stand. Only with the aid of his arms did he manage to pull himself up.

Lawrence, recognizing the symptoms, came over and leaned against the car, saying "Maybe we should rest a little before we play tennis."

David agreed, and after standing by the car for a few minutes, they walked slowly into the gardens near the tennis courts. There they talked about life, and lessons, and learning. Now David knew much more of his uncle, and had a strong feeling that—just as the judge had changed his uncle's way of life—so too had his uncle—changed his.

●

The Satellite

Astronomers like dark nights. Moonless nights make it easier to view the stars and the planets. On one such night, a group of amateur astronomers had gathered on a mountaintop in China. It didn't take them long to spot it and the news spread quickly from there. It appeared to be a satellite crossing the northern sky, flashing some kind of bright light every thirty seconds. A phone call roused a sleeping professor who alerted the world community.

Within a few hours, space agencies all over the world were busy asking each other, who launched this satellite? It was the Brazilians who first broke the story to the media.

"Today our scientists tracked and identified the mysterious satellite that has been baffling astronomers and space agencies for the last few days. We have determined that the satellite was launched by an individual by the name of Mr. Kopano Alotse. At the time of this release, no national or international space agencies seem to know who Mr. Alotse is. The satellite is broadcasting a message on 2402.186 MHz and is flashing a strobe light. The satellite is visible in many countries without the aid of a telescope."

TV stations around the world began interrupting

their regular broadcasting. "We interrupt this broadcast with breaking news. A previously unknown scientist by the name of Kopano Sputnik Alotse has launched a satellite into orbit. The satellite can be seen without a telescope and emits a flash of light every thirty seconds. The satellite is broadcasting a message which we will play for you at this time:

This is a pre-recorded broadcast from the satellite Alotse One. My name is Kopano Sputnik Alotse. This is my satellite and this is my story.

I was born in October of 1957. My father named me Sputnik after he heard on the radio about the Soviet satellite that was circling the earth. At the age of eight I met a U.N. volunteer who helped me to cultivate a love for outer space. When he left Lesotho, he gave me three books about space and space travel. Since that time, it has been my dream to become an astronaut.

A few years ago, in pursuit of my dream, I moved to the United States and attended college while working part time. For one of my classes, I wrote a paper entitled "High Altitude Balloons — An Alternative Door to Outer Space." My professor gave me a 'C+' and wrote in red ink that I should stick to more practical engineering methods.

A year later, I turned the paper into a detailed specification and submitted it to NASA. They showed no interest. A few years later, I decided that the only way for this idea to be tested was to do it myself. I built this satellite, the rockets, and the balloon launch platform with my own funds at a total cost of $6,783.45. If you are receiving this message, I have been successful — if not, I will try again.

For those of you who may be interested in this project, here are some details: The launch originated near Joshua Tree National Park when four hydrogen balloons lifted a lightweight launch platform to an altitude of one-hundred thousand feet. Then a fiberglass cannon launched a rocket horizontally. Fifteen seconds after the cannon fired, the rocket engines ignited. A few minutes later, it released this satellite.

Anyone interested in supporting future missions may contact me at 9988 Green Street, San Diego, California.

The gray-haired news anchor shook his head in amazement, smiled, and then said, "At this moment, we have news teams searching for Mr. Alotse in San Diego and near Joshua Tree National Park. We now return you to our regular coverage of the International Ice-skating Marathon."

"Isn't that something?" asked one of the many truck drivers gathered in the restaurant in the Canadian Rockies.

"Yeah, sure is," said another driver. "Change to the news station, maybe they'll have more about this guy."

A man in a white apron put one of the two coffee pots he was carrying on the counter and then reached up to the large TV and changed the channel. "In case you have just joined us, we are coming to you live from Thermal, California, where a Mr. Kopano Alotse has single-handedly launched the world's first individually-owned satellite. Mr. Alotse has captured the hearts of people all over the world and has raised interest in government circles. With the exception of the recorded message that the satellite is broadcasting, very little is known about Mr. Alotse. Here outside the Palm Motel in Thermal, a sea of reporters has gathered. One of the motel employees spoke to me earlier and said that Mr. Alotse arrived at the motel early this morning looking happy but tired. Now, it is ten o'clock in the morning here in the California desert and a team of FBI and NASA officials has already arrived. A short time ago, they spoke to the motel manager, and then they went directly to room 135 where we assume Mr. Alotse was sleeping.

"None of the officials would make any comment. So far, we have only one short video clip showing Mr. Alotse when he opened the door of his room and greeted the government officials. We still have little information on his background or the reason for the launch.

"Let's run that video clip again. There you see the man in the gray suit, knocking on the door. He is from the FBI. There you see Mr. Alotse. He sure looks happy—take a look at that big smile on his face!

"We hope to have more for you soon, but for now this is John Zimmerman CBC News reporting live from Thermal, California."

The truck drivers in the Canadian Rockies had to abandon their coffee and return to work. But, like so many other people all over the world, they felt just a little more hopeful than they did the day before. The truck drivers kept their ears open for more news, while they chatted on their CB radios about how a man named Kopano Alotse had attracted so much attention by simply following his dream. People around the world were talking about how the largest space agency in the world, which wouldn't listen to his ideas before, had now dispatched their best engineers to go and meet with Kopano Alotse—in a simple hotel room—in Thermal, California.

♦

The Silk Scarf

There were twelve of us in the class. Each and every one of us had a name, and most of the names meant something: a wish for divine blessings, a hope for the family, an attribute of the divine. Then there was Darahto. No one knew the meaning of his name. Darahto didn't know, our teacher didn't know, and if his parents knew—they weren't telling anyone.

Of course Darahto got some extra teasing for this, and we all took a turn at making up cruel names to use instead of Darahto. But after we saw the silk scarf flutter, and after he alone was able to explain the meaning, we used his name with respect.

Our school was at the home of our teacher. We came each day and learned to read and to write, and we learned a little mathematics and science as well. But mostly ours was a religious training. We tried hard, and our parents sacrificed what they could in order to keep our teacher clothed and fed.

One Monday morning our teacher announced we would take a trip. This was highly unusual and the excitement built fast in our eleven-and-twelve-year-old minds. Before we left, the teacher reached up into the tree above his head, and broke off a dead branch. He removed the small twigs until he had one straight pole about the height of a man. Then he tied a silk scarf of the color associated with certain religious beliefs to the top of the pole and waved it like a flag.

Next he announced something that struck terror in my heart. He looked at us all and said, "Today we are going to the rifle range." Having announced our destination, he opened the door of his courtyard and walked out into the dusty street, holding the flag high above his head.

Confusion ran around my brain like I had never felt before. My father believed that force was something to be used only very rarely—to protect the general good. He had selected this teacher because he thought he shared that same belief. Now we were going to practice with guns, and I was afraid. I considered running home, but something kept me in line with the others. The teacher started to sing and we joined him. The singing only added to my confusion. Father would not like this. I wanted to cry out for help. Sweat began running down my face. After an hour of walking, and thinking, and sweating, I began to hear the firing from the rifle range. We walked through the gate and then walked into a small wooden shelter with a number of men who were firing weapons at paper targets. When the operator of the range saw our teacher, he smiled, stood up, rang a bell, and shouted, "Cease firing."

The noise of the guns came to an immediate stop as the men unloaded their guns and laid them on the tables in front of them. The range operator then shouted, "All clear," and the men who had been firing walked out to check their targets.

My teacher walked over and embraced the range operator, and they exchanged words which none of us could hear. Then my teacher walked out onto the range carrying the silk scarf that had become our banner. He walked to a target that was not being used, and tied the pole so that the scarf hung like clothes put out to dry in the sun. The beautiful silk scarf danced in the light breeze. I kept wondering if I was sleeping and having a bad dream. I was hoping that soon my mother would call me to wake up and go to school.

Then our teacher came back to the small building that faced the firing range, walked over to the operator of the range, and took a big rifle and a handful of bullets. He walked back to where we were standing and instructed us how to load the weapon and how to fire it. He said the goal was to shoot a hole in the silk scarf.

The next thing I heard was a bell ringing, followed by the operator shouting, "Ready on the right, ready on the left—ready on the firing line." Then he shouted, "Commence firing," and the noise of the explosions of many guns surrounded us. Most of us covered our ears to protect them from the painful sound. Then, one by one, our teacher called us to the front and helped us to aim the rifle at the silk scarf fluttering gently in the breeze. Each time one of us fired, the silk scarf jumped a little, but there was no hole. After we all had taken our turn, he looked toward the operator, who rang his bell again and stopped the firing. Just as we were about to leave, the operator shouted, "The teacher has offered money for the man who can pierce the silk scarf." Then he shouted, "Ready on the right, ready on the left—ready on the firing line." Then after a short pause, he shouted, "Commence firing." The scarf began jumping as the deafening noise of many guns tried in vain to pierce what seemed to be a magic piece of cloth.

The teacher motioned that we should go, and we marched away from the firing range singing. We sang all the way back to our school where we gathered in two short rows under the shade of the tree. Then our teacher began to question us, "What did you learn today?" One by one, we struggled for answers.

"Guns are noisy."

"Guns are dangerous."

"If a man is dressed in the holy color, then no bullet can ever harm him."

We all tried. We all spoke—all except Darahto. For me, talking was a great relief—somehow it broke the tension. I was glad to be back sitting in the shade of the tree, with our kind teacher whom I had grown to love. Finally, Darahto raised his hand to speak.

The teacher turned his eyes lovingly toward him and said, "Yes, Darahto, do you understand the mystery?"

Darahto stood up slowly and with his eyes fixed firmly on the ground started to speak. "The color is not important. The silk scarf is a symbol to remind us how we should be."

"And how is it that we should be?" asked our

teacher.

"We should always be like the silk scarf blowing in the breeze. When the trials of life come, we should not cling to them. The silk is so light that even the force of the bullet cannot tear holes in it. If the silk were heavier, like a piece of canvas or a wooden plank, the bullet would make a hole. We must all be like the silk scarf. Problems in life will come and go. We cannot control this, but we can become like the silk scarf blowing in the breezes of life."

"Wonderful, wonderful. Come here, Darahto."

Darahto walked shyly towards our teacher as we all marveled at his wisdom. How could a boy who so rarely spoke see what we all had missed? Our teacher embraced him and then said, "Darahto, Darahto the Wise."

"We all clapped and stood up. We were all relieved to know that our teacher had not changed his position on the use of force, and we were thankful that today's lesson—so full of tension—was over. Beside all that, we finally understood the meaning of Darahto.

◆

The Sounds of Hidden Lake

Mina inhaled the late afternoon mountain air. She smiled as she climbed the wooden steps and glanced through Oma's screendoor. "Knock-knock," she called. "Oma, it's Mina."

A few seconds later the door opened and Oma exclaimed, "Mina, how nice to see you. Come in."

After a long, meaningful hug, they walked together to the kitchen. Oma put the kettle on the stove while probing the purpose of the unexpected visit. "It's so nice to see you. I thought you were in school.'

"I took a few days off," said Mina.

"Sit down. Is everything okay?"

"Well, nothing is really wrong. I'm still getting good grades in my classes, but I'm just not sure about things. I love engineering, but I have recently been playing more music, and have become interested in the education of children. I'm considering changing my major.

"The other day, while I was studying, I completely lost my ability to concentrate. It was the strangest thing—it was as if someone had flipped off the power to my brain and all the lights went out. I started mindlessly arranging the books above my desk. After some time Opa's last letter fell out from a book and landed on my desk. I sat back down and read it. At the end of the letter, he said that if I ever became confused, I should come for a visit and walk in the mountains. The way things worked out, by skipping one class, I could make a five-day trip out of it. So I packed and came."

"I'm so glad you did. The alpine air will do you good."

After a short walk together and a light supper, Oma asked about the small case that Mina had tied to the top of her pack.

"It's a violin. Would you like to hear some music?"

Oma agreed that she would, and for thirty minutes she was treated to a kind of music she had never heard before. They sat in silence for some time and then Oma spoke, "That's wonderful; did you learn that in school?" Mina explained awkwardly that it was her own composition. Shortly after that, they retired for the night.

The next morning, Oma was in the kitchen fixing breakfast when Mina walked in with her eyes sparkling. Before greeting her grandmother she said, "Oma, I had the most wonderful dream. In the dream, I was sitting in front of a small lake. It was very quiet, except for the sound of a small waterfall at the opposite side of the lake. Opa was there. He walked up to me, handed me my violin and said, 'Play, child, play the sound of the hidden lake.' I took the violin and played music I have never heard before. It was beautiful. When I stopped playing, there were animals all around me. All of them were staring at me. After a few moments, the animals drank from the lake, and then, one by one, they all walked away. That's when I woke up."

Oma reached for Mina's hand and led her out of the kitchen. "That's a wonderful dream," she said. "It reminds me of a letter that your Opa wrote to me two years before his passing." Oma sat down at a large wooden desk and started looking for the letter. "You know that he loved to walk in these mountains. Because of my knees, I couldn't go with him the last few years. We both knew how much it meant to him. He would go for two or three weeks at a time, but he would write letters and send them with people who were coming down the mountain. Sometimes, I'd get two or three letters on the same day and then nothing for two weeks. Ah, here it is. He was never the same after this. Let me read it to you.

Dearest Frau Ursula:

Today I am writing to you from the most beautiful place I have ever seen. I want to explain to you how I found this wonderful place, and what happened while I was here. Last Thursday, I was walking on a trail in the early morning when I met a young man who was absolutely radiant. I saw him walk from the forest and join the trail just in front of me. We both stopped walking and greeted each other. He seemed to be in a trance. He explained that he had discovered a small, remote lake with a waterfall.

Because of the intensity of his description I was seized

by a desire to find this place. I changed my plans and set out for this gentle place he called Hidden Lake. Two hours later, I entered this place from which I am now writing. I have been here two days , and I can honestly say that if it were not for my strong love for you, I think I would just stay here forever. Sounds echo around the lake and it is truly the most wonderful amphitheater that nature has ever created. On the first day here, I set up camp, ate lunch, swam in the lake, and then took out my harmonica and began to play music I have never played before.

I must have played for over an hour. Each note went across the lake and echoed off the walls of the surrounding stone. I was able to create the most wonderful harmonies as one note hung in suspense over the lake, while I sent out another one to harmonize with it. I was completely entranced until a small squirrel made a noise that brought me back to my senses. I looked around and there were a number of squirrels standing nearby. After I stopped playing, the squirrels all ran away.

Oma folded the letter reverently and put it back in its blue envelope. They both sat silently knowing that they had just experienced something miraculous. Mina finally broke the silence, "It sounds like my dream. Do you have any idea where this lake is?"

"Yes, I have a map. Opa went back there five times before he died, and since there was no trail, he wanted me to know where he was—just in case."

They both understood what came next. Mina studied the map for a few minutes, ate breakfast, and then packed.

Oma watched silently as her granddaughter walked down the same trail that her husband had taken so many times before. The violin case that was tied on top of the small pack, bounced gently with each hopeful step Mina took.

Just before she disappeared into the trees, Oma called out to her saying, "Give the squirrels my greetings and tell them you were sent by Opa!"

Story Tellers

I was near the edge of the hive and I could hear two lectures going on. The first one was, of course, my teacher. We were not ordinary bees; we were being trained to be storytellers. You probably have heard about workers and drones and queens. But most folks haven't heard about us. Our job, as storytellers, is to memorize the history of our ever-changing colonies in order to inspire the workers. Because I was near the edge of the hive, I could hear another lecture going on outside: "If you look over here in this macadamia tree, you will see a bee hive just under that large branch. The bees pollinate the tree and, in return, the tree gives up its nectar. Most people think that bees have a short and rather tragic life. By our standards of time, most live only about two months. But, it is my belief that bees don't perceive time the same way we do, nor do they perceive the cycles of life and death as we see them."

"Doctor Fielding, may I ask a question?"

"Certainly, please go ahead."

"Your ideas about bees …are they … um … widely accepted in the scientific community?"

I heard someone laugh and then the conversation continued. "Not exactly. Scientists cling to old ideas until they find evidence that forces them to new understandings. At this time, my research is still highly speculative."

I whispered to the bee next to me, "Do you know they are talking about us out there?"

"Who is?"

"I don't know. Some people outside the hive are talking about us. Can you hear them?"

"I hear some noise out there -- but I'm trying to pay attention to our teacher."

"You there...in the back. Can you pay attention to the lesson?"

"Yes, sir. I'm sorry."

Our teacher continued to explain the good things that happen as a result of the work of bees. He explained how children love to take a spoonful of honey and put it into their mouths; and how happy it makes people who live close to nature to find a beehive somewhere in a forest. He also explained how fruit trees are pollinated. He told us how billions of peaches and apples and mangoes are joyously eaten by people, in part because a worker bee did his job.

Then he went on to explain how our job, as storytellers, was to inspire the bees in the hive, to encourage them and help them to understand how important their work is. My mind drifted from the lecture of my teacher, and I started to hear the lecture outside the hive again. "As I mentioned to you before, I don't believe that bees see life and death the way humans do. They don't view the world from a selfish perspective, but rather as an organic-whole. I believe that they understand the importance of their service to the ever-advancing world. I think they see and understand their part in the universe and that makes their lives less stressful. I suspect that there is a group of bees, within the hive, that have the responsibility to preserve and share the collective knowledge—much like our teachers and educators do."

"Did you hear that?" I whispered to my friend, "He's talking about us now."

"Who is?"

"The guy outside the hive. He is talking about us—about us storytellers."

"Let's be quiet, I don't want to get in trouble again."

"You there, you in the back. Would you please pay attention? How do you expect to be a good storyteller, if you don't have any stories to tell?"

I apologized again to the teacher and then let my mind drift back outside.

"Um, Doctor Fielding, don't you think it's cruel to steal the honey from the bees?"

"If you look at it as theft, then it can only be seen as wrong. But if you look upon it as a gift offered by an all-providing universe, then you might consider it wrong not to harvest the honey. Let me ask you a question in return. Do you consider it wrong to plant wheat and then eat the seeds? Would you consider it stealing from the plant or from the soil?"

"I guess I see the point."

"Even when a hive is completely destroyed by the action of a bear, the bees swarm and make a new hive.

These are the processes of life."

My mind focused inside the hive again. I had lots to think over. On the one hand, I was learning to be a storyteller and memorizing all the good that bees do. On the other hand, I was starting to understand that not all creatures believe we are all working towards one and the same goal. I had a lot to consider. I looked for an empty cell, crawled in, and began my rest. Tomorrow would be my first day as a story teller, but for now there was much to think about.

⬤

The Sunflower Mug

"Click-clunk." Each time a pen was placed in the mug, it made a different noise.

"Hi."

"Hello there, welcome," said the yellow highlighter.

"Thanks, where am I?"

"We call this place the sunflower mug. We named it that because of the yellow sunflower that is on the front. Let me introduce you to everyone." Then, directing his attention to the older residents, the yellow highlighter said, "Hey, everyone, can we introduce ourselves to the new arrival?"

One by one, the blue pens, the black pens, and the pens containing red ink, gave a short history of their life before they became residents in the brown mug with the yellow sunflower.

After the others, the yellow highlighter spoke again. "Thanks, everyone," he said to the cooperative pens. Then directing his attention to the new arrival his said, "As for me, I am a yellow highlighter. I'm kind of the senior person around here; I've been here the longest and seen a lot of pens come and go—fountain pens and ballpoints, I've seen 'em all. Now, why don't you tell us a bit about yourself—you don't look like you just came out of the factory yesterday."

"That's a fact," said the new arrival. "I have been around a bit. When I first came out of the factory, I was a shiny, new, very expensive pen. A salesman bought several of us to give away, and that's how I found my first owner. I was used for a number of questionable things—but I had no control over it. I'm a little embarrassed to say that a number of shady deals were signed, using me. Not having free will as humans have, I figured I had to either cooperate fully or find a way to malfunction. I spent a lot of nights thinking about what I should do. Finally, I decided I must choose between two ideas for malfunctioning. The first was to leak all over the guy's shirt, and the second was to leave blank spots while he was signing his name.

"Believe me, I thought long and hard about the first option. In the end, I decided that it wasn't really fair for me to mess up his shirt, and on top of that, I was afraid I'd get tossed straight into the wastebasket."

"So, you went for option two?"

"Yes. I would hold my breath sometimes—just when he was signing his name on a contract or something important. The last time I did that, he said something I didn't understand, looked at me, glanced at the wastebasket, and then dropped me into a side pocket of his suit. Later that night, he pulled me out and gave me to his wife. I thought that was pretty strange, but I didn't complain. Life with her was much better—mostly making shopping lists and signing credit card receipts—stuff like that."

"How long did that last?"

"Maybe a year or so."

"Then what happened?"

"One day, she didn't close her purse carefully and I dropped out in a big parking lot. A homeless man who saw me fall, picked me up and ran to return me. But the lady was scared of him and rolled up her car window and drove away. She didn't even see me when he was holding me up outside the window."

"That's pretty strange."

"Yeah, I thought so too. But I have to admit, life became pretty interesting after that. I traveled all over the U.S. and Canada. There was lots of fresh air and a few cold nights, but generally speaking—life was good. A lot of times he'd just take me out of his pocket and show me to his friends, and then tell the story about how I fell in the parking lot."

"And how did you get on this side of the Atlantic?"

"Well, that homeless man was helped by a nice lady in a shelter. She found him a job and a place to live. He wasn't exactly rolling in money, but he had enough to pay his rent and eat regular meals. He went back to the lady in the shelter and he gave me to her as a present. He said something like he didn't know how to properly thank her for all she had done, and he wanted her to have the pen he'd been carrying for the last ten years.

"Then, that lady traveled to a conference in a place called Sweden, and she gave me to another lady. I think that last lady, the one who put me here, I think her name is Adelaide."

There was a low rumble that echoed around the mug as all the diverse pens recognized and spoke the name of Adelaide. The yellow highlighter spoke again, "Yes, that's right, Adelaide is the lady who keeps us all here in this nice brown mug. The town we are in is called Uppsala."

"That sounds familiar—I think I must have written it once."

"Well," said the yellow highlighter, "on behalf of us all you are really welcome here. We are all glad to meet you and to hear the stories of all your adventures."

"Thanks, thanks very much. What's it like here? I mean, how do you folks spend most of your time?"

The yellow highlighter spoke again, "Well, it's pretty low-key here. This is an office where Adelaide does a lot of reading, writing, and meditation. She writes letters to people all over the world. Her letters are very sweet and encouraging. If you ask some of the other pens, they'll tell you what a joy it is to see the words she writes flow out of them. As for me, I don't get a lot of use—most of the reading she does is in religious and self-improvement books. She doesn't seem to want to use the highlighter for that. Oh, here she comes now, let's quiet down a bit—hey, she's picking you up—see you later."

Adelaide wrote several letters, between which she ate lunch. Around two in the afternoon, she finished and replaced the new pen in the slightly-cracked brown mug.

"Click-clunk."

"Hey, you're back!"

"Yeah, I wrote a few letters. Like you said, nice, sweet letters to people all over the world. It was a real joy to be part of it."

"That's what they all say—she's real special."

"Can I ask your opinion on something?"

"Sure, anything."

"Do you think Adelaide can hear us when we talk?"

"I don't think so—why?"

"Well in one of the letters I wrote, she talked about all the pens in her favorite old coffee mug. Each one of the pens had a story, and she told them all. But what's most interesting is that all the stories you folks told me earlier—they were exactly the same as the stories she wrote in the letter."

The highlighter paused for a few seconds, shook his head, and then said, "Well it beats me. But then what would I know? I'm just a yellow highlighter!"

●

The Swallows

Being thirteen is tough no matter where you live—but being thirteen and being a girl in my school seemed especially hard. In my head, I knew that my tormentors were just jealous but that didn't make it any easier in my heart. One Thursday afternoon, after an especially rough day of being teased at school, I was walking home past the park when I noticed a large gathering of swallows playing in the sky. I stopped to watch and then was drawn to a picnic table where I sat down. The weather was odd. Small, puffy, cotton clouds were suspended from the otherwise gray sky. The swallows seemed to love it.

Suddenly I felt an overwhelming urge to sleep. I rested my head on my books and immediately started to dream. In the dream, I saw swallows—many swallows. One of them seemed faster than the others as they circled the sky above my head. I followed the faster swallow as she circled around the park and then flew over an ocean. The swallow flew faster than any bird I had ever seen. In seconds, we had crossed a great ocean and then started to slow down. We passed over mangrove trees as we neared land. Many swallows were flying in the mangrove swamps, but they all looked different from us. We began to fly over houses, and apartments, and factories. Finally, we started to circle a college campus with a large sign that said, "Welcome to the National University of Singapore."

We flew into a large hall and sat on steel beams high above the students. The professor was just beginning his lecture. "Today we will learn about genetics and transformation." The students seemed serious and were busy taking notes. "We will begin with a short video on the life of a swallow named Jamilah." The students continued to write as the lights dimmed. A large screen came to life behind the professor.

The video was a documentary on the life of Jamilah, who was described as much faster and much smarter than ordinary swallows. It described her emotional problems as she tried to adjust to being different in a world where so many were trying to be the same. It seems that one day Jamilah just forgot she was different and was no longer troubled when the other swallows called her funny names. She acquired compassion for them as she began to understand the nature of their problem. As it turns out, Jamilah was the first of a new species of swallows, which were especially adept at eating mosquitoes. As a direct result, all mosquito-bearing diseases had been completely eliminated from Singapore and the surrounding islands.

My guide started flying in circles in the room, and I followed. A student opened the door and we flew out. We flew around the university, back through the mangrove swamps, back across the ocean, and ended up right back in the park where my dream had begun. Suddenly my guide looked at me and spoke in a very loud voice. "Oh, Jamilah, you can be part of something new and special, or you can remain just another swallow chasing insects. The choice is yours. But, for now, wake up and take shelter under the big tree."

The emotion and the sound of the swallow's loud voice woke me up. I opened my eyes and sat up. Above me, there were hundreds of swallows, dancing in the wind. They seemed to be playing under the clouds that were hanging like large balls of cotton. The loud voice of the swallow in the dream echoed through my head. I stood up and walked obediently to the large tree I had seen in my dream. The shade was refreshing. The strange gusts of wind increased to a roar. The swallows played underneath the cotton clouds. Suddenly the wind got even stronger and the swallows all flew away. It started to rain. Large, spitting drops were hitting the ground like fruits dropped from the heavens. Then the drops turned white and became larger and larger until the ground was covered with hail the size of golf balls. The sound was peaceful—but deafening. The atmosphere changed from hot and sticky, to cool and comfortable. Suddenly I felt a great sense of relief—but did not understand why. The hail lasted no longer than a minute and then I walked home, pondering the dream, thinking about my life, and wondering about the nature of transformation.

◆

Trying Too Hard

It had been a long time since I had seen Uncle Hakim. He had been so close to the family and he always showered us children with such love. I never did understand what happened between him and my parents. After a while, he stopped coming to our house, and we stopped visiting him.

Now, some ten years later, I had my own family problems. I needed a friend and in my desperation, I thought of Uncle Hakim. I took the bus to the harbor and then walked to the docks where I remembered he used to moor his fishing-boat. It was ten in the morning. As I noticed that most of the boats were gone, my heart sank. Nevertheless, like an obedient child I walked toward the only remaining boat. A tall man stepped off the white, orange, and brown fishing boat and started walking in my direction. My spirit soared as I recognized him. It was as if all my problems were suddenly solved. "Hakim," I shouted. A now-much-older-than-I-remembered-Hakim looked at me as if he was peering into the night. "It's me, Cantara," I said.

Hakim stopped, as I continued to walk toward him. His eyes squinted. Finally, he seemed to recognize me and said, "Cantara? The little girl who used to sit on my knee?"

"Yes, Hakim, it is me."

"Please take off the sunglasses, so I can see your eyes."

Reluctantly, I removed the sunglasses that helped protect me from my painful world. Hakim's face changed to a mixture of pity and compassion. "Oh, Cantara, what has brought the little girl who was so full of joy—so much pain?"

I burst into tears and then blurted out, "That's why I came."

"Let's sit on the boat," he said. "We'll be alone for a while."

We walked back to his boat and sat near the piles of fishing nets. I explained how painful and complex my relationships had become. I told him how trapped I felt and spoke openly of all the options I had considered.

After listening for a very long time, Hakim started to speak, "Oh, Cantara, my heart is bursting for the suffering you have gone through. If I had a magic wand, I would wipe your tears away forever; but the best I can do is—to help you—to help yourself. No one should ever be so bold as to think they can totally understand what you are going through, and you should be very careful about following the advice of friends or foes. Do you understand?"

"Not really, but I trust you."

"Be careful who you trust. Trust should always be earned and never assumed." I nodded my head as Hakim continued. "Here is what I'd like to suggest. Go for a long walk every day—at least for an hour. Don't think too much during that time. Don't dwell on your problems. Let your mind focus on the trees and the birds, and the sound of your walking, and the rhythm of your breathing. Next Tuesday, come back and see me. I'm always here on Tuesdays—that's the day I do the maintenance on my boat."

I thanked Hakim, put on my sunglasses, and walked away. For the next seven days, I walked every morning. It was hard not to think about the problems that surrounded me, but I tried my best to follow the advice that Hakim had given me. On Tuesday, I went back to see him again. Just like the previous week, Hakim asked me to remove my sunglasses and I obeyed. He looked deeply into my eyes and asked, "How are you today?"

I shrugged my shoulders and looked down. I knew I would cry if I looked for too long into his loving eyes.

"And did you receive any 'messages' while you were walking?" he asked.

Not knowing quite what to say, I told him what I thought. "I suppose I should be more patient ... and self-sacrificing ... and maybe ..."

Hakim interrupted me saying, "Cantara, you're trying to hard. You're telling me things you have read; I'm looking for messages. Sometimes it takes time to clean out the cobwebs. We have to clean our ears before we can hear the messages. They will come—don't worry. Just walk for another week and then come see me on Tuesday. I'll be here waiting."

When I visited him the following week, it was the same routine. Hakim asked me to remove my sunglasses, and then asked how I was and if I had received any messages. I responded with words about love and patience and again he said, "Cantara, you're still trying too hard. You're telling me things you remember from school, and from your parents, not what comes from your heart."

The next week I began to relax and enjoy the walking. I was able to shut off the normal flow of thoughts and to forget about my problems. Halfway through my walk on Saturday, I felt like a torrent of water gushed through my mind. Suddenly, it all seemed clear; the messages that Hakim had promised rushed into my head like a summer storm. Everything that had seemed so confusing before—now seemed so clear. I wanted to see Hakim right away; I didn't want to wait for Tuesday. I turned quickly and walked toward the bus that went to the harbor. It was crazy to expect Hakim to be there. He was a fisherman and it was far too early for him to have returned. Still, I had a strong feeling that he would be there.

As I got off the bus and walked toward the dock, I saw only one boat. Flashes of white and orange penetrated my sunglasses. I started to run. My heart was bursting with joy. Uncle Hakim stood up and stepped onto the dock. As I got closer, I removed my sunglasses, greeted Hakim, and then started to explain. As I spoke, Hakim kept nodding his head and smiling. Every once in a while he would say, "Now, you've got it."

When I had finished sharing all that had happened, I asked, "But, Hakim why were you here today? Don't you normally fish on Saturdays?"

He smiled, looked deeply into my eyes, and said, "I got a message; today—I got a message."

Victoria Falls

The rapids below Victoria Falls left me with one of those special once-in-a-lifetime experiences. Now, after a night's rest, I had a sunburn, sore muscles, and hopefully a few photographs to help me remember that I had really been there. I asked around and finally located 'Mos-Oa-Tunya Photo Studio,' a small shop, on a small street, in a small town. I walked in, as a bell attached to the back of the door announced my presence.

The place felt as unique as the falls themselves. A number of beautiful color photographs decorated the walls. A rack of stunning postcards gave me comfort, in case the film in my camera had been damaged. After a few moments, a tall, dignified-looking man emerged from behind a curtain and said, "Good morning."

"Good morning," I said in reply.

"I'm sorry I delayed you. I was in the darkroom and had to finish what I was doing before I could come out."

"It's okay, I was looking at the beautiful photos. Did you take them?" I asked.

"Yes!" he said, smiling. "Victoria Falls, according to some, is one of seven wonders of the natural world.

It's a photographer's dream!"

"But these are not the work of an amateur," I added.

"I studied photojournalism in college."

"Really—how did you end up here?"

"It's a long story. If you have time, I'll share it with you later. But for now, how can I help you?"

I opened my camera case, and handed him my Pentax. I stared anxiously into his face, searching for a positive sign.

"Is there still film inside?"

"Yes, after the boat hit the rocks—I didn't touch it."

"Well you need at least a new UV filter, but then you already knew that much. Let me take it into the dark room, pull the film out, and then we can take a closer look."

He disappeared behind a curtain, as I continued to look around. On the wall, there was a photocopy of a check from *National Geographic*. It was made out to Mr. Chenzira Chikwanda. In the display case I noticed a number of cameras for sale and wondered how badly damaged mine was. A few minutes later, he returned with a roll of film in one hand and my camera in the other.

"Let's see," he said, setting the roll of film down on the counter. He opened the back of the camera and then, aiming it towards the window, cocked and released the shutter several times.

"What do you think?" I asked.

"I think you are a lucky man. If you buy a new filter and a short roll of black and white film, we can find out for sure."

I paid for the filter and the film, and then left the shop in search of something to photograph. It had been a long time since I had used black and white film, and I enjoyed the change. A man on a bicycle and a woman selling tomatoes became the subjects for my test. When I returned, there was another customer in the shop. As the other customer departed, the shop owner extended his hand and said, "By the way, my name is Chenzira Chikwanda, what is yours?"

"Charles Mohajer—from Toronto."

After we shook hands, he asked about the origin of my name. I explained that my father was from Iran and my mother was Canadian. My curiosity about the check displayed on the wall came out awkwardly, "What's with the check? Did *National Geographic* buy a camera from you?"

He smiled, glanced toward the frame on the wall, and then asked if I wanted to hear the story. I nodded my head as he removed the frame containing the check from the wall. Holding it fondly, he started his story. "Ever hear of the photographer call Ba-Tu?"

"Yes, I have; he is originally from Burma. He works for *National Geographic*—in the U.S."

"That's the one! Well, I was attending San Francisco State—studying photojournalism. In my final year, we had a seminar that was outstanding. There were fifty students divided into groups of ten. The school had arranged a number of world-class photojournalists as guest speakers. They also acted as short-term mentors. The mentoring program was set up so that you drew a name at random, and then you spent a whole day with the person you picked."

"And you drew Ba-Tu's name?"

"Yes, and I got more than my one day with him. Actually, I followed him constantly for three full days."

"That must have been something."

"Yes it was, and during that time, several things happened. First of all, he sat me down, eyeball to eyeball, and asked me if I really had the desire to be a photojournalist. Then he told me a story about focus—not focusing your camera, but focusing your life.

"He took me to a racetrack, and introduced me to a friend of his in the stables. He showed me a pair of blinders and told me I needed a pair. Not understanding, I asked him what he meant. He said if you want to be good at anything, you need blinders. He told me that blinders keep a horse focused so he is not distracted by things that happen to the right or to the left."

"Interesting," I commented.

"Then he told me that when he goes out every morning, he always goes with his camera, and symbolically he always puts on his blinders. He said you must take risks, and you must focus quickly when a story is in front of you. He promised we would return to the racetrack later that day. As it turns out, he was shooting a series on racing—not horse racing, but racing in general. Those three days we were together, we went to dog races, horse races, stock car races, sprint car races, and we even caught the end of a marathon.

"During the sprint car racing, he leaned through a hole in the fence that over looked the speeding cars. He told me to hold his feet as he leaned out over the track in order to get photos of the drivers as they sped by. As I held his feet, I realized that the real story was Ba-Tu. I turned to a rather large woman who was seated nearby, and asked for her help. As she took one leg, I let go and grabbed my camera. When I let go, she shouted something, and then quickly grabbed the other leg. I started shooting pictures of Ba-Tu. I even got a picture of him as he looked at me with a bit of shock on his face, realizing that I was no longer holding his legs. I got another picture as he bent his head around to see the smiling face of the lady in whose hands his life had now been entrusted.

"Over the next few days I continued to take photos of him as he worked. I ended up with about fifteen rolls of film and about a dozen really nice shots.

"Using Ba-Tu as a contact, I submitted the photographs to *National Geographic's* freelance desk, and they used them a couple of years later. They did a large section on photojournalists, and my picture of Ba-Tu hanging over the sprint car track was used on the cover."

"Wow, that's something. So, what happened to you and photojournalism — didn't you like it?"

"I loved it. But it required a lot of travel, and I really wanted a family. Here, I can close my shop anytime and take photographs of the world's largest sheet of moving water -- and I can still see my family in the evening. I sell postcards to the hotels, and take photos for weddings and other events."

"You sure picked the right spot for it," I said.

"Nowhere else like it in the world. Now, enough talk about me, let's see how your photos came out."

I rewound the film, removed it from the camera, and handed it to him. He disappeared behind the curtain and a few minutes later, returned with a strip of wet negatives. He smiled and said, "One hundred percent—looks like your camera is okay and the content is great!"

I breathed a sigh of relief, thanked him for his time, and bought a handful of his beautiful postcards. As I walked back toward my hotel, I thought what a lucky week this had been. I had experienced one of the seven wonders of the natural world, and during the same week experienced one of the wonders of the human world. On top of all that—I was still able to use my now much-more-experienced camera—to take pictures of it all.

The Watermelon and the Rose

"Naseem, dear, wake up. The first lights of the morning will be here soon. Please go to the garden and bring a cutting from the finest rose."

Naseem dressed quickly and went to the garden, while her husband Amir went and picked the finest watermelon. They met again in the small courtyard just outside of the kitchen. They could hear the sound of Amir's cousin with the camel outside the gate. In a few hours, their families, Shiraz, and the rising sun, would all be behind them. Amir looked upwards toward the fading stars, asking that this journey be blessed and his family kept safe. Then, with the aid of a small, sharpened stick he punctured the thick skin of the watermelon and stuck the cutting from the rose into the small opening. That's when the conversation between the watermelon and the rose began.

"Ouch"

"I'm sorry about the thorns."

"It's okay, we both know it's for a good cause."

"That's true, but still I'm sorry for the pain."

"You also felt the sting of the knife this morning."

"Yes, but I will grow and bear beautiful flowers

again soon."

They rode for days together, the one giving necessary life to the other. They listened at night as Amir and his cousin spoke of their families and their hopes for joy and happiness and long life. Each night, before sleeping, they listened to the poems of Hafiz and Rumi.

Both the watermelon and the rose were cool at night, but very hot during the day. It was just a matter of patience. In a month, they would be separated and life would change yet again.

"I will be forever grateful to you for your sacrifice," said the rose.

Quoting Rumi, the watermelon replied:

...may your soul be happy, journey joyfully. You have escaped from the city full of fear and trembling; happily become a resident of the Abode of Security...

With that, the rose shed tears of love for this humble watermelon. Darkness passed, and they only spoke again on the morning of the next day.

"Oh, humble watermelon, in honor of you, I will explode in spring with the most fragrant roses ever smelled by man. When little girls play nearby, I will draw them close and entrance them. And when the nightingales perch nearby, I will tell them of the sacrifice you made—that I could live on forever. Every rose will be named in your honor; and every perfume will carry your grace. And when the pious come to ponder near my blooms, my sweet scent will tell them only stories of you."

After this wonderful tribute, there was silence as they rode in the heat of the sun and treasured the taste of the sweet words. After a time, the watermelon replied, "Your tribute, warm and sweet, penetrated to the very core of my being. But we are one, and sacrifice is only an exchange. A few weeks ago, you were part of a branch that was making wonderful roses for Naseem and her children. Now, you journey to the East to adorn a new place with your beauty. Though you were cut away from the place you had grown to love, you understand you will live again, and will never really die. The admiration you feel for me is because you drink my sweet juices and think that by this sacrifice, I die. By giving life to you, I will now live many lives. Part of me will forever be a rose and my seeds will still give joy to many children. Each will sing the song of change, and tell the stories of long ago."

Three months later, long after the rose cutting had been separated from the watermelon and was standing in warm soil, and long after the watermelon seeds had been dried and stored safely away to await the coming of another spring—Amir and his cousin returned home and were sitting in the small courtyard outside the house of Amir.

Naseem went to the kitchen to prepare them sweet tea, while her eldest son collected a ripe watermelon from the garden. A short time later, all the children had gathered around the two travelers. As the children begged for stories and sweets, Amir and his cousin enjoyed the luscious, red watermelon, and while laughing and smiling and feeling happy to be back home, the two men disposed of the watermelon seeds as children have done—through all of time.

♦

West Street

Excuse me, excuse me, everyone. My name is Andris, and I'm your M.C. for this evening. I hope you enjoyed your meal. I want to thank all of you for the food you brought tonight and give a special thanks to those who arranged the canopies, chairs, tables, and the sound system. After this evening's poetry, Scott is going to give us a little pitch about the petition to have the street renamed.

"As you know this is the last in the series of events that have honored all the residents of West Street. We have heard music of many forms and enjoyed dances from South America, Africa, and from China. We have heard about the research being done by the two eminent scientists living here on West Street. We have listened to stories about the late Bruce Fulton and heard about his sacrifices as a fireman. I think I can safely say that we all wish we had taken the time to get to know him better.

"This process of getting to know our neighbors here on West Street began when Nora Roberts, whom we all know as Mama Nora, started to make contact with all the people on this very special street. After some time, we discovered that there were no average people on this street. As the process of getting to know each other moved forward, we found that every single person living here has something they have accomplished, or something special they are currently working toward. There are no boring people here. That's why we signed a petition to have the street renamed.

"As you know, tonight's program is primarily for poetry, so without any further introduction let's hear from someone who has lived here for only six months, Elie Kalinsky."

The applause was both warm and genuine. The crowd of about two hundred were grateful for such a sweet introduction and were eager to hear the poetry that would follow. Andris sat down as Elie walked up to the microphone.

"Hallo everyone. I wish you forgive my language. I still learning. My first poem called, 'Blue Sky.'"

Elie took a deep breath, cleared her throat, stood up straight, and then began to read from a paper she held out in front of her.

Blue Sky the day of my birth, and sunshine all around;
And on the day of marriage, there was sunshine all around.
And on the day of our child's birth, the sunshine was around.
The day we came to West Street, the sunshine on the ground;
But the day we meet Mama Nora was the finest all around.
She welcomed us with flowers, ones she said—that she had found;
She welcomed us with Blue Sky and sunshine all around.
Yes, the day we met Mama Nora—was the finest—all around.

Elie then looked at Mama Nora, walked over, and

gave her a big hug, as everyone else was clapping for the wonderful poem, filled with wonderful thoughts. After that, Elie shared two other poems both in her native language. You did not need to understand the words to feel the power of her poetry—and many were moved to tears. Many looked at each other with tears in their eyes and questions on their faces, wondering how a poem, in a language they did not understand, could move them so deeply.

After Elie sat down, there were poems from Carlos, Dawn, Helen, Loret and from Farahmarz. Then Scott and Rosemary Pederson recited a beautiful poem together. The poetry touched every heart, and the residents of West Street were all asking themselves, why they were so very lucky.

Then the M.C. introduced Crystal and Natalie, who stood up and walked to the front. Natalie opened a black case and removed a violin and a bow. After a little tuning, she started to play a heart-wrenching melody. After Natalie played for about a minute, Crystal took a step toward the microphone and started to recite a poem about the love and joy of sharing with people of diverse backgrounds. By the time they were finished, most of the two hundred listeners were completely entranced.

After they sat down, Andris thanked all those who shared their gifts on this special day, on this very special street. Then she asked Scott to come back up and talk about the project to rename the street. Scott walked up slowly holding the petition in his hand.

"Dearly loved friends and neighbors," he started,

"we have witnessed nothing short of a miracle here. Every adult on this street, of whatever age, race, or background, has some special quality, and primarily through the work of Mama Nora, we have found these special talents and have been able to bring them to light so that all may see and appreciate them. And we haven't even thought about how this might affect our children. Think about the blessing of being a child, raised here on West Street. It is truly a miraculous thing that we have all witnessed.

"As you know, this street got its name because it lies west of almost everything else in town. Many of us started talking about the idea of renaming the street because we were convinced that there was no other street like this in the world and that 'West Street' was just too plain a name to be used for a living miracle. We considered many options like 'Special Street' and 'Magic Lane,' and we were so convinced that this was the right thing to do that we contacted the Town Council and then circulated this petition."

Scott held the petition high for all to see. Many smiled, and some cheered; some even started to chant, "Ma-gic-lane, Ma-gic-lane, Ma-gic-lane." Scott smiled and then resumed his talk.

"What finally changed my mind was not how many signed the petition, but those who had not. You know, friends, there are 202 adult residents on this street; I have 201 signatures on this petition. The one signature that is not here is the one that made me rethink the whole idea."

The residents of West Street became very quiet.

They all felt the winds of change blowing and they were trying to remain open. Then Scott spoke again, "I would like to ask Mama Nora to come up and talk to us a little about this petition."

There was a round of restrained applause as Scott took a few steps back, and Mama Nora with the assistance of her two canes, made her way slowly to the microphone. No one tried to give her assistance, they had all tried before, and they all knew how independent she was. Everyone became very quiet as they tried to anticipate what Mama Nora might say. She tapped on the microphone once and said, "Hello, hello…is it working?" She glanced behind her at Scott, who respectfully nodded his head, indicating that everyone could hear her fine.

"My dear children," she started, "how can I ever hope to put into words the love I have in my heart for each and every one of you?"

The residents all smiled that bright—radiant—genuine, baby-like smile that a child shines on its own mother.

Mama Nora continued, "I have thought deeply about the idea of renaming the street for a number of weeks now. Something bothered me about it. I asked myself why? Was it because it might attract attention and introduce a strange dynamic that might spoil the magic we have here? Or was it because it seemed a bit like bragging? What finally convinced me that it would be wrong to rename the street was the thought that every street might be a magic street. In order to test the idea, I started spending my afternoons at Bluff

View Park on the east side of town. Each afternoon, I'd take the same bus that I take to go shopping, but continue until I reached the park. I spent many afternoons there. I got to know quite a few people living near the park. What I found there was: poets, heroes, and musicians, and wonderful mothers, and fathers — people just like us — living over there near Bluff View.

"After about three weeks of this, I became convinced that we were just lucky. We discovered our own special nature; we discovered our magic."

With that, Mama Nora walked slowly back to her seat and Scott stepped forward to the microphone. After a few awkward seconds of silence, Scott started to speak, "Ah, ... um... friends, I don't know what to do. I feel I have a responsibility to you all. You signed this paper, and I signed this paper. If it is handed to the Town Council, they will, without doubt, change the name of the street." With much emotion, he looked out towards his friends and toward his dear wife Rosemary and then blurted out, "What should I do?"

There was a long period of silence. Then, finally, Rosemary broke the tension. Without speaking, she raised both hands above her head, looked directly into her husband's tear-filled eyes, and started making motions with her hands as if she was tearing a paper. Suddenly with only the faintest of sounds, others started making the same motions with their hands. First only a few women, then a few men, and then finally, every resident except Mama Nora made the sign to tear the paper. Mama Nora just smiled and radiated love for all. Finally, Scott, who was almost completely overwhelmed with emotion and tears, raised the petition high above his head as if he were about to tear it but couldn't quite find the strength. Finally, Scott's three-year-old daughter broke the emotionally-charged silence with the words, "Tear it, Daddy."

That was all it took, and to this day, West Street is still called West Street—but it is all the more magical—than it ever was before.

●

The White Flag

Freman had been under pressure for years. How often I had secretly wished he would quit this madness and do something else—anything else. But Freman was not a quitter. I'd seen him single-handedly move a boulder that was bigger around than he was tall—because it was in the middle of where he wanted to make a road. He dug a big hole right next to it, and with a long steel bar, rolled the boulder into the hole and then buried it. As I said before, he was not a quitter and neither was his father, nor his father's father. I had known them all, and the phrase "give up" was never used.

Freman, though still part owner of the business, had long ago lost control of how things were managed. He had totally lost faith in the direction in which things were moving. The day his father's letter arrived was at the end of an especially bad week. It was late in the evening by the time we sat down to eat dinner. Already knowing the answer, I asked, "How was work?"

Freman looked at me as if he had just hobbled off a battlefield—he may as well have been bandaged and walking with a cane. With two very sad eyes he looked at me and said, "Pretty normal." He took a deep breath—like it was the first air he had inhaled all day. It pained me to see him suffer like that. There was nothing in this world that I wanted badly enough that could justify all this pain. "Freman, you know I'd rather be homeless than have you suffer like this."

"Please don't start," he said.

"There's a letter for you. It's from your Dad."

"I'll read it after supper."

He poked at his food as if he might discover some hidden treasure buried inside it. I knew in my heart that one day this would all end, but I was powerless to control the timing. After supper, Freman took the letter and sat in his favorite chair. I cleared the table and thought about happier times.

Suddenly I heard Freman sobbing. I looked at his stress-worn face; there were tears streaming from his eyes. It appeared as though someone had opened up two large dams that had been filled far beyond their capacity. This was not a common occurrence in our house, and I was utterly unprepared to deal with it. I walked over and pulled his head toward me, not knowing quite how to comfort a pain, the cause of which I still didn't understand. I glanced at the letter, which was already streaked with the tears that had fallen on it.

Suddenly he stood up straight, like a tall tree, and announced, "I need to walk." With that, he handed me the letter and headed for the door. I sat down in his chair and began to read.

Dear Freman,

This work you are doing is causing you and your family great pain. I know that you once had a vision of where this was going, but it seems that vision has long ago faded. You have lost all faith in what you are doing. You are walking like a dead man, still putting one foot in front of the other, though you know in your heart, it is a big waste of time. The battle was lost long ago.

I know that you are not a quitter. I have seen you overcome many difficult situations. Eventually you always find ways to make things work. I have seen you take dreams that I thought were crazy and create wonders. But there are times when things become so intolerable that even the best of generals must surrender. That time has come. Find a piece of white cloth, tie it to a small twig, and wave it high above your head. Walk away, turn the page, and don't look back. Chalk all this up as experience gained and move forward. Find new dreams and new horizons.

Of course, this is just a father's opinion. You are your own man. You have a family to consider and a spiritual partner to consult. Think about it, Son. Please think about it.

>   *All my love,*
>   *Dad*

Now it was my turn to cry. What was Freman doing now? What torment was he going through? How could I help? Many thoughts began racing through my mind.

An hour later, Freman returned. There was still pain in his face, but it was different. Some faint rays of hope shone through all the pain.

"What do you think, Lynnette?" he asked.

I started to give my opinion, but remembered how many times I had done so before. "It's your decision, Freman. Whatever you decide is fine with me." Those were the hardest words I had ever spoken. I wanted to shout out, "For the sake of the whole universe—end this madness—quit this insane-gone-out-of-control thing." I turned and walked quickly back into the kitchen, hoping and praying he would do what was best. I was beyond caring where the idea came from, I was just happy to have hope—that this nightmare might end soon.

When I awoke in the morning, Freman was already up and dressed. It had been a long time since I had seen him awake and ready for the day so early. I wanted to ask, but I knew I shouldn't.

I was anxious all morning. Then, just after lunch, I heard the car. My heart began racing. Freman came in with an expression I hadn't seen in a long time. His face vibrated with a new sense of faith—sprinkled with just the smallest touch of joy. He walked up and gazed into my eyes in a way he had not done in many years. Then he smiled and said, "I did it. It's over, the nightmare is over."

◆

Who Are You?

If you have ever flown on long flights, you know how hard it can be. Well this time, I had planned everything. I had a couple of apples, a nice fresh sandwich, a few health bars, and a new book. The flight from LAX to Tel Aviv lasts eleven hours. My plan was to suffer less and maybe learn something. The book was something you could get your teeth into on a flight like this: *The Spiritual Growth and History of the Middle East* by George somebody or other. The last name was hard to remember. Anyway, I was all set. I arrived at the airport in plenty of time, fully prepared to be patient.

A few hours later, I was on the plane and settled in seat 48A. I don't remember exactly why, but I had asked for the window seat. I watched anxiously as the plane filled up, wondering who might sit next to me. After a few minutes, a lady in her fifties smiled, said hello, and then sat in the aisle seat. As she fastened her seat belt, I pulled out my new book and placed it purposefully on the seat between us. I made it a point not to start a conversation, because I didn't want to get stuck listening to somebody's life story.

After reaching cruising altitude, the pilot switched off the seat belt sign and told us about the weather in

Tel Aviv. I leaned my chair back and picked up my book. Just as I opened it, the lady in the aisle seat spoke, "So, who are you?" Panic struck, as I feared this might go on for a while, and I would end up doing a lot of listening and not much reading. The question did strike me as odd. Normally people say, "My name is so-and-so," and then you answer with your own. Only later do they ask any other details.

I gave her my name in reply.

She asked, "Do you live in L.A.?"

"In the foothills of L.A.," I said, smiling.

"Do you have a family and children?"

"Yes, I am happily married and have three children." I felt awkward holding the book open, so I closed it. I was sure that since she was mostly asking questions, the conversation wouldn't last long.

She was a pleasant person and had a very gentle voice. When she asked questions, I felt relaxed. I guessed she was a schoolteacher at first, but later figured she was a psychologist, and at one point, I even thought she might be some kind of a spy. I soon forgot all this and was telling her about my job as a manager at the factory, and about my dog, and that I was an avid reader. She was an attentive listener and seemed to have a genuine interest in the things I was telling her.

After some time she said, "You have a very interesting life, but I'd like to understand who you really are."

I must have looked a little blank as I took the book from my lap and placed it back on the seat between us.

She went on, "For example, your name, your job, your children, these are all important aspects of your life, but they are external things. They are things about you, but these things are not-who you are!"

The statement seemed a little bold for a person I had only known for a few hours, but she seemed trustworthy and wise. I paused as I considered her question. I felt a bit confused. The airplane shuddered slightly as we passed through some turbulence. I paused so long that I thought maybe our conversation had reached its end. I considered looking out the window or opening my book again. Still, her question and her comment-intrigued me.

She spoke again, "For example, when you go through a major change, or when a crisis strikes, what comes to your mind; or when you are falling asleep or standing in the shower, what do you dream about?"

The questions seemed a bit personal, but the sound of her voice and the look in her eyes conveyed only trust. I thought for a moment, and then I had the strangest sensation. As the airplane shuddered again, I felt like I was a piano, and someone with large warm hands had just picked out the right notes and was playing a very soothing chord—the chord of my heart.

It all started to come out. "Well, I love music and sometimes I imagine myself sitting down and just playing. Playing with lots of feeling and emotion, hitting all the notes at just the right time, and expressing a piece the way I'd like to hear it. Silly, isn't it?"

"Not at all. These things are of the heart. They are your inner wishes," she said clearly.

The captain switched on the "Fasten Your Seatbelt" sign and announced something about turbulence at high altitudes.

I felt like I was in a trance and continued, "At times, I see things in nature like sunsets and I melt into them." I looked to see if she was still listening. She nodded. "I would like to share these things with others. I want to help people to see sunsets, and sunrises, and flowers. I yearn to find a way to encourage people to meditate on the beauty and warmth of a never-to-be repeated sunset."

She smiled intently and nodded. Her face was radiant. I felt tears coming to my eyes.

"And I love to work with my hands. I love to make things of wood." I could tell that my voice was straining. All the talk, all the emotion of trying to talk loudly enough for her to hear, but softly enough that others would not, was taking its toll on my voice. In spite of all this, my heart was bursting with joy. I couldn't remember when I had last felt like this.

As the plane landed, she smiled and said, "So that is who you are!"

Finally beginning to understand, I smiled and replied, "Yes! I guess that's who I am."

As the plane pulled to a stop, she said, "It's been nice getting to know you." It felt like a dream. People were getting up, gathering their belongings, and walking off the plane. I looked at her again. I could hardly speak. She smiled warmly and said, "I wish you all the best in life." And with that she turned and was gone.

I sat back down slowly, and waited for most of the people to leave the plane. I picked up my book, and placed it carefully back into my bag. Then I stood up slowly and walked off the plane. It was strange—I felt I knew her so well but I hadn't even asked her-what her name was.

The Wooden Wheel

I pulled the blanket over my shoulder, turned on my side, and drifted off to sleep. Dreams came and went—seeming of no consequence. Then a very old man appeared. His face was like a well-worn piece of leather, his smile gentle and radiant. He seemed familiar, but distant; he looked a bit like my grandfather— but not quite. I felt a great sense of peace and security as I gazed on his face.

In that special way we ask questions in dreams, I asked him who he was. He smiled and said in a gentle but firm way, "My name and relation to you will be discovered in time. For now you may think of me as your past and your future." In the dream, this all seemed reasonable but now, hours later, as I write these words in my journal—it makes little sense.

As the dream continued, I realized that this man was standing next to a large wheel. The wheel was made of wood, and it looked very old. In places, the grains of the wood were opened so wide that light streaked through from some source behind it. The wheel was slightly taller than the old man himself, and was connected to some unseen force that made it turn. The light, filtering through the cracks, seemed to come from this same source of energy.

He said, "It's time to play," and the wheel began to spin, sometimes slowly, and sometimes more quickly. The wheel had three pegs stuck in the front of it and an arm hanging down from above it. As it turned, each of the pegs struck the arm and made a deep, magical, resonating sound. Each peg made a different sound. As the wheel turned at different speeds, the sound of the wood made musical phrases, like some mystical music from the heavens.

The old man then looked into my eyes and said, "In order to play you must tell the wheel when to stop."

Not knowing the game, I said, "Okay, then, stop!" After a few more musical phrases, the wheel stopped. The arm pointed to some words, carved deep into the wooden wheel.

As I strained my eyes to see, the old man said in a loud carnival-like voice, "The wheel stops at kindness." Then in a softer voice, he looked at me and said in a rhyming tone, "Kindness is good, everyone should be kind, but it is not enough; why not try again?"

As he said this, the wheel started to turn again. I watched the wheel move and listened to the magical sounds as the pegs passed by the wooden arm. Then, I said, "Stop," and the wheel slowly came to a halt.

Then, the old man said, in a loud, announcer-like voice, "The wheel stops at radiance." Then in a softer voice directed at me, he said, "Radiance is good, everyone should be radiant, but it is not enough. Why not try again?"

As I watched and wondered about this strange game, the wheel started to revolve. Once more, the music of the wood returned as the wooden arm struck each of the pegs in turn. I felt I was beginning to understand this game and said, "Stop" and the wheel slowly obeyed my command.

As the wheel stopped, the old man said, "The wheel stops at purity." Then directing his eyes to mine, he said softly, "Purity is good, everyone should strive to be pure, but purity alone is a lonely place to be. Purity must be shared, and in order to be shared, you need kindness and radiance."

Then he directed his voice to others whom I could not see, and said, "Step right up, spin the wheel, win the prize and get all three." The wheel began to spin, the notes making their sounds as the old man sang out, "Step right up, spin the wheel, win the prize, and get all three."

As he continued to sing, I looked closely into his eyes. They seemed to be my father's eyes, his face my father's face, then my own eyes, and my own face. The sound of the wooden wheel, and the music it made, became louder, then softer, and my eyes fluttered open. I lay still on the pillow, thinking and wondering.

I glanced up from my journal. Staring out the window, I fell into a trance-like state as I remembered that long-ago dream. Looking back down, I realized it was exactly ten years ago today that I had that dream and wrote those words. How strange and marvelous this life is. We never know what tomorrow will bring. We can't control our dreams at night, and much of what comes to us each day is just as mysterious.

Your True Colors

Who would have thought my own grandfather would start something in the middle of the West Siberian Plain that would attract tourists from all over the world? Newspapers began referring to it as, "The Garden of Peace," and "The International Flag Garden." I was very young when it all started so I don't remember much of the early days. When I was six years old, we went to visit him. I remember Grandpa waking up every morning, walking into his garden, and then raising colorful flags on tall, white flagpoles.

It was during a later visit that I asked him what it was all about. "Peace will only come with understanding," he said. "After the last great war, I started trying to understand the causes of these conflicts. I found that associated with every war there was misunderstanding, fear, and prejudice. I began to read about other countries and found many positive things about every one of them. I started buying flags from each of the countries I had read about.

"Then I started the practice of raising these flags every morning at dawn. Each time I do this, I recite a few facts that are special and unique to that country. It is a purely personal practice—just my own little contribution to world peace. I had no thought of it becoming a tourist attraction—it was just something I was moved to do. The more the tourists came, the more this little town prospered. Hotels were full all year 'round, and restaurants multiplied. At the same time, I had to spend more and more money replacing flowers that were trampled by excited little children. Finally, I met with the City Council and the Chamber of Commerce. Both of them encouraged me to quit my job and to devote all my energies to the gardens. They both offered financial help, and I began to charge a small fee for admission.

"Now, it's grown to what you see today. I have 171 flags now and add one or two each month. I only add a flag after I discover a few special things about that country. Then I memorize those to say aloud each morning when the flags are raised."

That was what Grandpa told me when I was sixteen. Five years later, I got a good job near the town where Grandpa had his Peace Garden. I spent many evenings asking him questions about life and absorbing as much of his unique wisdom as I could.

I had been there about a year when I asked him for advice about my situation at work. I told him that I worked hard every day, but they didn't want to increase my salary. I explained all the sacrifices I made for the company and how hard I worked.

Grandpa sat in silence, looking at the flags blowing in the late afternoon breeze. Finally, he spoke, "Come tomorrow at dawn. Help me raise these flags and I will share my thoughts with you."

The next morning, I arrived in the Peace Garden after Grandpa had already started to raise the flags. He was reciting the special things he'd discovered about each country. It was a very moving experience. It was his gift to the world, his own special ritual, his own practice, his own garden of peace. As I walked up, he was raising the red, yellow, and green flag of Bolivia. "Oh, Bolivia," he cried out, "You are isolated and preserved. Your cultural wealth and high mountain landscapes are a beauty saved for a dedicated few."

Then he moved a few steps to the next flagpole and unfurled the blue, black, and white flag of Botswana. Then he started again, "Oh, Botswana, like the priceless diamonds found deep in your desert sands, your people too are like diamonds."

After all the flags had been raised, we sat down on a bench. Then he looked at me with his deep, steel-gray eyes and asked, "Why do you conclude that your employer doesn't want to raise your salary?"

I was a bit taken aback. I thought it was clear. After seeing that I had no new information to share, he pointed to the flags flapping against the blue sky and then started to speak. "It's like these flags; you have to share your true colors. You have worked hard for a year and you think you deserve a raise. I hope your working hard is not because you want more money, but rather because you feel it is the right thing for you to do."

I listened as he continued, "Now, you have shown them your true colors by the way you work, but you have not shown them that you want to make more money. Working hard does not automatically raise that issue—it's a separate thing. They may appreciate your efforts and wish that all their employees worked as hard as you do. But there are all kinds of possible reasons why they have not given you a raise, but they are all speculation—unless you ask.

"What is needed now is for you to ask, without expectations. Don't assume they will say, yes, and don't assume they will say, no. Don't make plans for what you will do if they say, no. Be content to show them your true colors. Just tell your boss that you work hard, and that you would like to make more money. And then stop and look at him without emotions or expectations. Listen to what he says. Let him show his true colors. Then think about his reply, evaluate it and see if there is any new action you wish to take."

Since that time in the Peace Garden, I have followed Grandpa's advice three times. Twice I was given a raise, and once I was not. But the lesson he gave me began to affect every part of my life. My level of anxiety dropped. When faced with difficult decisions, I found them to be far less stressful than before.

It's now twenty years since my grandfather passed away. The City Council has turned his home into a historical monument and the little town in the center of the West Siberian Plain, fueled by my grandfather's love of peace, continues to thrive.

In my case, I wake up each morning at dawn and raise a small purple flag in his honor. He loved purple, and often asked me why I thought more flags didn't have purple in them. He showed the world his true colors and taught me about showing mine.

◆